# THE WHOLE OF THE MOON

RUSH LEAMING

## BRIDGEWOOD ENT.

ISBN: 978-0-9997456-3-2

Front cover image "Flight of Icarus" used with permission by: Abner Recinos
Copyright 2010
Inside photos: Parts 1 & 2 C.Portney;  Parts 3 & 4 CanStock Photos
Cover design by Bad Doggie Designs

SPECIAL THANKS
Blair Lott
Jane Speight
Starr Waddell
Quiethouse Editing
Bad Doggie Designs

"You were there at the turnstiles

With the wind at your heels

You stretched for the stars

And you know how it feels

To reach too high

Too far

Too soon

You saw the whole of the moon"


—The Waterboys

THE WHOLE OF THE MOON
Words and Music MICHAEL SCOTT
Copyright@ 1985 DIZZY HEIGHTS MUSIC PUBLISHING, LTD. (PRSI
All Rights Administered by WB MUSIC CORP.
All Rights Reserved
Used By Permission of ALFRED MUSIC

*For Kathy, Kathy, and Pumbu*

# THE WHOLE OF THE MOON

It had been almost a year since we had seen TV, live TV anyway. The tiny villages where we had been living, deep in the interior of the country, had no roads, no electricity, no running water, and certainly no TV. So, as we sat in the café at the American embassy in Kinshasa, a place that tried so hard to be everything that was not Africa, that was not roiling and dusty like the city beyond those high whitewashed walls, but instead was a clean bar with green tablecloths and clean ice that we were told was safe to drink (they even had posters on the wall of the NFL schedule for 1989), the images that flickered on the two TVs above the bar were mesmerizing. The Berlin Wall, thousands of miles away in Europe, lay crumbled in pieces on the ground and swarms of people crammed the once divided streets, singing and cheering.

"When? When did that happen?" I asked.

"A couple of days ago," Doc Peters said. "While you guys were down near the coast."

Sheila, who had been silent the whole time, and who had rarely lifted her eyes from staring at the floor, glanced up at the images. "Incredible," she whispered. "We've been in the bush so long…"

"Yes," Doc said as he took a pen from his shirt pocket and opened a brown file folder. "Crazy things going on everywhere."

My face hurt. The cuts and scrapes beneath the bandages on my forehead itched and burned, and the deep bruise on my cheek still throbbed and echoed with the errant punches that had created it. I didn't want to be there. I wanted to be hundreds of miles to the east, back in my mud hut.

"Anyway," Doc said. "I need to go over the details of what happened in Matadi."

I looked out the window of the café. A man and woman, each wearing perfectly clean white clothes, played tennis on a perfectly clean court. "We've spoken to the police," I said. "We've spoken to the director. Do we really have to do this again?"

"Yes. I'm approaching it from a medical angle and my report will be final, will determine what ultimately happens to him."

"Where is he?" Sheila asked.

Doc jotted something in the file. "We got him yesterday. He's at my place… He's lucky he's not in jail." He looked up at Sheila and me. "So are the two of you."

I lit a cigarette, a very strong local brand called Okapi, named after the striped phantom deerlike animal of the northern jungles. "He didn't mean for any of this to happen. None of us did. Things… just got out of control."

"Obviously."

"He wasn't like this when we first got here," I said, my voice cracking, my face getting flushed. "Not at all. He was much different. He just… bit by bit… He changed." Sheila reached over and gently placed her hand on my forearm.

"That's exactly what I'm here to find out," Doc said. He dangled his pen above the stack of papers in the file, ready to continue writing. "So… Why don't you go back to the beginning, a year ago, when you all first got here. Tell me about how he changed."

The smoke burned my throat as I sucked it in and nearly finished the entire cigarette in one deep drag. I looked out the other window of the café where half a dozen people, their eyes shut, sat in vinyl lounge chairs beside a sparkling, pristine blue swimming pool. A roar came from the TV, and I turned to see those crowds in East Germany rushing around piles of concrete left from the fallen wall. Many grabbed chunks of the rubble and held the pieces above their heads. Some of them jumped up and down, shouting and pumping their fists in the air, then ran away with their souvenirs or stuck them in their pockets.

I looked at Sheila. She nodded her head just once. "Ok," I sighed out. "Yeah. Maybe that's the best thing to do." My hands shook as I put a new cigarette in my mouth and lit it off the end of the other. "Start from the beginning," I said. A string of images flashed in my mind, jumbled and quick, scattered events from the previous year. "Maybe that will work… Maybe that way it will all somehow make sense."

# PART ONE: BUKAVU

# CHAPTER ONE

There are certain people who sizzle and burn. Gabriel was one of them. I first noticed him sitting near the front of a twin-engine prop plane as we made our descent into Bukavu, Zaire, long before the wax on his own wings would begin to melt. Those tiny foam chairs could barely contain him: you can't wrap a seat belt around a pulsar. In his lap, he held a boom box that played a cassette tape of fast-beat African swing, and he moved his body back and forth to the music. At the same time, he twisted his neck in all directions, looking out the windows at every road, river, or tree that passed below us. He was like a Tesla coil, firing in all directions. For six weeks, I had occasionally glimpsed him around our training sessions along the South Carolina coast back in the States, but this was the first time I really noticed him, really noticed anything or anyone, the previous month and a half having been a deep gray blur. It was actually at that moment, on that plane, that I first woke up.

We flew over Lake Kivu on a crystalline, cloudless day. Rolls of sharp mountains, covered in thick canopies of palm and banana trees, poked in and out of the shimmering blue-brown water. It was my first time in this part of the world, my first time ever outside of America. All my life, since childhood, I had had bizarre recurring dreams of exploring other planets, of drifting through deep space and being dropped into other worlds far from our own. In those dreams, the awe and the fear, the shocking thrill, and the dark oblivion mixed and mingled into a conflicting anxiety. It was the same thing I felt at that moment as we fell from the sky, deep into Zaire, Africa—the Congo— moving like a foreign blood cell through Joseph Conrad's infamous *Heart of Darkness*. It was the limitlessness of the exotic; it was the danger of the wild. It was exciting. It was sinister.

We landed in a red-dirt field next to a tin shack, and all sixteen of us crawled out of the plane, stiff joints popping and cracking. Gabriel was tall and long-limbed like a basketball player. He had shaggy brown hair, and his clothes were full of holes: shirt with holes around the collars and in the pits, pants frayed at the cuff and holes in the knees. The wind blew red dust through those holes, blew dust over everything and all of us as we pulled our duffel bags and backpacks from the belly of the plane and watched two cargo trucks arrive.

A skinny man with a thick orange mustache carried a clipboard and leapt out of one of the passenger seats to herd us forward. "Future fish heads! Welcome, welcome," he said. "Pick a truck, any truck. Throw your bags in the back, climb aboard, and hold tight. Not too many paved roads where we're going. Better get used to it."

I stared at his T-shirt, a drawn outline of a yellow fish against a white background with black lettering that read: Pensez Poisson.

"You like it?" he asked. "If you make it through the rest of training, you'll get one."

*If I make it through.*

The two trucks left the airstrip and plunged into the thick mountains. Up and down they clanged along the dark-red dirt roads, each jagged bump knocking us side to side. The air was cool and wet—mountain air—and the wall of trees greener and more dense than anything I'd seen before. A young woman with strawberry-blonde hair sat across from me. I watched her face soak in our new world. Her hair was cut just below her chin, and she wore no makeup nor did she need to. Her gray eyes lit up when a group of three young Zairian boys jumped out of the forest. They yelled *"Mzungu! Mzungu!"* and tried to chase the truck. She reached out her hand and, for a quick second, touched fingertips with the fastest boy.

———————•———————

Our training compound was a sprawling school of half a dozen arched buildings made of sandstone and granite, built sometime in the early twentieth century. It stood at the top of a hill that looked down to the lake and down to the center of town. We arrived just before sunset. In the clean air, it was easy to see across the water all the way to the other side.

5

Orange-Mustache Man pointed to the rolling skyline. "That's Rwanda over there," he said. "Great place for hiking. Lots of us go there on the weekends. It's a bit calmer. Good place to unwind."

We carried our bags and stood in line at a table where we waited to get our room assignments, keys, and a per diem envelope stuffed with the multicolored cash notes of that country. Gabriel couldn't stand still, jumping up and down like a kid on a pogo stick. Twenty-Four-East was my room number, and I followed the crowd into the long dormitory building, down the stone hallways to my single room: bed, table, chair, white mosquito net hanging from the ceiling, and a window overlooking the water.

No one stayed inside for long. The courtyard was lit up at night with strings of multicolored lights. There were tables full of fried plantains, roasted peanuts and corn, slices of pineapple and mango, small cheese-and-avocado sandwiches and glass bottles of filtered water or cold Fanta soda. Crooning African music, slow and aching like blue ice, swirled from a tape deck. Over a hundred people mingled and chatted, some standing in groups bouncing hacky sacks off their feet, others tossing a Frisbee. Most, like myself, looked like they were straight out of college.

After completing the next six weeks of training, we were supposed to eventually spread out into towns and villages all across Zaire as well as in other nearby countries like Cameroon or Zambia. For two years, some of us would work as teachers, others as nurses, and some would work with farmers; I had come here to help people raise fish. I knew nothing about fish.

I stood at the edge of the lawn with a small cup of coffee in my hand, and that's when the fluttering began, when my breathing got faster and my skin started to sweat in the cool night air. The lights of the town, pushed into the dark hills down below, blinked and blazed brighter in my eyes. All those people all around me, people I didn't know, turned my head dizzy. Snippets of conversations floated my way:

"...at least Reagan's gone..."

"...Dukakis blew it..."

"...Guns N' Roses best new band..."

"...I'm gonna miss football..."

"...Glad I'm here. Eighty-eight's been a crappy year in the States..."

I wanted a cigarette but saw no one else was smoking so I watched the fat leaves of a banana tree shift in the wind, and then I saw Strawberry-Blonde standing by herself as well. She had an inviting face, comforting eyes. I thought she'd at least be polite, so I walked over to her.

She smiled and watched me approach without any glimpse of hesitation. She seemed to be genuinely ready to speak to me, but as I arrived right in front of her, Gabriel rushed in from the side and wrapped his arms around her waist.

"There you are! Let's go down to the lake. I heard people singing down there. Singing!"

She exploded in laughter. "All right. All right."

Gabriel looked into my face for the first time, his dark-blue eyes burning and piercing. "Hey, come with us."

"Um, sure. Ok." I fumbled with my coffee cup and put it down on a tray. I followed the two of them to the edge of the courtyard, the edge of the electric lights, where we passed a medium-built guy with a bowl haircut.

"Where are you guys going?" Bowl-Hair asked.

"To the lake!" Gabriel shouted.

"Cool."

The four of us ran across a wide dark field, the bulbs giving way to blazing moonlight. Gabriel leapt and cartwheeled in the thick grass and even did full body flips, impressive considering his size.

We reached the shore of the lake and found a small dock jutting into the black-ink water. A fat, full moon rose above us. We settled in a row on the dock and just remained silent for several minutes. The water lapped against the planks of wood. The air was crisp and smelled like coffee. Then, came the sound of low, rhythmic voices, calling out a song in another language, a language whose words we didn't yet know. Two silhouettes, two fishermen rowing by themselves in two wooden canoes, singing in unison, cut across streaks of moonlight on the lake water.

"Isn't that amazing?" Gabriel whispered.

"Mm," Strawberry-Blonde said and started to wrap her arms around his back.

Gabriel jumped up. "Can you imagine the things we will see and do here these next two years?" He stretched his long arms up to the night sky, laying both hands on each side of the full moon. He mumbled something to himself, ignoring the rest of us, then came back down to earth and sat on the dock.

"Ahh… I just came here for the women," Bowl-Hair said.

Strawberry-Blonde swatted his arm. "Stop!"

"Hey. What's your name?" Gabriel asked me.

"Michael. Michael Shaw."

"Gabriel Moss."

"Sheila Vonn," Strawberry-Blonde said.

"Robert," Bowl-Hair said. "Just Robert… like Madonna."

"Well, welcome to all of you… Just look at this. This moment, right now… I've been waiting for this all of my life," Gabriel said. "Nothing can stop me. Nothing can stop *us*."

Water lapping, fisherman singing, sparkling fat yellow moon: I ran my hands over my face and through my hair.

## CHAPTER TWO

"**M**ichael!"

I pressed my back into a large tree trunk and tried to keep from passing out. It was the next day, and I was in the middle of an endless forest—green, green, surrounding me and closing in on me. The tangled trees and vines seemed to crawl right up to my neck. The rest of the group was on the hiking trail, but I couldn't move. I couldn't peel my back from that tree.

"Michael," Gabriel said. "What are you doing? We are all waiting on you. We need to keep moving."

I had come to take a quick leak, but everything else had collapsed. The mountains wanted to swallow me up. I couldn't stop breathing in and out. I couldn't move, I couldn't disappear. Those people out there, those people waiting for me, I shouldn't be here, I can't do this, they know that...

"Michael? What's wrong?"

"I... I... ok." I forced myself to leave the wet bark. I grabbed my backpack and moved forward, the sky blurry, the ground feeling like a sponge.

"You need help?"

"I'm all right."

Gabriel led me back to the main trail, and the eight of us kept moving through a narrow wall of trees. We were led by Sarah, one of our trainers, and a Zairian man named Kunga who carried a machete and occasionally hacked away at a branch or shrub. We came to a clearing in the forest and saw three perfectly shaped rectangular fish ponds lying in a row, with grass planted on the banks, and the water inside each a greenish-brown color.

An old man with a long gray beard sat waiting in the shade of a thatched shelter, and two young girls of around five or six, one in a tattered blue dress, the other wearing an old red T-shirt, played along the edge of the ponds. The girls were tossing small rocks in their hands and grabbing sticks off the ground in what looked like a version of jacks. Below them, the pond banks dropped sharply away into a churning river. The brightness of the clearing filled my eyes.

Sarah stood beside the man and introduced him to our group. "This is Molo," she said. "One of the best fish farmers in all of Zaire." She translated to him in Swahili. He smiled and shook his head no. "Ah, he's too humble. But seriously," she continued, "he is what you shoot for out here. He has been doing this for six years, and now teaches others what he has learned. I want all of you to walk around and make careful observations about how this farm is set up. We'll discuss afterwards."

Everyone else seemed to know exactly what to do. They all fanned out, taking out notebooks and scribbling away at things I had no idea about. I could hardly breathe again, the bright field was spinning around me, my legs ached, and my hands were tingling and going numb. I walked backwards along the edge of one of the ponds, the river below me, the sky above me, my head turning round and round.

I saw Gabriel looking at me from across one of the ponds; I saw his mouth open, and I guess he was trying to say my name, trying to warn me before I tripped and my body fell violently onto a small ball of flesh. It tumbled down and splashed into the river. Then came shouting and screaming, and I saw the little girl in the blue dress flailing her arms in the swirling water, her head sinking quickly. Two large bodies ran past me and jumped off the side of the pond. Gabriel and Kunga crashed into the river below. Gabriel dove for the girl, reached under the surface, and pulled her to his waist. Kunga took her legs and they carried her to the nearest bank. She spat out water from inside her chest and began to cry while Kunga cradled her head in his hands.

Everyone surrounded them to watch. Sarah pushed through the crowd. "What the hell just happened?"

Gabriel's chest heaved up and down, and he wiped his wet hair from his forehead. He looked straight at me, into my eyes. His face froze for a moment and then he turned toward Sarah. "I'm sorry," he said. "I wasn't watching where I was going."

"Jesus Christ, Gabriel. You've got to be more careful," she said.

Gabriel nodded his head. "I will. I promise."

Sarah explained to Molo and Kunga what had happened.

They indicated they understood and appeared to forgive Gabriel for something he didn't do. The girl seemed shaken, but otherwise ok.

Sheila knelt beside Gabriel and placed her hand on his back. He rose to his feet, glancing at me once again, and then the rest of the crowd, except for me, slowly disappeared, going back to what they had been doing before. I stood alone at the edge of the river and stared into the swirling brown water.

---

I knocked on Gabriel's door.

"Come in."

I opened it and saw him and Sheila sitting on his bed playing chess.

"Oh. Sorry," I said and began to back away.

"No, it's ok," Sheila said and held out one finger. "Just a second… checkmate!" She sat straight up and smiled.

Gabriel mulled over the board. "Damn. Good move."

"Ha! That's three in a row!"

"Rematch tomorrow?"

"You bet." She stood up and gathered a pile of notebooks and gave Gabriel a quick kiss on the cheek. "Goodnight."

She walked past me, smiled, and briefly touched my arm.

Gabriel looked at me a moment as I fidgeted in the doorway. Out of his window, I could see the streaks of moonlight falling across the surface of the lake. He pushed out his wooden chair.

"Have a seat."

I sat down in front of the bed, and he offered me a bottle of water but I refused.

"Do you mind if I smoke?" I asked.

"Yes. But go ahead. You look like you need it." He put an empty coffee saucer on his mattress in front of me.

I inhaled and continued to poke my eyes around the room and out the window.

"I'm sorry," I finally said. "And thanks."

"It's ok. What happened to you out there today?"

I shook my head. "I don't know."

"Has that ever happened before?"

"Kind of, but not that bad. A few times in college. I went to the health clinic, but they couldn't find anything wrong. I just... I get so I can't breathe; I get dizzy..."

"Sounds like a panic attack."

I fidgeted with my hands. "Really? The clinic said there was nothing wrong. Probably allergies."

"They sound like they weren't too thorough. My sister used to get them. Anxiety attacks, same thing... You should speak to Doc Peters about it. Maybe he can help."

"Yeah."

"If it happens again you should tell someone instead of pushing through it. That girl could have drowned."

"I know. I know... I couldn't believe what was happening. It was like I was standing beside myself watching it all."

Gabriel didn't speak. His eyes examined me as if he were

trying to decide just what in the world to do with me.

I nodded and stood up. "Anyway, thanks for covering for me. You didn't have to do that."

Gabriel grimaced. "You're right. And you're welcome."

I began to leave the room.

"Hey, you play chess?" Gabriel asked.

"A little."

"Wanna play? I just got my ass beat, and I'd like a chance to redeem myself."

"Um… ok. Sure."

"Great," he said and began to set up the board. "But no more smoking."

"Got it," I said and stubbed out the cigarette in the saucer.

We began the game in silence.

---

After the game, which I lost, I went back to my room. I tried reading my training manuals, but the pages blurred and I couldn't concentrate. Out the window, on the lake, I could hear the old fishermen paddling their canoes and singing their songs.

It was near midnight, but I slipped on a pair of sandals and decided to walk around for a bit. The long stone hallway was quiet, empty, and dark except for a single light coming from underneath one door on the west end. I went down the central staircase to the ground floor and out the front door into the crisp night air. I smelled charcoal burning; in fact, everywhere one went in that country one could catch wafts of that smoky, soothing smell, a smell that brought me back to weekends on my middle-class street, where every other house would light up a grill in the late afternoon.

I walked alone in the grass in the front yard, around the rows of circular thatched-roof gazebos, or *paillotes*, that served as some of our classrooms. Below a small hill was the long dining and recreation hall, the *réfectoire* (I was slowly beginning to pick up these French words).

Just a few days ago, I had never even been outside the southern US except for a trip one summer to Connecticut to visit relatives. Now, I was strolling along the grounds of these old buildings constructed when this country was a colony. It was a dictatorship now (though, for the moment, a peaceful one), in the center of a distant continent, where almost every single thing I saw and heard was completely different than anything I had ever known. The tropics, jungles, deserts, Alpine vistas, or ancient temples—those things had been two-dimensional my entire life, existing only on the pages of books or on the screens of movies and TV. Now my skin, my eyes, my breath could soak it in every direction I turned. It was a stunning shift in perspective.

I walked past the vegetable garden up to the front gate where two Zairian sentries in red overalls sat around a tin pot of smoldering coals. I offered each a cigarette and they eagerly accepted, but when I reached in my pocket, I realized I had left my matches in my room. One of the men pushed a stick into the pile of ash until the end turned orange. He pressed it against the cigarette dangling from my mouth.

"Thank you," I said. "*Merci.*"

He shook his head. "*Bien sûr.*"

"It's cold," I said and illustrated by rubbing my hands over my arms.

"*Oui, c'est vrai. Il fait froid,*" said the other.

I wanted to say something else, but that was the extent of my language skills at that moment. They looked at me, smiling and waiting. I simply nodded and continued on my way across the silent courtyard.

Over the past few weeks, I had kind of lost track of time, but then remembered that Thanksgiving was coming soon in the States. Was it in one week or two? Then Christmas would come, then 1989 would arrive, then birthdays of family and friends, and all those events back home would happen while I was here, in this country. It made me wonder if being so far away was like when a tree fell in a forest and no one was around to hear it: did it really make a sound?

I lingered a few more minutes in the calming solitude of the night air, the thick, cold grass around my toes, and the stone archways rising behind me. The deep sky above me was now the Southern Hemisphere, showing a whole new set of stars and constellations I had never seen before: infinite galaxies, infinite pathways of light and dark, and just like those dreams I had as a child, infinite new worlds to discover. Which ones would I find?

# CHAPTER THREE

I woke up the next morning late. Very late. Past 11 a.m. Language class had begun at eight thirty.

I had a deep sleep when I got back to my room around 2 a.m., the best in months, but I failed to set the alarm on my Casio watch. I scrambled out of bed, slipped on a sock on the floor, and hit my head on a chair. I got back up, threw on a shirt, khaki pants, hiking boots without tying the laces, and ran down the hallway and jumped down the stairs. All the circular *paillotes* in the yard were full of students and teachers. I found the one I was supposed to be in and collapsed into a chair.

"Very good. That's all for today," said Ilunga, our teacher, a young Zairian man in his twenties, wearing a shiny silver and orange shirt.

Everyone stood up to leave. I closed my eyes and shook my head.

A flat hand slapped me in the chest and grabbed my shirt. I opened my eyes to see Gabriel and Sheila standing behind me. "Come on," Gabriel said. "Follow us." He half dragged me to my feet.

"Where are we going?" I stumbled behind them and pushed through the crowd of all the other students filing out into the grass.

"On an adventure!"

"What? Doing what?"

"We're going on a hike," Sheila said.

"No. Not today…"

Gabriel pulled the strap of my backpack. "Stop bitching. It'll be fun. Let's go see what's out there."

I surrendered. We walked out the front gate, down the hill to the edge of town. It didn't take long for the insular quiet of our training compound to give way to the full assault of the city of Bukavu. Diesel fumes poured out of every vehicle and singed the air with a slightly sweet, tarry smell. The asphalt roads were covered in red dust, and indeed layers of dark-red dirt stains ringed the bottom of each concrete and cinder-block building. Rickety wooden tables lined the sidewalks with single vendors, either old women or young children, selling everything from batteries, cigarettes, tins of sardines, to roasted peanuts poured into paper cones.

Sheila and I stopped at one table, run by a teenage boy whose name we found out was Chicoe. I shelled out two hundred Zaires of my per diem for a pack of Okapi cigarettes (the brown-and-orange stripes against a yellow background on the package meant to mimic the fur of the rare forest animal), and she bought two packs of mint Chiclet gum for twenty-five Zaires apiece.

We continued toward the main street in the city, passing by petrol "stations," which were basically ramshackle stacks of plastic jugs of gasoline, next to piles of half-worn rubber tires. A taxi or other car would screech to a halt, and one of the young gas jockeys would jerk the red or yellow cans of fuel to his waist and precariously tilt the nozzle into the car, often spilling as much on the ground as what went inside the tank. Zairian music blared from nearly every shop: the fast-paced, jangling electric guitar rhythms with staccato bursts of horns, pushed full blast at a distorted pitch through rumbling box speakers. It would be a few more weeks before I would be able to identify specific singers and songs and before I started to like the local music, but it certainly created a vibrant soundtrack to our surroundings. Bright advertising banners hung from every possible wall and street corner, emblazoned with brand names such as Primus Beer, Nestlé, Orangina, and Ambassade Cigarettes, just to name a few.

It was a sensory explosion, to say the least, and for a few moments, I felt myself getting a bit overwhelmed by it all, my heart racing, head tingling. Then Sheila came to a stop in the center of a stretch of buildings lining the main thoroughfare. She looked at a three-story, somewhat art deco–style building, painted half-white and half-green, with white iron gates covering arched windows. The name said: L'Hôtel de la Reine de l'Afrique.

"Ooh! You know what this is?" Sheila said.

"A McDonald's?" I asked. "God, I'm really craving a Big Mac."

She swatted my arm. "Gross. No, it's The African Queen Hotel. From the movie. It was built specifically for Humphrey Bogart and Katharine Hepburn when they came here in the 1950s to make the movie."

Gabriel squinted at the building in the bright sunlight. "Oh yeah," he said. "I remember reading about that before I left. The final scene was filmed here on the lake, right?"

"Yep. When they sink the German boat. Right out on the lake. They stayed here." She turned to me. "Ever seen it?"

"Bits and pieces," I said, thinking back several years to a day when I stayed home sick from middle school, flipping channels as I lay on our sofa.

"Oh, *The African Queen* is a classic," Sheila said. "I love old Hollywood movies. I wonder if we can find a videotape of it here in the city. Maybe we could have a movie night for everyone. There's a TV and VCR in the rec room back at our school."

"Sounds like a plan," I said. I peered past the front gate into a courtyard lined with ferns and with tables of reposed white people drinking from tall glasses of beer.

Sheila rummaged through her blue-and-gold-colored backpack, embroidered with the logo for UC Davis. "Fuck," she said. "I forgot to bring my camera."

"Language, language," I said, teasing her a bit.

"Sorry. I've got a sailor's mouth. I wanted to get a picture of the two of you in front of it. Note to self: always pack your camera."

"I'm sure we'll come back another day," I said. I looked a few feet down the sidewalk at a Zairian woman in a traditional wrapped and folded dress (called *pagnes*, I'd later learn) made from typically kaleidoscopic, multicolored fabric. She had a pleasant, smiling face and stood beside a blue plastic table. On her table was a large wooden bowl. She waved me over several times, saying: "*Kuja! Kuja!*" I slowly stepped closer, and she kept pointing to the bowl, saying: "Yummy!" I finally reached the table, peered inside, then immediately jumped back.

"Aye!" I shrieked. In the bowl was a large mound of what appeared to be fried crickets, their legs and wings all tangled together, their crispy black eyes looking up at me.

The woman burst out laughing. "*Ahh, Mzungu! Mzungu!*" she yelled and stomped her feet in pure joy.

I ran back to Gabriel and Sheila. "What's *mzungu* mean?"

"It's Swahili for *white person*," Gabriel said.

"She got you good," Sheila said. "What was in the bowl? Snakes?"

"Bugs! Crickets, I think." I hurriedly reached for a cigarette. "Seriously, is there no place to get a cheeseburger around here?"

Gabriel smirked at my wishful thinking, then turned and looked across the road. He snapped his fingers at Sheila and me. "Check that out," he said and pointed to the other side of a traffic circle, where a large mural of the Big Man himself, the president of the country, Mobutu Sese Seko, glared down on the city. He was Big Brother in a tall leopard-print cap, plastered against the green, red, and gold hand-holding-a-torch flag of Zaire. The paint on the wall may have been somewhat chipped and fading, but his influence, we were warned, was not.

"Jackass," Gabriel mumbled under his breath.

"Shh," Sheila said. "We can't say that. Remember what they told us?"

"I *whispered* it," he said, then put two fingers to his mouth, whistled, and waved down a taxi. Sheila looked at me, rolled her eyes, and shook her head.

A rusty little gray Toyota Corolla pulled up in front of us. Gabriel spoke to the driver in broken French, and the three of us crammed our bodies on top of the shredded vinyl seats.

———————•———————

The taxi drove along the outskirts of the city to a secluded cove along the lake where another mountain rose into the sky. We each chipped in a one-hundred-Zaire note to the driver, and then Sheila and I followed Gabriel. We found a trail near the shore and began our ascent through a maze of banana trees and thick underbrush, with the shimmering lake water to our backs. The entire time Gabriel led the way, pushing through branches and thickets, always humming some strange, nameless tune.

"Do you happen to know where we are heading?" I asked, halfway up the mountain, my smoker's lungs starting to cause my breath to disappear.

"No," Gabriel said. "That's part of the fun. See where we end up."

I turned to Sheila. "I suppose you're in on this, too?"

She smiled. "Hey, I'm a passenger just like you. I'm just along for the ride."

After another ten minutes hiking up the mountain, the red-dirt trail opened up to a small clearing with two small mud huts topped by thatched roofs. A pile of cold ashes sat between them, and a rack made of thin branches held two gourds tied off by dried vines.

Gabriel called out: "*Jambo! Bonjour!*" He waited for a response that didn't come. "No one here."

"Thanks, Mr. Obvious," I said and took a canteen of water from my pack, pouring a long sip into my dry mouth. I looked around the edges of the trees. "Maybe a pack of wild baboons carried them off. This is a very small village."

"Probably just a day shelter," Sheila said. "Whoever owns it is probably out in the woods farming or hunting."

Gabriel kept pacing around. "Yeah, but isn't this so amazing? Think about where we were just a week ago, back in the States, and where we are now. We're here dropping into someone else's life. A completely different world."

"Maybe they don't want us dropping in," I said, then felt a sharp urge and slide in my stomach and bowels. My body definitely hadn't yet gotten used to the local food, most of which was cooked in buttery, but very heavy palm oil. "Uh oh. I gotta go. Soon. What do I—"

"There," Sheila said and pointed behind one of the huts to a small outhouse covered in dry leaves.

"That? What do I do with that?"

"What do you mean, what do you do?" Gabriel said. "You squat. You never used an outhouse before?"

"No, I grew up with electricity and indoor plumbing, thank you." Another sharp shift in my stomach left me no choice. I pulled open the door, which was nothing more than branches tied together with vines, to reveal a series of wood planks surrounding a hole in the ground. Stuck in the crevice of one of the walls was a roll of bright-pink bath tissue (the only kind that seemed to be sold in that country), so at least I wouldn't have to use leaves. I looked back wistfully at Sheila and Gabriel. They both grinned as they watched me. Sheila had her arm wrapped around Gabriel's shoulder, and she jiggled her fingers at me in a half wave. "Good luck," she said.

I entered the "room" and shut the door. The wood planks creaked ominously as I shuffled my body, hunched down, and got into position. A few flies buzzed around my head, and after several minutes, I finished my business, cleaned up, and got ready to depart.

Suddenly, the door flung open and a tall Zairian man was in front of me, shouting and waving a machete. I jumped back in fright, then the inevitable happened: one of the wood planks gave way and my left leg went crashing through, half my body followed, and I grabbed onto the back wall to keep from completely falling into that hideous hole. The entire outhouse bent and shook as I tried to raise myself up, but my foot and leg sunk deeper, hitting the disgusting wet mess at the bottom of that hole.

The man kept pointing the machete at me saying, *"Mzungu! Mzungu!"* and then Gabriel appeared next to him, began speaking to him in a mix of French and Swahili, apologizing over and over again. Eventually, the man calmed down, a smile crept across his face, and the two of them looked at me as I desperately held onto the last branch on the back wall.

"A little help here?" I said. "Please?"

Gabriel and the man reached in and helped pull me back up to standing, but my left leg from my shin to my foot was covered in… well… all *that stuff.*

---

I had to take my pants and left shoe off, so as we climbed down the mountain, I had the unfortunate opportunity to be wearing only my boxer shorts. I followed Gabriel and Sheila as we came to a small cliff jutting out over the lake. They kept looking back at me, their lips quivering, jaws clenched tight, trying to hold it back, but finally, they both burst out laughing.

"Ha, ha. Very funny," I said.

That did nothing but send both of them into further spasms. Gabriel wrapped his arms around his stomach and fell to the ground, rolling from side to side as the laughter poured out of him. Sheila had tears streaming from her eyes, and every time she looked at me, she quickly turned her head.

I sat down on a patch of grass. "I'm glad I'm here to entertain you all."

"Stop… Stop…" Gabriel squeaked out in between gasping for breath. "Oh my God, you're killing me."

"How is it you were able to talk to that guy already?" I asked. "We haven't even been here a week."

Slowly their laughter petered out. Gabriel propped himself up on one arm. "You're welcome, by the way."

"Thanks," I said.

"I bought a pack of Berlitz tapes a few months ago. Cost me nine ninety-nine, local Waldenbooks."

"Of course you did."

Sheila looked at me, wiping away the last of her tears. "Seriously, are you ok?"

"I guess." I took my soiled boot and tried to clean it by rubbing it in the grass, but a hot ball of anger, frustration, and embarrassment rose up inside me. My teeth clenched, my face tingled and turned red, my hands suddenly wanted to hit something. I slammed the boot down on the ground as hard as I could. "MOTHER FUCKER!" I screamed, as long and loud as possible until it felt like I was about to split my throat in half.

Silence followed. Gabriel and Sheila stared at me. "Language, language," Sheila whispered.

I bent my head down and took several sharp breaths. "I need to go," I said.

"We are," Gabriel said.

"No. I mean home. Back to the States. I don't belong here."

"What?" he said and sat upright. "What do you mean? We just got here."

"This isn't right for me... I don't know what I'm doing here. I don't understand all this stuff we're supposed to be learning. Languages? We have to learn, what, two different languages, at least. I can't do that. I can't do any of this. I'm not right for this. I just need to go home." I reached into my backpack for my cigarettes and quickly lit one. Again, Gabriel and Sheila sat in silence for a moment and watched me.

Gabriel cleared his throat. "Ok... but before you decide anything, let's talk through this. What made you come here in the first place?"

I took a deep drag off the cigarette. "I don't know. I just, I wasn't going anywhere with my life back home."

"What were you doing there?"

"Nothing. After college, I was just hanging out, in Columbia, South Carolina. Working part-time in a stereo store. One night in a bar, I saw an ad on TV. People smiling and running around in a jungle. Looked fun. I had never been anywhere in the world. So I wrote for an application. I never thought I'd get accepted."

"What did you study in school?" Gabriel asked.

"Biology."

"Well, there you go. That's a good fit for what we're trying to do."

"Yeah, but that's the other thing, technically I never actually finished school."

"What do you mean by technically?" Sheila asked.

"I ran out of money. My last semester. I couldn't finish. It was mostly PE classes, but I was about four credits shy."

"Oh, for fuck's sake," she said. "Just because you didn't take Racquetball 101, that means you're not qualified? That's bullshit. Hey, at least you studied a science degree. I was an art history major. You're better qualified for this fisheries program than I am."

"I can help you," Gabriel said. "We both can. Sheila is good with languages."

"That's right. I am," she said. "Pick 'em up like candy."

I looked out at the shiny lake water, the clear blue sky, the mountains rising all around us. I shook my head. "I don't know."

"What is it you don't understand?" Gabriel asked.

"Everything. All of it! Teaching people how to raise fish? I know nothing about that."

"It's not that hard," he said. He took his hand, stabbed it into the ground, and pulled up a chunk of soil. "You take dirt. You dig a hole. You can do that, right?"

"Yes, of course," I said.

Gabriel continued: "Well, then you fill it with water. You put fish in it. They grow and make more fish. It's that simple. Then we take this out to these villages, these places in the middle of nowhere, where there are no roads, no towns, where people are barely getting by with what plants and bugs they can pull from the ground, and you inject more protein in their diet, and you give them another source of income. We can change a person's life." Gabriel suddenly jumped to his feet as if he had been sitting in a pile of fire ants. "Whole families! Whole villages! Whole valleys of fish ponds! As far as the eye can see. Whoo-hoo!"

"Whoo-hoo?" I said.

"Yeah, man, that's what I came here to do." He kicked off each of his shoes, then quickly unbuttoned his pants and pulled those off, down to his boxers.

"What the hell are you doing?"

"I'm showing solidarity with your plight, my brother. Plus, I'm getting ready to do this…"

He turned and ran and leaped off the cliff, yelling all the way to the lake water below. Sheila and I shouted after him, scurried to the edge of the cliff, and looked down. Gabriel came to the surface and shook his wet head side to side. "Yes! That was awesome!"

"Are you fucking insane?" I shouted down to him.

He splashed around in the water. "Maybe. But it feels great! Come on, Michael, jump in. You must cleanse yourself. You smell like an outhouse!"

Sheila suddenly wriggled out of her khaki shorts, down to her underwear. She looked at me, her eyes gleaming, then grabbed my hand.

"No…" I said.

"Oh yes," she said, and with a surprising amount of force for her slender frame, she yanked me with her. The two of us tumbled through the air until we smacked into the cool water. There was a brief second when I first sank below the surface, my eyes closed and my body motionless, that I wondered if I was dead. Then I came up for air.

Sheila screamed. "That was great!" She splashed water at me

and Gabriel.

The three of us were in a narrow cove, tucked away from the main part of the lake. We had the late-afternoon sun drifting down upon us, thick curtains of palm and banana trees surrounding us. For a brief moment, it felt like we had the entire country to ourselves.

Gabriel surged up, grabbed both Sheila and me on the top of the head, and gave us a proper dunking. Sheila and I returned the favor, then we all flipped and floated, spun and tumbled, over and over again.

Sheila drifted on her back. "I'm swimming in the same water as Katharine Hepburn!"

"Zaire, Africa!" Gabriel shouted to the sky. "Here we are! Get ready!"

"Hey, wait a minute," I said and stopped swimming, looking from side to side. "There aren't any crocs around here... Are there?"

# CHAPTER FOUR

I was able to master the vast complexities of setting the alarm on my watch, so for the next couple of mornings, I made it to language class on time. I decided, at least for the immediate future, not to give up and return to the States.

We all had immersive French instruction in the mornings up until noon, and I had class with Gabriel, Sheila, as well as a half dozen other volunteers from a health program. Eventually, depending upon what part of the country we were assigned to, we would all have to start learning a second language as well. There were nine regions in Zaire and five official languages. French was the language of the government and spoken in most cities and large towns. Swahili was spoken in the region of Kivu (where we were training), Shaba, and other eastern areas; Tshiluba was spoken in the two Kasai provinces (East and West); Kikongo in the region of Bandundu; Lingala in the capital Kinshasa as well as the provinces of Bas-Zaire and Équateur... *Plus*, we were told there were over two hundred tribal languages in addition to all that. It made my head spin trying to comprehend it all.

Our teacher, Ilunga, was certainly nuts—in a good way. Very high energy and interactive, he had us speaking nonstop from the moment we entered our open-air *paillotes* until we left. He always had a huge smile stretching between his large ears, always wore shiny, multicolored shirts, and had a funny habit of pronouncing the French word *oui* in an elongated, slurry fashion so that it came out sounding like: "ahh, *weeeesh*." It was a far better and more entertaining way to learn a language than the monotonous note-taking, memorize-it-for-the-test-then-immediately-forget-it method I'd had for two useless semesters of college German.

The shakiness and nervousness still came and went, mostly when I was in a crowd, such as when the lawns and courtyards filled up with people in between classes or when I stepped into the dining and recreation hall. If Gabriel or Sheila were there, their now-friendly faces helped to ease my anxiety a bit, but I decided to take Gabriel's advice and make an appointment with our chief medical officer, Doctor Peters. He was based out of the capital Kinshasa nine-hundred and fifty miles to our west, but spent most his time traveling the country, visiting the various posts and programs.

When I first stopped by the small infirmary at our compound, tucked under the long stone wall that separated the dormitory from the administrative offices, an elderly Zairian nurse told me I'd have to wait until that following Sunday when he was due back from a trip to Lubumbashi, a large city to the south of us.

So, to help calm my nerves, I (unfortunately) leaned heavily on cigarettes and chewing gum during the intervening days.

That Sunday, as I sat on the exam table in his cluttered office, I looked at the walls covered in anatomy posters one would typically find in most any physician's room, as well as alternating layers of beautifully ornate hand-carved African masks. His desk had teetering stacks of file folders, a manual typewriter, and a rotary phone that I noticed was unplugged. Above the useless phone was a wall calendar, *Best of The Far Side,* opened to November 1988. The cartoon for that month had a scraggly man staring out a window, his back to a table where several pieces of paper lay scattered about with titles such as: "The Tell-Tale Spleen," "The Tell-Tale Kidney," "The Tell-Tale Duodenum." The caption beneath the drawing read: "Edgar Allan Poe during a bout of writer's block." I smiled briefly, and then the doctor entered the room.

"Hello, Michael," he said in a Midwestern American accent that was immediately comforting to hear. "Nice to meet you. I'm Jon Peters. You can just call me Doc. Everyone else does. Not very original… but effective."

He stuck out his long weathered hand, and as I shook it, I glanced again at the calendar.

"You a fan of *The Far Side*?" he asked.

"Yes," I said. "Reminds me of—"

"Home?" Doc said and looked at me. He opened a brown file folder and took a pen from the pocket of his short-sleeve khaki shirt.

"Well, yes. College. I used to have one of those calendars in my dorm room freshman year."

"My sister sends me some every year. I have a few different offices in this country," he said and began writing. "When I get the new ones for 1989, I'll save one for you."

"Thanks, that would be great."

I watched as he continued to fill out a form in the folder. He was tall and rangy—definitely *rangy*—he looked (and sounded) like he'd be right at home on a ranch in someplace like Oklahoma, herding cattle and tossing around bales of hay. He pulled up his wheeled desk chair next to the exam table, sat down, and for several seconds just looked at me. I looked back at the wall calendar.

"So," he said. "How can I help you?"

———————•———————

**A**fter thirty minutes of poking, prodding, squeezing, and peering, Doc made several more notes in my file.

"I think Gabriel is right," he finally said.

"Really?" I replied, half-surprised, half-relieved.

"Yep. I'm not a psychiatrist, I'm a general practitioner, but I'd bet my left thumb that what's going on with you is you're having anxiety attacks, sometimes severe. You said they started a few years ago in college?"

"Yes."

"And it seems to happen mostly when you are in crowds,

especially crowds of people you don't know? And when you're in unfamiliar situations?"

"Yes, I guess so. I went to a big state university—"

"Where was that again?"

"University of Georgia."

"Go dawgs," said Doc, repeating one of my school's mottos. "You from there?"

"I was born there, but grew up in South Carolina."

"So what is it that's going on in your head when you feel this way? Do you feel threatened? Like someone might hurt you?"

"No, it's not that. It's not like I think someone is going to leap out and stab me with a knife or anything." Doc handed me a cup of water, and I took a sip. "It's more like... I feel I don't belong. Like everyone is looking at me saying 'Get him outta here!' Like I've got a big sign on my forehead. Like I'm an impostor or something and I'll soon be found out."

"And the worst of these attacks was a few days ago? When you were visiting that fish farm?"

"Yes."

"Well, if it helps, as far as the program you came here to do, you shouldn't feel like an impostor. I've seen your report from the first six weeks of training, back in the States. You've got high scores."

"Really? How is that possible?" I tried to think back to those weeks we spent along the South Carolina coast in between the towns of Georgetown and Charleston, spending days at this old plantation that had been converted into a research facility. I had only vague memories of waking up at 5 a.m., riding in a van crammed with others, and wandering around the woods and fields all day.

"Maybe it's because you are better than you think you are?" Doc said. "You should think about that when you start feeling that anxiety coming on again."

"Ok. I'll try."

"Remind yourself you do belong here. And everyone here is friendly, willing to help you, and, for the most part, nonjudgmental. We're famous for that, you know."

"Yeah. So I heard."

"And if it comes on again, just stop what you're doing and try to slow down. Slow your breathing down especially. That's what's causing the tingling and numbness. When your breathing gets going fast like that, you're hyperventilating, burning off too much carbon dioxide too quickly. I can give you a paper bag to carry around you can breathe into."

"That might look ridiculous," I said.

"True. You can also cup both hands to your mouth as well. You could also try making a very tight fist and squeezing your hand hard when you feel it coming on. That works for some people."

"Ok." I nodded.

Doc stopped a moment and gave time for everything he'd been saying to sink in. "I mean, I can give you some Valium to take, but you don't really want to do that during the day, especially if you're out hiking in the woods or, even more especially, when you're operating your motorcycle."

"Right. Of course."

"That can be very dangerous. Have you started motorcycle training yet?"

"This week, I think."

"I've been lobbying that we get rid of them. I've seen too many horrible accidents here. But I understand when you guys get out in the bush, there's no other practical way for you to get around and do your job. So if you're riding and you feel an episode coming on, stop immediately." He looked straight into my eyes. "Ok?"

"No panic attacks on motorcycles. Check."

"Good," Doc said. "You could also, *in the evenings*, try to relax with a couple of beers. That works for me. But again, not during the day and *never* on your bike."

"Yes, I know."

He smiled. "Ok. I'll be here for the next week before heading back to Kinshasa. I think we can find ways to get this under control, don't you?"

I took a deep breath and sighed out, shook my head and shoulders, trying to loosen them up. "Yes, I hope so. I think so."

"All right, because if it does keep happening, I'll have to consider sending you home, probably for good."

"No, I understand. I'll work on it. Feel a bit better already."

"Good. I'd hate to see you come all this way and not have things work out for you. You've got a lot going for you, remember that. You're *not* an impostor."

"Not an impostor. That's good to know," I said and stood up. "Ok, thanks for all your help."

"That's what they pay me the big bucks for." He motioned to the calendar on the wall. "And I'll send you a new *Far Side* when I get one."

"That would be great."

He put my file on the large pile of other ones on his desk and escorted me to the door. "By the way, you've been taking your malaria meds on a regular basis?"

"The chloroquine? Yes."

"Any issues with that? Any side effects?"

"No, not really."

"Good. Keep that up. You don't want to mess around with malaria. That's nasty business. We've been hearing reports of resistant strains popping up in places, so any problems, report them right away to your supervisor. We're tracking that."

"Got it," I said and stopped in the doorway. A large group of people was sitting on the lawn just outside his door, lounging in the sun like crocodiles on rocks. Some were sleeping, others reading, one girl was strumming a guitar.

Doc smiled and put his hand on my shoulder. "All right, Michael, take care… Knock 'em dead," he said and gave me a little push forward.

I walked out into the long green courtyard, looked up at the deep blue and yellow sky. I lit a cigarette and looked down the hill to the *réfectoire*. I could see, through the windows, that it too was crowded as usual with folks studying, talking, and playing chess and other games. I really wanted a cup of hot tea. I took a deep breath, squeezed my hand hard several times, then walked down the lawn and entered the swirling room.

# CHAPTER FIVE

The next afternoon, following language class and lunch, I met Gabriel for one of his promised one-on-one tutoring sessions, to help get me up to speed with all the technical stuff I should have been retaining in my brain, but which instead had been flowing in then quickly disappearing, sizzling away like drops of water on a hot stove. We walked up a hill behind the dormitory, through long gardens of corn, manioc, sorghum, and other plants used as training tools for the agricultural programs. Off to the side, near the far edge of the compound, was a medium-sized, rectangular fish pond, drained and currently empty.

"So, how did you turn in your final school transcripts if you didn't actually finish?" Gabriel asked as we came to a stop at the closest bank of the pond.

"I fudged it a bit. Created a false last page to make it look like I completed those classes."

He dropped his backpack to the ground and squatted down in the neatly trimmed grass. "Nice. An evil genius. I love it. So, if I ever need a fake passport, you're the guy I should see?"

I laughed. "Sure. I'll give you a good discount."

"Ok," he said. "So take a look around at this pond and tell me what you see."

"You sound just like the trainers."

"This is what you wanted, right?"

"Sure." I walked around the edge of the pond, looking down into the exposed muddy bottom. At one end was a compost bin made of tree branches tied together, the other end a fat bamboo pipe jutted out from the wall. "Uh, yeah. It's a fish pond. It's a rectangle."

"See, I could tell you *almost* finished college," Gabriel said. He then tossed me his walking stick, and I caught it midair. "Here. I made a present for you."

"A stick. You shouldn't have."

"It's a special stick. Look at the markings."

I saw it had been notched in three places, and he had carved the numbers twenty-five, fifty, and seventy-five at each mark. I still wasn't sure what to do with it and looked at Gabriel.

"Measure the pond," he said.

"Ahh, it's a meter stick. Got it."

"You're impressing me more and more."

I used the stick along the length and width edges, flipping it over and over, counting off the distance of each. "Ten meters by twenty," I said triumphantly.

"Right," Gabriel said. "Two hundred square meters. That's the standard size we want for what we're doing. Any smaller, the harvest isn't really worth it. And any larger, it becomes difficult to maintain. So what do we put in the pond?"

"I know this one: water."

"And…?"

"Fish."

"What kind of fish?"

"Tilapia, which I've never heard of by the way. What the hell is Tilapia?"

"You ever go bream fishing as a kid, with a cane pole and crickets?"

"A couple of times."

"Tilapia is like a tropical bream. They grow fast, resistant to disease. We do the initial stocking of the pond for the farmer. About one fingerling per one square meter, so for a pond this size, we stock it with two hundred fingerlings."

I stepped into the pond along the soft bottom. "Right, I remember that. The harvest cycle is six months?"

Gabriel nodded. "Yep. After six months, you'll have three generations. The initial fingerlings will be full-grown, then you'll have a midsize second generation, then you'll have another group of fingerlings. The whole idea is to make this self-sustaining for the farmer, so that he can keep that last group and keep restocking his own pond. The rest he can eat and sell." He motioned to me. "How deep is the pond?"

I put the stick in the ground, bent down, and saw the top was nearly level with the top of the pond bank. "One meter."

"Right," he said. "Now this is important: look at the sides, what do you see?"

All four sides sloped downward to the bottom at a long angle. "Ok, yeah. I know this. We dig the sides at a three-to-one angle. So three meters."

"Why?"

I stood and looked and looked at the dirt. My mind went blank. I shrugged my shoulders.

"Babies," he said. "That's where the momma fish will lay their eggs. They will use their tails and create small indentations in the sides of the pond banks and lay their eggs closer to the surface of the water."

"Fantastic," I said.

For the next half hour, we went over all sorts of things: soil types, water quality, algae blooms, pH balance, with Gabriel drilling me with questions over and over to make sure what he was telling me was actually sinking in. We came to a stopping point, and I grabbed my canteen out of my pack, took a sip, and offered some to Gabriel. I walked over to where he was, climbed out of the pond, and sat down on the bank next to him.

"It's not so hard, is it?" he said after taking a sip.

I groaned a bit. "I guess. It's one thing to sit here and talk about it and have you feed me the answers. Another to be out on my own..."

"You'll be fine."

"You study this stuff in school?" I asked.

"Kind of. I was wildlife management."

"Where?"

"Virginia Tech."

"Hokies. Nice."

"You?" asked Gabriel.

"Bulldawgs. UGA."

"Athens? That's supposed to be a great town. Lots of good music comes out of there. You like R.E.M.?"

"Yeah. My senior year, I lived next door to the drummer."

"Nice!"

He handed back the canteen, and we stayed silent a bit, a few dragonflies buzzing around our heads. "So what did your family say when you told them you were coming here?" I asked.

Gabriel didn't immediately answer and, instead, pulled a few blades of grass from the ground. "Well... My dad disappeared when I was about seven. Last I heard he was in prison somewhere in Ohio for attempted murder."

"Oh. Wow. Sorry."

"Yeah. And my mom, she's... Well, she tried, but she's pretty fragile. I don't see her much. My sister and I were pretty much raised by my aunt, near Virginia Beach. My sister didn't really get it. She's a telephone operator. Not the most adventurous sort. But my aunt was all-in. She's obsessed with *National Geographic*, the magazine. She has thirty years of issues categorized in her basement. I read almost every one growing up. Other kids were into Spider-Man and Batman. I was looking at maps and photos of cave dwellers and such. And that show on TV, *Big Blue Marble*—"

"Oh yeah! I remember that show. About how kids lived in different countries."

"Yeah," Gabriel said. "I was crazy about it. I knew since middle school I wanted to do something like this. Travel the world. After this project, I might try to get on with other groups, other places. I can see myself living the life of a permanent expat."

"That'd be fun."

"Yeah, I might not ever go back to the States. Nothing really for me at home anyway."

I nodded in agreement. "I kind of have the same situation. I—"

Before I could finish, we heard Sheila calling out for us from down the hill. Soon she, Robert, and our teacher Ilunga joined us beside the pond. Sheila came and wrapped her arms around Gabriel and gave him a kiss on the cheek. "You kids having fun?"

"I'm doing my best to whip him into shape," Gabriel said.

"We're heading into town. Ilunga is going to show us the main city market. Says he knows some great restaurants down there."

Robert chimed in. "Yeah, we're gonna get some stewed monkey balls or something."

"*Vraiment!*" Ilunga said. "No monkey balls. Maybe monkey brains."

"Mmm…" she said. "You guys game?"

"Sure," Gabriel said and stood up, brushing grass off his pants legs. "Mike?"

"How can I resist?"

Sheila reached out and helped pull me to my feet. "Did you

learn a lot?"

"More than I could have imagined."

"Hope you took good mental notes," Gabriel said. "There'll be a test later."

I laughed and rolled my eyes. All five of us began the march down the hill to the front gate.

"I'm serious…" Gabriel said.

---

If walking down the street in a city like Bukavu was an assault on the senses, diving into a raucous open-air central market in the middle of Africa was like an atom bomb going off. A wild, swirling, teeming, teetering, muddy explosion of color and noise; pungent scents of raw, bloody animal flesh—goat, cow, pig, boar, antelope, chicken, snake, and various mysterious types of bush animals—mixed with the soothing wafts of that meat roasting over a charcoal fire. The sour scent of manioc, the long bark-covered roots and flat green leaves both used as the main food staple in most villages, mixed with sweet odors of pineapple, mango, and banana. Dried beans, corn, peanuts, plantains. Rusty piles of spare car parts next to bicycle chains. Notebooks and pencils for schoolchildren next to piles of sardine tins and cans of evaporated milk. Stall after rickety stall sold bright fabric, hundreds of exploding patterns used for women's dresses and shirts for men. Some had tailors on-site who would cut and measure it for you. Side-by-side were stalls selling second-hand clothes mostly shipped in from the States. Robert and Ilunga stopped at one vendor, a young Zairian girl with big, bright eyes, selling dozens of T-shirts hanging from a cross branch.

"Hey, check these out!" Robert yelled. He pointed to a white T-shirt with the cartoon character Tweety Bird, next to a blue T-shirt for the rock band Van Halen, next to a red T-shirt for Ohio State University. "Van Halen? Seriously? In the middle of the Congo?" He quickly turned his attention to the pretty young girl, leaning his elbow on her table, stammering through a mix of broken French. Ilunga helped translate.

Sheila and I roamed through tables of souvenirs: carved figurines in dark black wood next to bright-green malachite, the brilliant soft stone formed into all sorts of trinkets like jewelry boxes and chessboards. She watched Robert flirting with the girl, smirked, and shook her head. "He's hopeless."

A few feet down an alley, Gabriel was surrounded by a circle of young kids, most of them barefoot with dusty clothes. He was telling them a story, shaking his body in wild gyrations that sent the children squealing and laughing. Several of them grabbed his hands and arms and began to lead him away.

"Gabriel, where are you going?" Sheila yelled.

He turned his head back toward us as the pack of children pushed and pulled him forward. "They said there's a python here as big as a house. They want to show me. I'll be back soon!" Gabriel turned down a muddy corner and disappeared.

Sheila smirked, again, and shook her head again. "He's even more hopeless."

"Yeah. He's nuts," I said. We slowly strolled past each table and came to a pile of carved masks, similar to those on Doc Peters' office walls. "How long you two been together?"

Sheila tilted her head up and squinched her nose and lips. "Are we together?" she asked, mostly to herself. "I guess we are... I don't know really. I guess we started hanging out near the end of the stateside training, before we flew here. To be honest, I don't really remember when exactly it started." She picked up a scowling wooden mask and put it to her face. "Whaddya think? Is it an improvement?"

"Definitely."

She swatted my arm and put it down. "You know, I'm sorry. But I don't really remember you from the training back home."

"Yeah, I kind of kept to myself. Plus, I was in the overflow group. I wasn't at the nice campground cabins in the woods like you were. We were the ones stuck at that rinky-dink motel in Georgetown."

"Ugh, the one next to the paper mill?"

"Yes, we had those lovely fumes to breathe in every day. Maybe that's why I can't remember most of what we learned."

"Ha! Yeah, that makes sense..." She looked down the alley for Gabriel, but he was still out of sight. "Who knows what will happen, though. With Gabriel. I mean, we might be stationed on opposite sides of the country."

We came to a table with piles of bags and hats made from woven tan-and-black dried straw called raffia. "Can't you request you guys be posted close to each other?"

"I guess… ooh! Hats! I need a good hat." A plump Zairian woman in a green-and-yellow dress sat at the table and gave us a warm smile. Sheila rummaged through the pile and found a wide-brimmed sun hat. "Perfect." She put it on and twisted her body from side to side. "What do you think?"

"Looks good."

"Need to protect our skin. Just because we'll be living on the equator for the next two years, doesn't mean I plan to get skin cancer. I told Gabriel he needs one, but as usual he won't listen to me… Here, you need one too." She dove her hand in the pile and pulled out one in the shape of a cowboy hat and plopped it on my head. "Looks good!" She turned to the woman and pointed at me. "*Oui?*" she asked her.

The woman smiled and nodded. "*Oui, c'est bon.*"

"I like it. You look like a Congo cowboy." She reached up and gently adjusted the hat on my head, her right forearm brushing against my cheek. She paused a moment. "Yes. Looks good." She turned to the woman and reached in her backpack for a wad of Zairian cash. "*Combien? Pour le deux?*"

"No, I can pay for it," I said and started to dig in my pockets.

Sheila reached out and grabbed my arm. "No, I got it. You can thank me forty years from now when your skin is still intact."

"*Quatre cents* Zaires," said the woman. Sheila gave her four orange-colored one-hundred-Zaire notes. The woman smiled and took the money. "*Merci,*" she said. She looked at me, then back to Sheila. "*Il a les beaux yeux,*" the woman said.

Sheila stopped and looked at me as well. For a brief moment, her face fluttered somewhat nervously. *"Oui,"* she said to the woman.

"What did she say?" I asked.

Sheila hurriedly stuck the leftover cash back in her bag. "She said you have nice eyes."

# CHAPTER SIX

**It's** hard to fathom that we were only at that training compound in Bukavu for six weeks. So much happened, so much was jam-packed into each and every day and night, that in retrospect it had to be an illusion, some kind of Einsteinian trick that bent space and time, stretching it way past the normal laws of physics into a quantum package of infinite reach.

Thanksgiving came and went. The Belgian nuns who ran the dining hall, under the strict supervision of their seventy-year-old leader Ma Suer, did their best to give us some kind of American-style feast that day, but with pheasant instead of turkey, and without football, gravy boats, and the Macy's parade, it just wasn't the same. For most of us, it didn't matter too much, so wrapped up were we all in the strange new land we had adopted for the next two years.

I started to get better acclimated to the food. Breakfast in the dining hall was usually simple fare like hard-boiled eggs, hot tea, and toast with homemade jam—either strawberry or orange marmalade. Lunches and dinners were a bit heavier, with chicken, rabbit, or goat cooked in palm oil and hot pepper sauce, often with sides of fried plantains, beans and rice, or stewed manioc greens. We were also getting introduced to the infamous *fufu* (or *luku*, depending on what part of the country we were going to), a giant spongy dough ball made from ground manioc flour. It came in large pale, grayish-white lumps in bowls, and we would tear off chunks in our hands, then dip it in whatever meat or vegetable dish we had in front of us, clamp the two together, and pop it in our mouths. We did often get fresh-made strawberry ice cream, however, brought from a Belgian abbey in the center of town. That was always a welcome treat.

In between meals, the *réfectoire* was the center of activity. It was wide, spacious, and comfortable, decorated simply with bright African cloth hanging from the tall windows. There were always crowds studying their training manuals, reading books, or playing old donated board games like Scrabble or Sorry.

Sheila was the reigning grand master in chess, as she remained undefeated the entire time we were there. I came the closest to knocking her off her throne, one evening cornering her king and battling her to a stalemate. It was also where she, and often Ilunga, met me to help with extra language instruction, quizzing me with vocabulary flash cards and pushing me with conversation practice.

The good news was that on the Monday after Thanksgiving, Gabriel, Sheila, and I found out that we had all been assigned to posts in the same region, the central-western province of Bandundu. So that meant the three of us would be together, not only for the rest of training, but for the next two years. It also meant that we had the great fortune to begin our second language class, Kikongo, learning from none other than crazy-fun Ilunga, who came from the city of Kiwkit, capital of Bandundu.

Gabriel was nonstop, focused, and driven to learn everything he could (and beyond) about our program: always reading, drawing plans, and building models of connected fish farm systems out of clay. Sometimes, he seemed to go days without sleep. On several occasions I got up in the middle of the night to use the restroom, and as I walked to the lavatory at the end of the long dark corridor, a light coming from Gabriel's room would often be the only thing shining in the hallway. I always wondered what genius things he was up to at those hours.

He and I met a few more times at the training pond, and he actually did give me tests. It was kind of annoying but worth it, for by the time all of us in the fisheries program had to do a mock pond stocking and a mock harvest, standing knee-deep in the water, running tests of pH, looking at compost bins, scooping up and sorting the silvery fish with handheld seine nets, those were the moments that I first began to feel that I actually knew what the hell I was doing.

But it didn't stop there: the process of getting us "post-ready"—ready to be dropped off in remote areas to live and work completely on our own—was multifaceted. We took frequent day-trips out to visit volunteers living in nearby villages, taking long hikes through the cool green undulating mountains to see some of the different programs people were doing and the different ways they lived. One woman lived in a mud hut in a tucked-away forest village, past long emerald fields of tea plants, near a short rock waterfall. Another volunteer taught at a high school and lived in a small town in a concrete house with part-time electricity spun by communal gas generators.

One of the most amazing and emotionally harrowing experiences was when each of us were dropped off alone in a village to spend the night with a local family. I was bouncing around in the back of one of the cargo trucks for a good hour and a half, not even sure which direction we had headed from our compound, the tires spinning around the edges of wide valleys, until I arrived in a flat clearing with about a dozen houses made of mud bricks and tin roofs. I was allowed to bring only one small bag of clothes and toiletries, which I clutched tightly as we came to a stop in front of the farthest home.

I was introduced to a middle-aged Zairian man named Kimbandu. He had large ears and a gray-speckled beard, and he seemed just as nervous as I was. I was told he spoke no French, no Swahili, no Kikongo, only his local tribal language, so that meant we would be unable to speak to each other; and that was the whole point. As the sun disappeared over a sharp hill, that truck pulled away and Kimbandu ushered me inside his sparse three-room home and showed me a short bamboo cot in the corner that would be my bed for the night. The pointing, grunting, hand signals, and awkward smiles between us began in earnest. He offered me a wooden mug of milky-white, sweet and sour palm wine, and then he took me on a walking tour of the village, beneath a deep-ink, moonless sky, until we arrived at what I assumed was the village chief's house.

Most everyone who lived there was sitting at a row of long wooden tables in the sandy yard, waiting for me to join them. As I approached and felt that familiar fluttering in my chest, I clenched my hands into tight fists just like Doc had recommended. It helped. My mini panic attack eased up a bit, and after I sat down, the villagers soon began to pass around bowls of *fufu* and red plastic dishes of stewed chicken in spicy peanut sauce. The cool mountain air rolled across the ground, and the only light we had was from the flickering yellow glow of two small cooking fires. I had arrived with a full pack of cigarettes; within about two hours, between smoking them myself and giving them to my hosts, it was completely empty, though they served their purpose to ease my anxiety as well as my guests'. It also made me very popular.

———————•———————

The other big issue we had to deal with was motorcycle training. All of us who would be placed in remote areas would be issued our own cycles, Yamaha 125-horsepower dirt bikes. We were told in most places outside major towns and cities there would be no paved roads, so we had to learn how to ride and navigate safely through various types of terrain: slick red clay or thick sandy roads or washed-out paths covered in deep mud. Quite a few times at our training fields, I hit a soft patch of sand only to have the front wheel of the bike come to an abrupt halt while my body kept going, flying over the handlebars, leaving me facedown in the dirt.

We also were taught how to completely break down the bike and take apart the engine, how to clean and fix it, and how to clear dirt clogs from the fuel line and sand from the carburetor. Like most everything we did, Gabriel breezed through it all while I struggled; and as always, like in most everything we did, he was there, ready, willing, and able to pound some knowledge into my shaky brain and help pull me through.

In the evenings after classes, I used some of the free time I had to read up on the history of this country that would now be my home. There was a robust lending library in the *réfectoire*, and on the shelves, I found what looked like a tattered old textbook from the late seventies called, appropriately, *Sub-Saharan Africa*. The section on the Congo/Zaire was one hundred and sixty pages long. I would sit on my bed in my room, windows open to let in the crisp night air (mosquitoes and malaria be damned) with the lake water shimmering far below. I read about ancient kingdoms, Portuguese explorers, Stanley and Livingstone, and of course the ruthless King Leopold of Belgium, who carved up this land for his own profit, following the practice of most all colonial occupiers by drawing arbitrary boundaries, trapping over two hundred different tribes speaking two hundred different languages in an artificially created country. I saw photos of piles of hands hacked off the arms of inefficient rubber-plantation workers, white managers in pith helmets standing proudly beside them.

I also read about the rise of the independence movement in the late 1950s and early 1960s and the epic battle between the two men who claimed this country for their own—Patrice Lumumba and the current Big Man, Mobutu Sese Seko. We had been told early in our training never to speak about it in public, never to mention the name of Lumumba, because we never could know who was really listening. I soon understood why. It was the Cold War in a microcosm. It was East versus West. The US vs. the USSR. It was the paranoia of the domino theory run wild, that if one African country went Communist the rest would soon follow. Lumumba was Socialist, left-leaning. Communist forces had invaded Angola to the south (and were still fighting a civil war up to that moment.) Mobutu had cozied up to the West and gone all-in that he would be coddled and propped up as a strongman counterpoint to Soviet expansion. He was right. Patrice Lumumba was assassinated in 1961. Many people claimed the CIA was behind it.

After that, the Big Man wasted no time in seizing total control, turning the vast country into his own personal fiefdom. The name changes started in 1966: Léopoldville became Kinshasa, Élisabethville became Lubumbashi, and Stanleyville became Kisangani. In October 1971, he renamed the country the Republic of Zaire. He ordered government officials to drop their European names, and Western attire, such as neckties, were banned. Men in positions of authority or power were forced to wear short-sleeve and pant combinations known as *abacosts*—shorthand for the French phrase *à bas le costume* ("down with the suit"). All power and all riches flowed directly to Mobutu and his family. Lavish presidential palaces were built in the middle of jungles. Enemies were killed or bought off. And the West turned a blind eye, as long as he let them play their political games.

That was the state of the country we had come to. At that moment, of course, none of us (including, I'm sure, *him*) had any idea that the Cold War as we had known it for the past forty years had only about a year left to live, and that the crumbling of the Berlin Wall twelve months later would eventually lead to the disappearance of his power and influence, followed by chaos, civil war, and death. Our job was to keep quiet, keep our heads down, and do what we could to help maybe only one person, maybe only one family, maybe only one village improve their lot as much as we could. That was the only way what we were doing made any sense. If you looked at the big picture, you'd kind of go insane.

———————•———————

As busy as we were, there was plenty of time to have fun. Doc was right: everyone was really nice. I can't think of a single unpleasant exchange I had with anyone I met while we were training, which went a long way to help tamp down much of my nervousness. Those last couple of weeks in Bukavu were some of the most relaxed and enjoyable I ever had in my life.

Music was huge. Music was everywhere. Walking through town, almost every shop, bar, restaurant, or roadside shack had *Musique Zairoise* playing nonstop and full blast. I started to get into it, and on one of our trips to the city market, I bought a bootleg mixtape from one of the music vendors (most all music there was bootleg—no Tower Records anywhere within a couple thousand miles). It was packed with songs from the big acts of that time: the two massively popular female superstars Tshala Muana and M'bilia Bel; the big soukous dance bands OK Jazz, Choc Stars, and Zaiko Langa Langa; the male Afro-swing kings Pepe Kalle, Papa Wemba, and the crooner Koffi Olomide (one of my favorites), whom some called the Congolese Sinatra.

Most songs were sung in Lingala, so I usually didn't understand the lyrics, but many of them incorporated the ubiquitous chant *"Kwassa! Kwassa!"* which basically meant "Dance! Dance!" It was a great time when we occasionally went to some of the clubs in town, and the dance floor, sometimes just a square patch of sand under an open night sky, would be packed with Zairians and expats alike, swaying and chanting along to the songs.

There was plenty of Western music around as well. Most everyone at the compound had brought a tape player from home, so a walk down the dormitory hallway past each room would be like strolling through a giant jukebox. American and British (and Australian) pop/rock was king, with The Cure, The Church, 10,000 Maniacs, The Waterboys, R.E.M., Eurythmics, Tracy Chapman ( I must have heard her song "Fast Car" four to five times a day), The Cult, Peter Gabriel, INXS, and as always, Bob Marley drifting out of each open doorway.

One of my last purchases before leaving the States was a dual cassette tape/shortwave radio combo I'd found at an Army/Navy store in downtown Charleston for about twenty-five dollars. One of the best investments I could have made as I was able to make taped copies of everyone's music for myself and Gabriel and Sheila. In a few weeks' time, once I was on my own in my village, I would realize how important that connection to home would be.

In addition to music, sports were big as well. Frisbee, soccer, kickball, Wiffle ball, volleyball—the large field below the *réfectoire* was usually packed in between and after classes with teachers and staff joining in with all the volunteers, mixing up teams. Ilunga never missed a chance to show off his athletic skills, and in fact, he was pretty much with us in everything we did. He was near our age, twenty-five years old, and loved spending time with us to help improve his English. Quite a few nights, he and I would hang out in one of the *paillotes*, drinking sodas and smoking cigarettes, and he would ask me about life in the States.

"Everyone here thinks the streets of America are truly paved in gold," he said. "They think it is like in the movies."

"Definitely not," I said. "I mean, there are lots of nice places. But to be honest, I haven't been to many of them. Spent most my life in only two towns."

"And you are from the South of Caroline?"

"South Carolina, yes."

"But black people there now are free?"

"Well, yes. I mean, it's not perfect, but better than it used to be."

"Still, a black man in America can become rich and powerful if he works hard enough. Muhammad Ali. Quincy Jones."

"Quincy Jones? Nice! How do you know about him?"

"I have seen 'We Are the World.' Here, it is not possible. Only if you are in the president's family. All the money goes to him. The rest of us are left with nothing."

I looked around the dark courtyard, making sure no one was lurking around. "We were told not to talk about stuff like that."

Ilunga laughed. "You are safe with me… But yes, when you are on the street, that is probably a good idea. Best not to discuss such things."

One weekend, Ilunga led us on a hitchhiking trip across the border into Rwanda, which lay on the other side of Lake Kivu. We took a cab to the edge of town, paid two hundred Zaires each for a one-day visa, then marched across and found a half-empty farm truck that was heading into the lush mountains. There was a park only about fifteen kilometers away, full of their famous golden monkeys. We hiked around in a forest of bizarrely shaped, twisted, and twirling trees—the Dr. Seuss forest, I dubbed it—and had a picnic of cheese-and-avocado sandwiches. The monkeys had absolutely no fear and came right up to us, trying to snatch the food from our hands.

We only spent half a day in Rwanda, but at the time we went, it certainly was quiet, clean, and almost quaint compared to the crazy dusty energy of Zaire. I could never have thought that six years after my trip, a cloud of pure evil would descend upon that tiny country and it would erupt into one of the most brutal waves of genocide and slaughter ever seen on earth.

———————————

But of all the things we did, learned, and experienced during those six weeks, nothing comes close to the afternoon we spent hanging out in the middle of the forest with a family of eighteen eastern lowland gorillas.

The day after Christmas, Gabriel, Sheila, Robert, Ilunga, and I hired a car to drive about an hour north of Bukavu to Kahuzi-Biega National Park. There had been a vibrant holiday party the night before, and most of us were hungover (except for Gabriel, who rarely drank). Rolling wisps of fog drifted halfway between the gray sky and brick-red ground. We stood at the entrance to the forest, while Ilunga negotiated a fair price for a guide to take us on a hike deep into the woods.

Though it was called a national park, it had no real structure like you would see in the States. There was a small wooden sign next to a narrow thatched shelter where two skinny men, barefoot, dressed in torn shirts and shorts, and each holding machetes, waited all day for someone to come hire them to go tracking through one of the last open preserves of the great beasts.

We each paid five hundred Zaires to a man named T'Chamba and his younger brother Layne. Before we started down the trail, they repeated several times to Ilunga, who translated to us, that there was no guarantee we would find the animals. This was not a zoo. There were no fences or boundaries. This was the real living forest, and it was the animals' home, not ours. We were guests; if we did find them, we had to respect them, and if either of our guides said it was time to get out, then it was time to get out.

Anticipation and excitement swirled in our aching heads. The worn footpath didn't last long, and soon we were deep into the woods where there were no trails, floating across thick green carpets of earth, surrounded by tall tangled trees. T'Chamba took the lead, hacking away at the thick brush, looking closely at the ground for what I supposed were footprints or dung markings. His brother Layne protected us from the rear. They said there were wild boars and lots of snakes to take heed of as well.

We marched for over an hour, seeming to zig and zag back and forth until we came to what looked like an impassable forest wall. T'Chamba suddenly stopped, turned, and motioned for us to be quiet. I swallowed empty air in my dry throat. He carefully began to cut away at the wall, chipping branches and trunks until he had created an opening about half the width of a normal door. He told us to get in a thin single line, and we followed as he turned his body to the side and bit by bit shuffled through.

Do you remember that moment when you first saw *The Wizard of Oz*? That moment after the tornado, when Dorothy— her world still in black and white—opens the front door, and there, in all its glistening Technicolor glory, was the world of Oz?

That's kind of how it was with us when, after we slithered through that narrow door in the bush, we were suddenly in a brilliant wide green clearing in the forest, and we saw, about twenty feet in front of us, a massive silverback gorilla. You could hear the oxygen get sucked out of each of our lungs. He was twice the size of Gabriel, with hands that could crush one of our heads like we could crush a grape. He simply sat on the ground, pulling leaves from a small tree sapling, chewing them in his gargantuan jaws. If he noticed us, at first he didn't seem to care.

Soon we saw three younger gorillas, thick balls of black fur, rolling on the emerald earth behind him. Then, we looked to our right and left and saw six more members of his family, different sizes, their long arms dangling and draping in the grass. Above us, we heard leaves rustling, and we looked up and saw a couple of mommas and six babies lounging and slowly swinging across the tree branches. One of the moms was straddling behind her child, her long fingers picking dirt and leaves out of the hair on the young one's back.

They were all around us, and as T'Chamba had said, this was no zoo. There were no fences or cages. We had entered their house, and we were right there, right in the middle, among them, beside them. Sheila carefully pulled a camera from the front pocket of her backpack and, as quietly as she could, pressed the shutter over and over again. The great silverback decided to move, rising to his thick legs and settling behind a bush, partially out of sight. T'Chamba walked on the tips of his toes to the bush and slowly cut a few of the branches to give us a better look at

Big Poppa. This seemed to be the first time he acknowledged our presence because he stopped eating, turned his head, looked right at us, then frowned and grunted. He rose to his haunches again and moved to another bush, so he wouldn't have to see us; and again, T'Chamba followed and clipped away a sight line so we could take pictures.

Poppa was not happy. The muscles in his shoulders and neck tensed and rippled. His fangs gleamed as he grunted, once, twice, then suddenly he roared and sprang to his feet, towering above us, beating his chest with his powerful fists, jutting his head toward us, his breath like a hot furnace blasting into my eyes. He seemed to block out the very light from the sky. Then he suddenly stopped, stood still, gave us one more angry scowl, and one more deep grunt of what was clearly disgust, before he turned and walked away from us, disappearing into the forest.

Message clearly received.

*"Hakuna zaidi!"* shouted T'Chamba. *"Hakuna zaidi!"* ("No more! No more!")

He quickly pushed us back through the jungle doorway we had come through.

"That's it!" Ilunga said. "Time to go home."

Eight of the most amazing minutes in my life.

# CHAPTER SEVEN

"Ok, you guys ready?" Gabriel asked. "We're on the homestretch now. Who wants to go first?"

It was near 10 p.m. on a drizzling night. Gabriel, Sheila, and I had taken over an empty corner in the dining hall to practice our final presentations, which were due the next day. It was basically our exit exam in language class. Ilunga had assigned each of us a five-minute lecture on a subject we had studied in school, but the catch was we had to give it twice, in both French *and* Kikongo. We were supposed to keep photos and other visual aids to a minimum. It was all about the words, grammar, and pronunciation.

We had plugged in one of the silver electric kettles, so we had hot water for tea. One of the young Zairian girls who worked in the kitchen had also been nice enough to leave us a pack of shortbread cookies before she knocked off for the night, and Gabriel had snatched a rolling chalkboard from the supply closet. We had spent the past couple of hours poring over our notes and putting the last touches on our speeches. Sheila had chosen to talk about Pablo Picasso. I had decided to explain simple genetics, dominant and recessive genes with blue and brown eyes. Gabriel was going to explain the standard ecological water cycle on earth—evaporation, condensation, and so forth.

"I'll go," Sheila said and stood up in front of the board. She shuffled her note cards and cleared her throat. I set the timer on my wristwatch, then gave her the signal to start. *"La vie incroyable de Pablo Picasso..."* she began, somewhat softly.

"Louder," Gabriel said.

Sheila's voice rose an octave, but she still stared at her notes. *"Il était un artiste majeur..."*

"Chin! Lift your chin, so we can see your face," Gabriel said.

She lifted her face and stared at him, her jaw grinding, her gray eyes slightly wounded. Gabriel silently raised his eyebrows as if to say: *Come on now. Get going.*

It felt like I suddenly had a glimpse of a deeply private moment between them. She started over, this time her head and body more open and her voice stronger. As she went through her speech, Gabriel continued to egg her on, shouting words of encouragement like "There you go!" and "Now you got it!" until, at the 5:01 mark, she came to a close.

"Great," he said. "Now do it in Kikongo."

She took several deep breaths and picked up a different stack of notecards. *"Pablo Picasso ikele artiste mbote mingi..."* she began. Sheila struggled a bit at the beginning, but Gabriel helped to correct her mistakes. Once she got past that, she really hit a groove and sailed through the rest of it. When she finished,

Gabriel leaped to his feet, ran over, and lifted her up in celebration, tossing her, not on purpose I was sure, a bit roughly.

Sheila pried herself free from his long arms. "Ok, Jesus. Thanks. I didn't just cure cancer, for fuck's sake," she said, then sat down at the far end of the dining table.

Gabriel turned his lightning-blue eyes on me. "Mike, you ready?"

I had several false starts and stumbled over some rough pronunciation, but I eventually got through both versions of my explanation of the various dominant and recessive combinations, BB, bb, Bb—*B* standing for brown and *b* for blue—and why a man and woman, each with brown eyes, can still have a blue-eyed child. Gabriel gave me a very hard high five slap, which left my hand bright red, as his vote of approval. Sheila applauded and said she actually learned something new.

We were the last group left in the entire *réfectoire* and now had the whole long building to ourselves. The rain outside had changed to a steady downpour, pinging off the red stucco roof. It was near eleven o'clock when Gabriel stood up to begin his presentation. He didn't use any notes. He calmly, confidently, almost flawlessly went through his speech in French. Without waiting, he then launched right into the Kikongo version, and I could have sworn I was listening to Ilunga speak, so perfect was Gabriel's accent and intonation. When he finished, Sheila and I just sat there, somewhat stunned.

"Whew! That was fun," Gabriel shouted and paced in front of the chalkboard. "But I can do better. I flubbed a couple of places.

Especially in the French. Don't have my rolling *r*'s down. Mike, set up the timer I want to go again."

"Gabriel, it was great," Sheila said.

"Yeah, but not perfect."

I reset the timer on my watch and gave him the signal, and like a whirling dervish, he tore through both versions of his speech again, and surprisingly, he was right: this time it was even better. At the end, he sat down on the dining table bench, for about twenty seconds, before he shot to his feet again.

"No. Still not right. Need to do it again. Mike? Count me off."

Sheila, who had begun to gather her things to leave, froze in place. She looked over at me, a mixture of annoyance and disgust. "Gabriel, it's getting late—"

"It's fine if you want to leave," he said and prowled the floor, shaking out his arms and hands like he was loosening up for a boxing match. "Mike? Tell me when?"

Sheila gave in and settled in her seat. I gave Gabriel the go-ahead, but this time, as he went through it, he started to stammer in places, started to lose track of what he was saying. Abruptly, he slapped the chalkboard and shouted both at himself and me.

"That was horrible! That sucked! Mike, start me over!"

I reset my watch again, and again he started off strong, the French version was pretty good, but not near as good as the first two times he did it. When he began the Kikongo version, he suddenly stopped moving and stared at the floor, his mind seeming to go blank for a few seconds.

"Dammit! No good. From the beginning. Mike?"

I looked at Sheila, whose expression had now decidedly turned from anger and irritation to shock and confusion.

Once, twice, three, four more times Gabriel tried to rip through his presentation, but each time they seem to deteriorate further. His agitation and anger continued to build, and it quickly turned inward; he started cursing at himself as he paced back and forth in front of us.

It was now just past midnight. "Gabriel..." I tried to reach him, but he ignored me. Wherever he was at that moment, he was in deep. His fast pacing began to slow. He turned away from us, facing the corner of the room, almost like a grade-school student being punished by his teacher. "Not good enough," he muttered. "I can do better. Have to do better." His whole body suddenly seemed to collapse on itself, his shoulders slumping. He leaned against the wall and ran his hands over his face.

Sheila and I stood up, knowing something needed to be done. I took a step, and then Sheila moved all the way across the room and put her hands gently on Gabriel's shoulders.

"Sweetie, it's fine. It's ok. You did... a great job."

Gabriel shook his head. "No, not good enough." His face, usually so robust and crackling with energy, now seemed sunken and pale. "I need to do better."

Sheila pressed her palms to his cheeks. "Tomorrow, honey. It's late. We have plenty of time to practice tomorrow. You did great. Michael thinks so as well." She looked over her shoulder, needing to reel in my support.

I took another couple of steps forward. "Yes, Gabriel. It was fantastic. Those first two were perfect. It's fine. You got this. You blew both of us away."

He continued to slowly shake his head in disagreement. Sheila ran her hands over and over his shoulder and neck, easing him down. Finally, he looked up at both of us, and it seemed, for a split second, as if he had to think a moment to remember who we were. He then let a long, deep sigh fly out of his chest. He kind of half smiled, somewhat sheepishly. "Yeah. Ok. It's late. You're right. I can work on it again tomorrow... sorry, guys."

"It's fine," Sheila said and took him by the hand, helping to pull him off the wall and over to the dining table. She glanced over at me, a nervous sense of accomplishment.

We gathered up all our books and notes, put the chalkboard in the closet and our tea cups in the kitchen. The wind and rain had been building over the past hour and a full-on thunderstorm was now pummeling the ground. We stood in the doorway a moment, hoping for a fortuitous break in the weather, but eventually we took off and made a mad dash across the courtyard, skidding and splashing through the wet grass until we dove through the stone archway and into the long dark dormitory halls.

# CHAPTER EIGHT

The next day all three of us gave our presentations, and everything went fine. Gabriel was his usual self, and in fact, Sheila and I quickly forgot about his behavior in the dining hall. We just chalked it up to him being so driven and a perfectionist, but the main reason was we all had much bigger and exciting things on our minds. It was finally done: training was over. A big ceremony was planned, and after that, the real adventure would begin: we would all spread out across this country or surrounding countries, living in towns and villages for the next two years, trying to teach others what we had learned.

The country director of our program in Zaire, a man named Cyrus Cole, and all the program coordinators for our organization flew in from our headquarters in Kinshasa for the event. The *réfectoire* was decorated in festival lights, empty oil drums were packed with ice and bottles of Fanta soda and Primus beer. Ma Suer and her team of cooks spent all day long roasting peanuts and ears of corn, stewing chickens, grilling steaks, and peeling and chopping potatoes to make large piles of crispy *pommes frites.*

Everyone dressed up; most all the American women by then had had at least one colorful *pagne* made for them, so they blended in with all the Zairian teachers and staff. Sheila wore a green, gold, and magenta dress wrapped around her slender frame. The Zairian men either wore an *abacost* short-sleeve suit or, like Ilunga, brightly colored custom-made shirts. Most of the American guys, like me, donned the only dress-shirt-and-tie combo they had brought with them from the States.

Director Cole was an affable man who looked like Groucho Marx in a three-piece suit. He took the time to mingle and strike up a conversation with each one of us, then right at 7 p.m., we all gathered together in the main hall. Gabriel and Sheila stood next to me. The director led us as a group in repeating the swearing-in pledge required by all US government employees, that if needed we would "support and defend the constitution from enemies foreign and domestic." That phrase irked some people, but I didn't care. I was fairly apolitical; I just wanted—after these past twelve weeks that seemed more like twelve months, after all the confusion, nerves, and doubt, after wanting to quit and run and hide—I wanted it to finally be official.

*So all together now, bring it on home.* We all chanted: "...and I will well and faithfully discharge the duties of the office on which I am about to enter. So help me God."

The faculty and staff erupted into applause. Big hugs and high fives all around. Someone cranked up a boom box, and the dance song "Kin Kiesse" by Zaiko Langa Langa rang out in the big room. Sheila wrapped her arms across Gabriel's shoulders and mine.

"We did it!" she shrieked and jumped up and down.

Gabriel reached out and messed up my hair. "Congratulations, Mr. Almost College!"

My smile couldn't have been any bigger. "Miracles do happen."

Director Cole and each of the program coordinators walked around and gave out different certificates to each of us, depending on which sector we had trained for. Not far behind them came Orange-Mustache Man (whose name was also Michael) holding a pile of white T-shirts draped over his arm, just like the one I had seen him wearing weeks ago in those first few moments after I stepped off the plane: a drawn outline of a fish and black letters surrounding it that said Pensez Poisson.

"Fish heads!" he shouted. "Gather round! Come and get your real prize."

I took a size extra-large. I held it up and looked at it. I had never wanted a T-shirt so freaking bad in my entire life. I immediately pulled it over my shirt and tie. Gabriel and Sheila wrapped theirs around their waists, and we dove into the crowd. The dance party wasted no time blasting off, with everyone swaying and swirling full tilt, reveling in our much-deserved accomplishments until well past the midnight hour.

———————•———————

Most of us didn't wake up until mid afternoon the next day. By then, it was time to pack and say goodbye. For those of us like Gabriel, Sheila, and I who were heading to the central and western provinces, a few cargo vans had been chartered to drive us to the larger commercial airport in Goma, about three hours north of Bukavu. From there we would fly across the country to the capital of Kinshasa, spend a couple of days at our headquarters, then split up and head to our respective posts. Those who had gotten assignments in the eastern half of the country would stay at the training compound for a few more days before they took off to their new homes.

It didn't take long to push everything into my two black duffel bags. I wrapped my tape player/radio in a towel and pushed my cassettes into several of my socks to keep the cases from cracking. I decided to wear my Pensez Poisson T-shirt for a second straight day, over gray work pants, and my olive-colored paratrooper boots; I also put on my Congo Cowboy hat Sheila had bought me and decided to carry Gabriel's gift, the meter stick/walking stick, onto the plane. I sat down on the bed, the bunched-up mosquito netting dangling above my head. I looked out my window at Lake Kivu, at the folding green mountains surrounding the water. It was another crisp and sparkling day. In a few weeks, once I was out in the flat sandy heat of Bandundu, I would badly miss the cool air that swirled down from those mountain peaks, and the idyllic, insular placidity of our training compound high on the hill. I thought back to those first nervous days when everything seemed so strange and overwhelming. I had left the States alone, uncertain, and half-asleep. I was leaving these long stone hallways befriended, eyes wide open, and far more confident.

About thirty of us met out in the courtyard to pack the vans and get ready to leave. You could see that mixture of excitement and sadness on most everyone's faces as they dragged their suitcases and belongings through the bright-green grass. The entire faculty and staff of the training compound were there to wish us well and say goodbye, and Ilunga helped Sheila lift her bags into the backseat. Once we finished putting away our things, Gabriel and I walked over to them and watched as Sheila gave him a big hug.

"Thank you so much for everything," she said to Ilunga. "You were the best teacher, *ever*."

"*Ahh, weeesh*," Ilunga said and reached out to grasp my hand and Gabriel's. "And you three were my favorite students ever." Ilunga then looked at me. "Especially when you managed to make it to class on time."

I held up my wrist and shook my watch. "I bought extra batteries in town."

Ilunga smiled. "Not just students. But friends. I'll miss you. I know you will all do great things. The people of my country are so fortunate to have you here."

"I hope so," Sheila said and wiped away a tear rolling down her cheek.

"You'll come visit us? When you travel home to Kikwit?" Gabriel asked.

*"Mais, bien sûr!"* said Ilunga. "I will come there this summer, maybe sooner, to visit my brother. We will see each other then."

"Ok, everyone, time to go!" Director Cole shouted.

Gabriel, Sheila, and I said our final goodbyes and climbed in the lead van, just behind the driver. I took one last look at the *paillotes* and the *réfectoire*; at the rows of banana and papaya trees lining the edge of the hills; at the houses and buildings down below us surrounding the lake. In a couple of days, a whole new group of trainees would arrive from the States, and the cycle would begin again. I imagined there would probably be another Michael in the group, someone who was lost and felt they were in way over their head. I just hoped he or she would find another Gabriel, another Sheila, and have the good fortune of Ilunga as their teacher, good friends like I had found to help pull them through. The van moved forward, and the other two vehicles followed us as we rolled down the hill, through the front gates, and away from that majestic old school.

The trip through town and to the north was uneventful. I watched the city disappear, melting into the thick countryside, and then I pressed my face against the window and slept the remainder of the way. We arrived at Goma International Airport near sunset, and Director Cole herded us into the large high-ceiling terminal, near a wall of dust-covered windows. We were booked on a 727 from Air Zaire, which had the unfortunate nickname of *Air Peut-Être* (translation: Air Maybe), not only for its spotty safety record but for its frequent last-minute cancellation of flights.

It was near 8 p.m., and the flight was scheduled to leave at 8:20. The crowd in the terminal continued to steadily grow and steadily move closer to the double doors leading out to the tarmac. The jet sat there, dark and motionless. Director Cole went around and gathered us in a group.

He hunched in front of us like a football coach instructing his team on the next play. "Ok, listen up!" he said. "So they overbook all their flights. That means it's first come, first served. We need to stay together and move to the edge of the runway. As soon as you see those airplane doors open and see them wheel the stairs up to the fuselage, you gotta run. If you don't get on, then you're out of luck. Understand?"

We all nodded. We gathered our things and tried to be inconspicuous as we opened the doors and inched outside. Others in the terminal, including a pack of six Belgian nuns, had the same idea and followed us.

8:05—a light came on in the cockpit, and a group of schoolkids joined us on the tarmac.

8:10—Director Cole adjusted the tie on his three-piece suit and took two more steps toward the plane.

8:15—the jet engine turbines spun to life, and I looked behind me to now see almost the entire terminal outside the building, a pulsating wall of bodies twitching restlessly in place.

8:20—and suddenly the passenger doors opened up, and workers in blue overalls pushed two sets of wheeled aluminum stairwells toward the plane.

"RUN!" shouted Director Cole.

The mad stampede was on. Gabriel and I sprinted to the front of the crowd, both of us laughing and yelling at the same time. We ran next to our director, when, like a pack of hyenas, those Belgian nuns, their sharp habits flapping in the wind, pulled even with us and split off our group. I looked over to see Director Cole trade sharp elbows back and forth with the lead nun, while his short little legs pushed forward as fast as he could. Gabriel swerved and drilled his shoulder into the poor old nun, knocking her off her pace, and sending her stumbling back into her other sisters. They bumped and tripped all over each other, their black-and-white gowns tangling together like bedsheets in a hurricane. A couple of sweet young schoolkids in their blue-and-white uniforms came running up on my left. I took my walking stick and jabbed them in the ribs.

Gabriel bolted ahead, his long limbs gobbling up chunks of concrete until he was the first to reach the rear stairwell. He slammed his body in front, blocking anyone else from getting on, and he spread his legs wide enough for us to crawl through.

"Go! Go!" the director shouted and helped push each one of us through Gabriel's body gate, up those stairs, and into the plane. The shouting and yelling from the mass of people behind us was almost as loud as the jets themselves, and once everyone from our group had safely made it through, Gabriel let go of the handrails, turned, and helped each of the nuns to scramble up the stairs.

When the plane doors shut again, with all of us in our seats, I looked out the window, down at the poor souls not quick enough to make it on, many of them angrily shaking paper tickets in their hands. Security guards came and pushed them away as the jet lurched forward. The passengers then burst into applause when the wheels finally lifted off from the face of the earth, and the jet veered westward, slicing through the night sky.

I settled back and lit a cigarette, flicking open the little square ashtray in my armrest. About three and a half hours from now we would touch down in the sprawling, raucous capital of the country. During our short conversation the night before at the graduation ceremony, Director Cole had asked me what I missed most from home. I couldn't think of anything profound or witty to say, so I had answered somewhat lamely (but truthfully) that I most missed cheeseburgers. He laughed and said I was in luck. A young couple from the States had recently opened an honest-to-goodness American-style diner in Kinshasa, only a few blocks from our residence house. He said they had fantastic double cheeseburgers, fries, and chocolate malts.

The inside of my mouth glistened at the thought of it.

# PART TWO: BANDUNDU

# CHAPTER NINE

"**W**hoo-baby! Congratulations! You guys are in the boondocks now!"

Vladimir Rasputin Goldberg, or Razz as he was better known, drove the truck down a very long stretch of empty highway. It was the only highway around, a single thin ribbon of black asphalt cutting through the wide, flat sandy earth. In the States, people talked about places like Montana and Wyoming as Big Sky Country; you could have said the same thing about where we now were. In the province of Bandundu, our new home, the sky seemed gigantic, heavy and low like it was right above our heads and easy to touch. There was nothing on the horizon, just dry grass and yellowish sand. No trees, no people, no buildings, no other vehicles on the road.

Gabriel, Sheila, and I were all crammed in the front cab next to Razz, with Sheila sitting on Gabriel's lap. The back of the canvas-covered cargo truck was full of my things: motorcycle, my duffel bags, a thin bamboo bed frame, a spongy foam mattress, table, desk, chairs, bags of dried beans and rice, pots and pans, and a big rusty barrel of gasoline. We were heading out to drop me off at my village for the very first time. Gabriel and Sheila were scheduled to be taken the next day, so they had decided to come and give me a proper send-off.

Razz lit one cigarette off the other as he drove. He was tall and wiry, with big muttonchop sideburns over his light-brown skin. He described himself as "Blewish"—half-black and half-Jewish from St. Louis, Missourah. He had completed his initial two-year program in water and sanitation, then extended for a third year to move into a leadership position, and was now in charge of all the volunteers in this region. He was in perpetual motion, always moving and doing things, talking nonstop.

"Make sure you guys take your malaria meds out here," he said. "And don't wear blue near rivers—tsetse flies are attracted to blue. They can give you sleeping sickness. Nasty stuff. And always hang your clothes to dry vertically. Don't lay them down flat on rocks or shit like that. Botflies can lay eggs in them, then those fuckers will burrow in your skin, and those maggots will eat away your flesh as they grow bigger, till they pop out of your body like that *Alien* movie or some shit. Had a couple of them. Bad news… So check this out: so on an island in Borneo or someplace like that, they sprayed a bunch of DDT to kill all the mosquitoes, but it also poisoned the flies and the geckos ate the flies, so then they got poisoned, then all the cats ate the geckos so then they died, so then the rat population gets out of control, so now they have to parachute cats back on the island! Ain't that some shit! Can you imagine that? A bunch of kitty cats flying through the air on little parachutes…!" He lit another cigarette and looked out the window at the desolate land flying by us. "You know they should plant some Chinese grass out here or something. Make it look nicer. We should have a landscaping program, or something like that."

We slowed down on the highway and came to a single crooked stick on the side of the road, with a couple of hand-carved signs nailed to it, pointing different directions. Different names of villages were listed with distances in kilometers. It was like something you'd see in a Bugs Bunny cartoon: Timbuktu 1000 miles; New York 2000 miles; Bunny Trail right here. We turned off the asphalt onto a narrow but very thick dirt road. The truck jolted back and forth, up and down.

Razz continued dispensing advice. "So they gave you motorcycle training, right? Gotta watch these roads. They can change overnight. Especially in the rainy season. And hey, this is very important. If you get in an accident, if you hit someone, or if they hit you, *even if it's not your fault*, get the hell out of there if you can. Don't wait around. If other people are nearby and they see it, man, they go crazy out here. They turn into a crazy mob or some shit."

"What are you talking about?" I asked. "Are you serious?"

"Fuckin' A right I am. They'll start throwing rocks and sticks, and they'll attack both of you, doesn't matter who. I've seen it, man. Some scary shit. Don't fuck around. Get out, and you can go back later when things calm down and try to figure it all out… Other than that, everyone out here is great." Razz glanced over at us a couple of times. "Gabe, you all right? Did I scare you with all that talk? You look as pale as day-old bird shit."

I looked at Gabriel and noticed that Razz was right. His face looked white and clammy.

Sheila pressed her palm to his forehead. "You do feel a bit warm."

Gabriel brushed her hand away. "I'm fine," he said, rather flatly.

"Ok, man," Razz continued. "So anyway, this kind of dirt road we're on now, this is normal. That highway back there, that's *it*, man. That is the only paved road in all of Bandundu. This is a place about the size of Georgia and Alabama combined, and that is the only road, except for the local ones in Kikwit. Cuts right through the region, cuts it in half. Ain't no phones out here. No electricity. No nothin'. You guys will be keeping it real out here, for sure."

Bit by bit, as we pulled farther away from the highway, the terrain began to change. More trees and vegetation began to pop up, and the ground began to rise and fall. We began a descent down a very long hill, into a deep valley. The sand turned to red clay and a forest rose around us, thick walls of trees that blocked out the fat sky. We followed the red road until we came to the edge of a wide but slow-moving river that seemed nearly black in color, like a giant oil slick.

The road stopped: there was no way to move forward. A rusty cable was attached to a steel pole and spanned the mouth of the river to the other side. All four of us climbed out of the cab of the truck, and Razz put two fingers to his mouth to whistle loudly. Across the water, we saw a man emerge from the shade of the trees. He waved a red shirt or some piece of cloth above his head, then he stepped onto what I had thought was a flat wooden dock, but the dock began to move forward, and I could see he was hand-turning a wheel and crank that pulled the flat barge along the cable.

"This here," said Razz. "Is your version of the Bandundu ferry."

Gabriel walked around the edge of the water. "Is this the same river that runs through Kikwit?"

"Yep," Razz said. "The River Kwilu. The heart of Bandundu. Cuts through the whole province. Now you three come here." We stood behind Razz as he pointed out at the water. "You see that?"

I looked at a diagonal angle to the other side, but all I could see were a few floating sticks and some bubbles. "No, what are we looking for?"

"Those two little bumps sticking out of the water."

"I think so," Sheila said, without much confidence.

"Exactly," Razz said. "It's hard to see them and that's the point. When you are on this river, it's what you have to be the most careful about. People think Africa, and they think lions and crocs are the most dangerous animals—"

"Are there lions around here?" I asked.

"Nah, no lions," Razz said. "But those two bumps, those are hippos. Eyes and ears. *They* are the most dangerous animals out here. They will fuck a person up. Snap 'em in two, even while they are in a canoe. And they can move fast over short distances. They don't *hunt* people, but they are fiercely territorial. If you get near their turf, 'specially if they got little ones around, they will kill you."

The barge had almost reached our side of the river.

"You got any cash on you?" Razz asked me.

I reached in my pocket. "Sure, how much?"

"Two hundred Zs is good. For the pilot. Make sure you always carry cash."

We carefully rolled the truck onto the barge and found space to stand near the edge. The pilot, a middle-aged Zairian with a speckled gray beard, introduced himself as Motongo. His long arms began to slowly turn the rusted handle of the pulley, and we moved along the cable, breaking free from the shore, swaying back and forth in the water. As I realized I would soon be seeing him on a regular basis, I used the opportunity to practice my Kikongo.

"*Ebwe?*" I asked. (How are you?)

"*Mbote,*" he said. (Good.)

"*Mbote,*" I said. (Good.)

He wiped sweat from his face with the back of his hand. "*Inki mbwala nge ta vanda?*" he asked.

I was still struggling with hearing the language in real time, so I turned to Razz for a quick translation. "He asked which village will you live in?" Razz said.

"*Mbangi Kitengo,*" I answered, giving the name of my yet unseen home, a name I had been practicing to pronounce.

"*Ayy, yo ikele mbote awa,*" he answered.

Once again I turned to Razz. "He said it's nice there," Razz said.

"*Mbote,*" I said to Motongo.

"*Mbote,*" he replied. "*Mbote mingi.*"

The word *mbote* in Kikongo was like *aloha* in Hawaiian: depending on the context it could mean hello, goodbye, thank you, you're welcome, beautiful, good, great, delicious, and it could end a conversation, in effect saying "That's it." I had no idea which one he was saying. I left it at that for the time being.

We looked around at the thick forest. There was a lush silence surrounding us, only the slight tinkling of the slow-moving water, and the squeak of the gearbox sliding along the cable. Lazy rays of sunlight broke through the trees and touched upon the river surface.

"It's beautiful here," Gabriel said. "I can't wait to get to my village."

"Tomorrow, big guy," Razz said. "Tomorrow is all about you."

"You feeling ok?" Sheila asked Gabriel.

He nodded and stuck his hand in the water, splashed some on his face. "Yeah," he said. "Just have to get used to this heat."

"Forget it," Razz said. "Been here three years. You never get used to it."

As we neared the other side, those two bumps in the water Razz had pointed out to us, about thirty meters away from where we were floating, suddenly rose up from the black river, the full, fat head of the hippo breaking free. His large body followed, waves of water splashing around it, and the big animal yawned, its massive mouth stretching wide, showing its pink inside and those thick powerful teeth. It then ambled over to the shore and disappeared into the trees.

Gabriel, Sheila, and I stood on the barge, our bodies frozen, our own mouths open in stunned silence. Razz turned toward us and smiled. "You sure ain't in Kansas anymore, are you?"

———————•———————

We came out on the other side of the valley, the truck rising up a craggy dirt road until we were back on top, now traveling through a savannah. This looked more like what I had always thought Africa would be: rolling fields of waist-high grass, punctuated by wide, flat-topped acacia trees.

There were a couple more signposts at a couple more forks in the road, and then after about twenty minutes, the truck took a sharp bend in the path and we came upon the outskirts of a village. A pack of children burst from the fenced-in yard of three red-mud huts and ran alongside the truck yelling: *"Mendele! Mendele!"* (White person! White person!)

As the truck moved forward, I could see people on all sides of us, young and old, dropping what they were doing to follow. The proper road came to an end, and soon we turned onto a wide, straight sandy avenue I estimated to be about a hundred meters long. Standing on either side were rows of more mud-and-straw houses, with neatly swept dirt yards partitioned by gates made from tree branches and vines. A dusty crowd poured into the path, gathering beneath mango, palm, papaya, and banana trees. A single wooden sign had been nailed to the largest of the trees, carved in black letters with the name Kitengo. This was finally it. This was my new home.

Razz pulled to a stop at the far end of the avenue, in front of a longish mud house with a corrugated tin roof. A trio of young men carrying different-sized drums scurried into place, sat down in the sand in front of our truck, and furiously began pounding away with their hands. The crowd parted, and like straw-covered aliens, two dancers in full tan-and-black-striped raffia body suits, faces covered by giant headpieces with bulging white wooden circular eyes, and hands disappearing into some kind of giant brown pom-poms, ran in front of the drum squad and began spinning and gyrating. The crowd clapped along and chanted words I didn't understand.

"Wow!" Sheila said. "What a reception!"

I couldn't quite grasp what was going on. "This is for me?"

"All for you, buddy," Razz said and turned off the engine. "Welcome home."

We got out of the truck. Razz faced the crowd and pointed to me, and then they erupted into applause. Several people broke free and came up to greet us. The first was a distinguished-looking man with gray eyes wearing a dark-blue *abacost* suit and carrying an ornate walking stick, carved with figures of elephants and snakes. He nodded at me and grasped my hand.

"He's your *mfumu!*" Razz shouted over the drums. "He's the chief of your village. First thing tomorrow, make sure you go visit him. Very important!"

I nodded and said "*Mbote.*" As soon as I did, a very thin old man with silver hair and eyes clouded metallic-blue from cataracts took my other hand as well.

"He's Mutamba, your landlord. He's also the local witch doctor. So, you know, make sure you pay him on time!"

My head was spinning as several more people approached and Razz made more introductions, until a slightly built man with a wide-set, pleasant face and wearing a very Western outfit of khaki pants and a red polo shirt came from around the back of the house. Razz put his arm around the man's shoulder and led him to me.

"And this is Pumbu. He's gonna be your assistant. He moved from another village to come work with you. Great guy! He's worked with our organization for several years. He knows the drill."

Pumbu smiled and nodded. "Hello, Mr. Michael," he said in English with a soothing African accent. "It is a pleasure to meet you."

"You speak English!" I said, rather joyously.

"Yes, pretty good. I am hoping it will continue to get better."

"He's gonna stay in your spare room for a while until he builds his own place," said Razz. "He's a gem! You'll love him… Ok, let's unload your things."

We grabbed the first round of boxes and bags from the truck, and Razz led me to the front door of my house.

"Hey, check this out," he said. "You've got a door with four actual windowpanes! That's rare out here." He tapped on the bottom quadrant and the glass immediately broke. "Oops. Make that three real windowpanes."

"I will find someone to fix it," Pumbu said. He opened the door, and I entered the house for the first time. There was one main room in the center and then four smaller adjacent rooms, two on each side. The floor was sand, the walls were red mud, but they had been plastered and smoothed in most places, covering up the tree-trunk frame.

"Wow, five rooms," Sheila said as she carried in a box of pots and pans. "This is bigger than I thought."

"You're livin' large," Razz said. "Let me show you the backyard." He opened up the rear door, and we walked out into a very large sandy yard, divided off by a fence made of bamboo. Beyond the fences were wide, seemingly infinite fields of savannah grass. Two large palm trees stood on the left side of the yard. "Tons of space! You can build yourself a *paillote* out here, or a chicken coop. Pumbu can help you." He pointed to the far edge where a straw-roof outhouse stood. "And there is your own private privy."

I walked over and took a peek inside, saw the central hole was surrounded by suspicious-looking wood planks, and I shuddered. "Yeah, we're gonna change that."

The drumming and dancing out in the street continued as we brought in tables, chairs, shelves, and bags of imperishable food.

Gabriel and I hopped up into the truck to lift my motorcycle down to the ground.

"This is amazing," he said as we twisted the front wheel back and forth. "I hope my place is as nice."

"I'm sure by the time you're done with it, people will want to buy tickets to visit it." We rolled the bike to the front of my house, and I popped open the kickstand.

He stood up straight and wiped sweat from his forehead. "Yeah, I've got some big ideas..." Suddenly, his long legs gave way and he collapsed to the ground.

"Gabriel! Razz, come here!"

Razz and Sheila poked their heads out of my house, and when they saw Gabriel on the ground, they ran over to us.

"Oh my God, sweetie," Sheila said as she knelt in the sand. "What is it?"

Gabriel's face looked white and his whole body was shaking. He was sweating but his teeth were chattering as if he were lying in a freezer.

Razz took one look at him and knew. "Oh shit," he said and placed his hand on Gabriel's head. "You're hot but cold at the same time?"

Gabriel nodded yes.

"You got a horrible headache? Right between your eyes? It comes and goes? Your insides feel like hot coals rumbling around?"

Gabriel nodded yes to all of them.

"Congratulations," Razz said. "You just popped your cherry.

You got your first case of malaria."

"But he's been taking his meds," Sheila said. "I made sure of it."

"There's resistant strains showing up 'round here. Meds don't always work."

"Yes, Doc Peters mentioned that to me in Bukavu," I said.

"Ok," Razz said to Gabriel. "We're gonna get you to the hospital in Kikwit."

"But I'm supposed to go to my village tomorrow," Gabriel said.

"That's gonna have to wait, big guy. Come on, lie in the front seat while we finish unloading Michael's things." Pumbu came over and helped us lift Gabriel to his feet and lead him over to the truck. The drumming and dancing had stopped, and the large crowd watched silently as Gabriel collapsed inside the cab of the truck.

"I'll stay here with him," Sheila said. She dug in her backpack, pulled out a yellow bandana, poured water from her canteen on it, and placed it on Gabriel's forehead.

Razz turned to Pumbu and me. "Ok, let's move quick and just get everything off the truck. You'll have plenty of time to arrange stuff later."

We worked fast for the next twenty minutes and just piled up everything in my front yard. The last was the big heavy drum of gasoline that took all three of us grunting and cursing to get it off the truck bed and onto the ground. Razz then reached inside behind the front seat and pulled out two large manila envelopes.

"Here," he said, handing me the first one. "I almost forgot. Doc Peters sent you this from Kinshasa."

I opened it and pulled out a new 1989 *The Far Side* calendar, as well as recent issues of *Newsweek International* magazine. The next envelope Razz handed me was full of Zairian cash in five hundred and thousand notes.

"That's ninety thousand Zs in there. Your stipend for the next three months. Two thousand each month goes to your landlord Mutamba. Six thousand each month goes to Pumbu here. The rest is for you, though nothing around here to spend it on. I advise you let Pumbu hold it and hide it for you. He can be your private banker. You can trust him."

"Sure. Of course," I said and gave Pumbu the envelope.

"Ok, time for us to make like a gorilla and break wind. Wanna get Gabe back to Kikwit before dark."

I walked to the passenger door and looked at Gabriel. Sheila moved out of the way so I could speak to him. His eyes darted back and forth: he looked scared, confused. I never thought I would have seen those expressions on his face.

"Hey, buddy," I said. "Hang in there. I'm sure you'll get over this fast. If anyone can, you will."

His face and jaw still quivered as he spoke. "Yeah. Been waiting my whole life for this. What's a few more days, right?"

"There you go. That's the spirit."

"Hey, Mike, don't forget everything I taught you."

I smiled. "No way. That's impossible." I patted him on the shoulder. "I wouldn't be here without you."

He nodded and I climbed out of the truck. Sheila was near tears. "Ok, I'll write you and let you know what happens," she said. "Note to self: write Michael a letter."

"Thanks. Take good care of him."

"I will," she said and gave me a long tight hug before climbing into the front seat.

Razz started up the engine and I walked to his side. He reached out and shook my hand. "You'll do great, buddy. Listen to Pumbu here. He knows everything. See you in Kikwit in three months!"

And with that, he rolled the truck forward, headed back down the avenue, made the sharp turn, and was gone. I continued waving at the truck for several minutes after I couldn't see it. Then, I turned around and stood before the large silent crowd, all of whom stared back at me. I pumped my hand into a tight ball several times and reached for a cigarette.

The two straw-man dancers shuffled quietly in the sand, their shoulders drooping, their straw pom-poms hanging limply by their sides.

# CHAPTER TEN

Eventually, the chief of the village told everyone to go back to their houses to allow me time to get settled. He spoke mostly in their tribal language, Pende (a third language for me to learn!), so Pumbu translated and we made plans to visit him and the other village elders the next morning. I looked at the pile of stuff in my front yard. I was a bit shell-shocked, had no idea where to even begin. I kept seeing Razz and the truck disappearing, leaving me all alone.

Pumbu wisely suggested that our first order of business should be to put together my bed frame so I would have a place to sleep that night. We set it up in the left-rear side room, with four bamboo poles as posts, and over those posts, we stretched my mosquito netting, with a nail on the side to tie it off when not in use.

"So you've been working with other volunteers?" I asked him as we dug small holes in the floor to steady the legs of the bed.

"Yes, four years now," said Pumbu. "Two with Miss Angela Stuart. She was a teacher in my village. Then when she left, I worked with her replacement, Mr. Jeffrey Waterson. They were very nice. They helped me a lot with my English."

"And you wanted to leave your village? To come here?"

"Yes, well, the chief of this village is my cousin. He offered to give us a larger piece of land to build our house."

"Us?"

"My fiancée and I. Yes."

"You're engaged? That's awesome. Congratulations."

"Thank you, Mr. Michael," Pumbu said and briefly bowed his head. "There is more space for us here in this village, to raise a family. I hope you do not mind me sleeping in the front room until we build our new place."

"No, of course not. Take as much time as you need. I'm sure it will be very helpful to have you here. Especially these first months. Razz speaks so highly of you."

"Yes, Mr. Razz was very excited when I accepted to come here."

"Mr. Razz is always excited about everything."

Pumbu laughed. "He has a lot of energy, doesn't he?"

"That… is an understatement."

We slipped the bed legs into each hole, then filled them in. I lifted the foam mattress in place and sat down, shifting from side to side to test for any shakiness. It felt solid. "I think we got it."

We spent another hour putting together shelves and chairs, and then we rolled the big barrel of gasoline from outside the house into the corner of the front-left room. The other half of the room would be good to use as a pantry, and within a couple of weeks, Pumbu said he would build a small kitchen as an addition to the house, to keep the fire away from that giant drum of flammable fuel sitting on the other side of the wall from my bed. In the rear-right room, we decided to set up a place for me to bathe. We nailed two planks in the wall to hold a soap dish and shampoo bottle, and Pumbu dug a small fire pit in the floor where I would be able to heat pots of water and use a large plastic cup to dip in and pour over myself. Eventually, I would pay a local craftsman to weave a couple of bath mats I could lay down and keep my feet from getting muddy.

From that very first day, I found it very easy and comfortable to talk with Pumbu, like we had been friends for years. Looking back, I can't imagine how much more strange and nerve-wracking those first few weeks in the village would have been without having had that instant connection, not to mention his wisdom and experience working with Americans before.

We took a break from moving furniture, and he showed me how he brewed coffee over an open fire, using a straining net and adding half a can of condensed milk. Then we sat in the main room and each enjoyed two large orange plastic mugs of the strong but sweet drink. He told me he had recently turned thirty, and his fiancée, whose name was Neva, was twenty and planned to be a teacher when we heard a loud knocking on the front door.

I opened it, and standing there was a short, thin man with a big grin on his face. He had a narrow mustache and large ears that were almost pointy—Spock ears. He bowed his head and greeted us.

*"Mbote mingi. Zina na mono ikele Vitesse."*

I was able to understand his introduction, though I was surprised at his name. "Vitesse?" I turned to Pumbu. "Did he say his name was Vitesse?"

"Yes," Pumbu said.

*"Vitesse* means speed in French. His name is Speed? I love it!" I turned to my visitor. *"Mbote mingi, Vitesse. Ebwe?"* (How are you?)

*"Mbote. Mono ke zola nge kudia nzo na mono sesepi y konso kilimbu."*

I caught only part of it and again turned to Pumbu.

"He says he wants you to eat dinner at his house tonight and every night."

"Every night? Well, I… That is very generous. Can we accept for tonight only?"

Pumbu translated, and Vitesse shrugged his shoulders to agree. He then pointed behind me, at my radio sitting on my desk. "He wants you to bring the radio with you," Pumbu said.

"Sure," I said, then spoke to Vitesse. *"Mambu ve."* (No problem.)

I was, in fact, very hungry after the long day we'd had. The three of us left my house and went to the main avenue just as the sun was setting, and I had to stop walking. The sky was simply breathtaking, vibrant orange, red, and purple streaks of color against a golden sky, surrounding the village, lying low over the flat fields of savannah grass. The air smelled like a fresh mixture of mango and smoky firewood. As we walked down the avenue, past all the houses, most families were out in their yards with their children, cooking over piles of orange coals, getting ready for their evening meal.

Vitesse's house was four down from mine, and we entered through his small gate into a clean and recently swept sandy yard. His wife was leaning over two cooking pots in fire pits, and she stood when we arrived and greeted us with a warm smile. She was taller than Vitesse, and like most village women, she wore a faded *pagne* wrapped around slender but well-toned limbs—arms and shoulders muscled from the hard work of village life. Her name was Jackie, and sitting on the ground behind her were two young children around five and six. She introduced the boy as Kanga and the girl as Naya. They were drawing pictures in the sand with sticks.

His house was a three-room mud hut with a straw roof, and Pumbu and I helped Vitesse bring out a wooden table and chairs to place in his yard. Vitesse brought two large gourds and put them on the table. Jackie handed him a small blue plastic bowl, and Vitesse poured water from one of the gourds into it. We sat down, and each of us dipped our fingers in the bowl to wash them. Then Jackie and the two children brought over our supper: a large bowl of *fufu*, as well as three smaller bowls of side dishes.

Pumbu walked me through the meal. The first dish was stewed manioc leaves called *saka-saka*, a staple eaten at most every meal, similar to collard greens in the southern States. The second dish was a pile of ground-up squash seeds in a hot pepper sauce called *mantete*. When I looked in the third bowl, I struggled to keep a straight face: it was layers of what looked to be black salamanders sitting in a yellowish-orange sauce of palm oil. Vitesse had that grin on his face the entire meal, as he watched me tear off a piece of *fufu* and try each dish; and I have to say, each one was truly delicious, even the salamanders, which tasted like spicy sardines. I kept repeating *mbote* over and over.

After the meal, Vitesse brought three plastic mugs, and from the other gourd, poured milky-white palm wine, known as *malafu*, into each. We raised our mugs in a toast, using the French word *salut*. I offered a cigarette each to Vitesse and Pumbu, and then we all three settled in our chairs for a post-meal smoke.

Night had fallen by now, and much like the daytime sky, the sky at night seemed huge and right above our heads, with millions of stars that seemed low enough to touch, like we could reach up and pick them off as cherries from a tree. We didn't speak a whole lot, but I found out Vitesse was a palm oil merchant and that Jackie was pregnant with their next child.

Vitesse motioned for me to turn on the shortwave radio, and after fumbling with the dial, I came across a station out of Gabon broadcasting in French and English. The program we found was *The Marlboro Hit Parade*, and we sat under the stars, next to the fire, no electric lights, no cars, no other sounds, except the American and British top-forty songs they played by people like Madonna, Michael Jackson, and UB40. Hearing those songs drifting out of those tinny speakers, songs that connected me to a home so far away and so completely different from the place I was now, was both comforting and strange at the same time.

Vitesse hummed along to the melodies, then asked me if I knew Zairian music. I told him I had some cassette tapes at my house I would bring with me next time.

"Tomorrow?" he asked in Kikongo.

I looked around, the mug of palm wine in my hand, a shooting star streaking across the sky above me, and I felt a deep sense of relaxation. "Yes, tomorrow," I said. "I'll definitely come here tomorrow."

# CHAPTER ELEVEN

So that was my first day and night in my village. Not too bad. Once I hit my spongy mattress and pulled the mosquito net around my bedposts, deep sleep actually fell upon me fast and hard; I was so exhausted by everything. I awoke early the next morning, just past sunrise. Roosters were crowing, pigs grunting, and as I lay in bed, I could hear the steady pounding of the neighboring women as they used large wooden mortar and pestles to smash dried manioc roots into flour in order to make *fufu*. I took a careful trip to my outhouse (it would be another couple of weeks before I replaced those old wooden boards with solidly packed dirt) and found Pumbu already up and dressed, brewing coffee over the fire pit in our backyard.

I still had to metaphorically pinch myself a bit as I sat in a chair sipping the coffee, looking around at the sun climbing higher in the huge savannah sky. Mornings had a slight cool tinge to them as we were at the tail end of the dry season, and a breeze circled my face and lifted up the fronds of the two palm trees in my yard. It was a wonderful way to start a day.

Before I had a chance to finish my coffee, Mutamba, my landlord and his oldest wife (of three) known simply as Mamma, came walking around the house, carrying covered dishes for Pumbu and me to eat. The largest bowl was of course *fufu*, freshly boiled as steam still rose from the lumpy ball, and the two side dishes were *saka-saka* and a nice plate of fried palm grubs. Now palm grubs, to the uninitiated, are basically giant maggots, the size of a human thumb, that burrow in the trunks of palm trees. They are fat and white, with ridges on their bodies, and a brown cap, like a small shell for a head. They look horrible, like something you would see in your worst nightmare, but Pumbu promised me they would be good. I bit into one particularly juicy one, and I have to say, it wasn't bad. Kind of like bacon fat. Kind of. That would have been the closest thing to breakfast food I would find out there—no Egg McMuffins, no doughnuts, no French toast to be had anywhere nearby.

Soon after, I fired up my hot "shower"—a pot of water over a pile of burning coals in the rear room of my house. I took a large plastic mug and dipped in and poured it over as much of my body as I could, and used the bottle of Johnson & Johnson baby shampoo I had found at a pharmacy in Kinshasa to wash my hair. Shaving wasn't a priority, so once I had slipped on one of my four pairs of gray khaki work pants, white T-shirt, paratrooper boots, and the cowboy hat Sheila had bought for me, and grabbed the walking stick Gabriel had made for me, I was good to go. Throughout my time there, that would pretty much be my daily uniform in the village, only occasionally varying the color of my

T-shirt (but staying away from blue, and hopefully tsetse flies, as Razz had advised).

First stop was the chief of Kitengo's house, for my official welcome meeting. I was never told his name, and Pumbu said just to address him as *mfumu*, which meant leader. We sat in chairs in a semicircle in his front yard, myself, Pumbu, the chief, Mutamba, and three other elderly village VIPs. It was not yet nine o'clock, but tradition dictated that mugs of palm wine be poured and shared.

I was living with the Pende tribe, one of the oldest and largest tribes in central-western Zaire (and northern Angola). They had their own language, and Pumbu explained to me that while everyone also spoke Kikongo, the leaders preferred to only use Pende in public out of respect to their ancestors. So Pumbu did most of the talking for me, explained who I was and what I was there to do. The chief sat silently, his taut face, shiny and dark brown, not showing any emotion beyond nodding a few times.

After a while, he called inside his large hut, and a teenage boy came out carrying the same walking stick I had seen the chief with when I had arrived the day before. The chief took the stick and motioned for me to come forward. Pumbu followed and said the chief was giving this gift to me in gratitude for my coming to live in his village and trying to help his farmers. He said this stick, deep-black, ebony wood, with a metal tip, and covered by ornately carved images of a cobra, two elephants, a lion, and a gazelle, would forever protect my house from thieves and others who wish to do me harm.

As I took that stick in my hands, I was humbled and moved, to say the least. I felt embarrassed that I had not brought him a gift as well, but Pumbu assured me that it would not be proper, the chief would not accept anything, and again my very presence in that village was all the chief desired. He motioned for us to sit again. The teenage boy then reappeared holding a tall wooden container, about the size of a tin of flour. The chief dipped his hand in and pushed some type of food in his mouth. At first, I couldn't see what it was.

The boy made his way around the semicircle, and each man stuck his hand in and quickly ate what was within. The boy came to the last village elder who sat next to me, a tall, lanky man with bushy eyebrows and wearing a white cotton sweater. As he brought his hand to his mouth, I saw live termites crawling between his fingers. He pushed his hand between his lips, but a couple of the termites escaped and ran furiously around at the corners of his mouth. His tongue, like a toad's, suddenly shot from inside and captured the bugs off his face, and then he swallowed them down. He looked at me and smiled, and that's when I noticed two of his front teeth had been filed into sharp fangs.

I began to pump my fist in and out of a tight ball, and I felt my chest flutter and my head swoon. The brightness of the sun suddenly seemed to explode in front of me, and I had trouble focusing my vision. I felt a stabbing pain in my stomach, and a tightness in my throat that made it hard to breathe. The teenage boy came to me and held out the container. I looked in and saw

116

those hundreds of termite legs and bodies throbbing and pulsing on top of each other. I turned to Pumbu, my eyes wide in desperation, and he clearly read my silent plea. He very politely spoke to the chief and explained that in my culture, we do not *usually* eat insects that are alive. The chief cracked a slight smile, then waved the boy away and back into the hut.

My throat and jaw were still trembling as Pumbu and I walked back to my house, and a few times, I had to reach for his shoulder to steady myself. The bugs were disturbing and I hadn't been prepared for that, but what really freaked me out was that man's smile and those fangs staring me in the face.

"What was that?" I asked. "The man next to us. His teeth? Did he do that on purpose?"

Pumbu, as always, was so calm, talking in a tone like he had just come out of a deep meditation. "Yes. He is paying respect to his ancestors."

"Respect for what? Did they eat people? Do people here eat people?"

"Yes. But it is rare."

"Rare! You mean it still happens today?" *Get me on the next flight out of here!*

"I'm sorry. My English was not good. I meant to say…"

I watched his face and waited for him to finish. "What? You meant to say what?"

His eyes still searched, and then he nodded. "Yes. I meant to say *extinct*. It is extinct. People do not eat each other anymore."

We arrived at the front door to my house. I reached in my

pocket and quickly pulled out a cigarette. "You sure?"

"Yes, of course. That was a long time ago. Before white people... mostly."

I struck a match and sucked the smoke deep into my lungs, as far as it could go.

"Trust me," Pumbu said, in a voice that was nearly impossible not to. "That is one thing you do not have to worry about."

I leaned against the outside wall and nodded. "Ok..."

Pumbu said he would soon start cooking some rice and beans for lunch, and then afterward, he would take me down into the valley, where I could meet with some farmers. I went inside and sat down on a chair in the main room. I inhaled the rest of the cigarette, tossed the butt on my dirt floor, and stepped on it, and then I placed the walking stick the chief had given me in the corner near the rear door. I cupped my hands and brought them to my face. I took several deep breaths and let my body ease down from that nervous rocket ride it had just been on.

I leaned back in the chair, my head now settled, my vision now clearer. The stick looked amazing, the metal tip catching a ray of sun coming in from the window, the carved animals looking back at me with a strangely comforting gaze. I didn't know it at the time, but I would in fact keep it with me as the chief had intended. I would carry it with me across continents and oceans, all around the world, and as the chief had said, in the dozens and dozens of places I would eventually call home, not once would anyone (or anything) ever invade, disturb, or steal from where I lay my head at night.

Midafternoon, after a brief rest from lunch, it was time to go meet some farmers, time to start doing the job I was sent there to do. Part of me wanted to curl up under my mosquito net and never leave, but I told myself enough was enough. I was sure if Gabriel were around to see me he would have metaphorically (or perhaps literally) slapped me upside me head.

In the village of Kitengo, like most villages in that area, the people lived in the flat, dry, sandy savannah, but most all their work was done at the bottom of deep valleys. That is where they had their farmland, their hunting grounds, where they gathered their drinking water; that is where they cut trees to build their houses. The valley below Kitengo was substantial. I'd describe it more as a small canyon. There were two main paths that cut through the back of the village through the savannah grass. After about fifty meters, the earth simply dropped into wide, cavernous yawns, deep red cliffs that plummeted to lush fertile land far below. It took about thirty minutes to walk down to the bottom of our valley, and about forty-five minutes to climb back up, depending on how much firewood or food or jugs of drinking water you were carrying in your hands or had perched on top of your head.

Pumbu came with me, and I was drenched in sweat by the time we reached a stretch of partitioned farmland. There were long plots of manioc, followed by corn, then various types of squash and other gourds. He showed me the primary stream that ran through the valley, some sections covered in deep shade from the forest, others exposed all day to the brutal Bandundu sun. Several groups of women stood at the edge of the stream, washing clothes with rocks and bricks of cheap green waxy soap that was sold in every market and roadside stand. Other groups were pulling manioc from the fields, stripping the tough brown bark off the roots, so they could soak the white tubes in water to leach out the natural cyanide within before they took them to the village to grind them into flour.

He also took me farther into the forest to the natural spring that was the source of the stream and the main source of their drinking water in the dry season, when collecting water in rain barrels was useless. The water flowed steadily from a wall of granite rocks, and I captured some in my canteen. It tasted fresh and clean. Pumbu had brought two five-liter red plastic jugs to fill up and take back to our house.

He then led me to a clearing where a small thatched day shelter had been constructed. In the shade of the shelter sat two men that Pumbu said owned land near the stream. He said he thought they might be good candidates to start a fish pond. As we approached them, I pumped my fist a few times and twirled my neck around in circles, trying to loosen it up.

The two men stood up and Pumbu introduced them to me. We exchanged "*mbotes*" back and forth. I guessed they were mid-thirties in age. They wore cut-off shorts, and the tallest one had a T-shirt from the heavy metal rock band Judas Priest that showed a screaming eagle, claws out to attack, against a bright-yellow background.

"Judas Priest," I said and nodded at his shirt, then stupidly added, "Nice. Rock on."

The farmer just stared at me and tilted his head.

"Your shirt," I said in Kikongo.

It was obvious he had no idea what the shirt meant. He briefly looked at it. "Yes. Good," he said, then stared at me again.

I looked at Pumbu for support. He just raised his eyebrows and shrugged. I cleared my throat and addressed the two men in my still-struggling Kikongo. "So, I want to talk to you about how to grow fish."

"Grow? Fish?" the shorter farmer asked.

"Yes. I mean, how to grow a lot of fish. I want to show you how to build a fish-house." *Fish-house* was the direct translation of the word *pond*.

Mr. Judas Priest twisted his eyebrows in knots. "A house?"

"Yes," I said.

"For fish?"

"Yes," I said.

"A fish-house?"

"Yes. To grow fish."

The two farmers looked at each other and burst out laughing. They shook their heads repeating: *"Mendele, mendele."* The short guy put his hand on my shoulder. "The fish already have a house," he said in Kikongo. "It is called the river. Come, let us show it to you."

He pulled me along into the forest. Again, I looked back to Pumbu for help, but he just shrugged his shoulders. He followed behind as the farmers led us to a smaller river deeper in the trees, and Pumbu tried to explain to them more about the project I was sent there to do, but they would have none of it. They enjoyed laughing too much, and once we got to the riverbank, they pointed at the water and said all the fish there were very happy with their current home. From my backpack, I took a flip chart, with colorful drawings of happy people, that tried to explain what it would be like to dig a pond and stock it with baby fish and then in a few months, have hundreds, maybe thousands, but the farmers just politely nodded and smiled and soon went on their way.

"Well, that didn't go well, did it?" I asked Pumbu as we cut across a field, heading back toward the trail leading out of the valley and up to our village.

"You have to understand, most people here, they let their animals walk free," said Pumbu. "They don't understand the idea of keeping animals in one place to control them. Especially fish. You will have to explain it many times, I'm afraid."

"Appears so. How was my language?"

Pumbu held out his hand and tilted it back and forth. "So-so," he said.

"Ok, then here is the new deal between us. During the day, you and I only speak in Kikongo or French. To help me get better. In the evenings, we can speak in English. To help you get better."

"Yes, that is good. That is what I did with Miss Angela. She improved very fast that way."

"Good." We reached the beginning of the valley wall, and I took my next step into a patch of thick grass, when suddenly Pumbu slammed his hand against my chest, and I saw a flash of shiny black rise from the ground.

"Stop," he said in a forced whisper. "Do not move."

My foot was about two inches off the ground, and about three feet in front of us, a thick, silver-black snake, with a sharp triangle-shaped head, rose up and coiled its tail. They had shown us pictures of it in training. There was no mistake: it was a black mamba. I literally felt the blood drain from my face. Pumbu and I managed to completely freeze our bodies as the snake's head twisted and darted in the air a few times. It probably only lasted a few seconds, but of course, it felt like several minutes went by before it finally lost interest and disappeared in the opposite direction, into the thick grass.

We both exhaled, and I nearly collapsed to the ground. I had just about stepped right on top of one of the most poisonous snakes in the world. One bite from that, and within about forty-five minutes, I probably would have been dead. Even the little snakebite kit I carried in my backpack would have doubtfully done much good. The only chance I would have had would have been the thick canvas netting of my paratrooper boots I had wisely bought at a supply store before I left the States. The shopkeeper told me they had been designed specifically to deflect snake fangs. If it would have tried to bite my feet or ankles, I might have escaped, but had it risen a few inches higher, sinking its fangs into my calf, that would have been, as they say, "all she wrote."

We continued on the trail in silence, climbing up the steep valley walls, with the sun now fading at our backs. Pumbu balanced one of the jugs of water on his head, and I could hear it sloshing around with every step we took. Just before nightfall, we got back to our house, and there was Vitesse waiting at the front door. I grabbed my radio from inside, and we walked down to his hut, pulled the table and chair into his yard, and washed our fingers. Jackie gave us a big bowl of *fufu*, another bowl of *saka-saka*, and this time for the other two dishes, we had fried plantains and a plate of mystery bushmeat, grayish-black chunks in spicy oil, that Vitesse said he had caught himself that day and described to us as some kind of forest armadillo. I wasn't sure exactly, but I was starving and it was pretty good, a bit gamey like venison.

After dinner, we had our post-meal mug of palm wine, our post-meal smoke, and listened to our post-meal radio program *The Marlboro Hit Parade*. That night they featured some new group called Milli Vanilli, another called Salt-N-Pepa, and of course, more Madonna.

Around ten o'clock Pumbu and I returned to our house. We had one final cigarette, then he said goodnight and went to his room. I carried a petrol lantern into my bedroom, and as I pulled back my mosquito net, I saw a swirling pile of yellow and white slither across my sheets. Another snake! A python! Sitting in my bed waiting for me. I screamed Pumbu's name at the top of my lungs. He came running through my door, machete raised over his shoulders, and as soon as the snake dropped to my dirt floor, Pumbu hacked off its head.

The next morning we fried it up and ate it. A little palm oil and some hot peppers. It was pretty damn good. And yes, it did taste like chicken.

## Chapter Twelve

So that was my second day and night in the village; two out of a planned ninety before it would be time to head to the regional capital of Kikwit for our quarterly break. Certainly not every day was as adventurous and interesting as those were. Like everyplace one lives, eventually I settled into a routine, and there were many forgettable, uneventful days; but the proportion of unusual, strange, exhilarating, mind-blowing, "Is-this-really-happening-to-me?" moments to normal ones was much higher there than any other place I ever lived.

Kitengo was a medium-sized village. I conducted an informal census during my downtime and counted sixty-four family dwellings. The average-size family was around five to six people so that meant a rough population between 320-380 people. Most of the inhabitants had spent their entire lives in the village, never venturing beyond the dirt roads that circled the savannah, marching every day down in the valleys, to scratch out an existence from whatever food they could grow or catch.

There was a small part-time school at the edge of the village, a single-room thatched hut, run by a young man named Allone and his wife Nolanda. They mostly gave math and French instruction a couple of days per week, and they were looking forward to Pumbu's fiancée moving there and joining them so they could turn it into a full-time endeavor. Sometimes they invited me there as a "guest lecturer" for some basic English lessons and tales about the magical, wonderful United States. One of the strangest things to get used to was when some of the children would come up and put their hands on me, then look at their own skin to see if my white color had rubbed off on theirs.

There was a tiny kiosk, about the size of a fat phone booth, that sold basic supplies such as matches, canned milk, sardines, cigarettes, soap, and some scraps of fabric that the owner would bring about twice a year from Kikwit. That was pretty much the extent of regular commerce in that area.

My territory for my fisheries program extended beyond Kitengo to four other neighboring villages, each similar in size and makeup, all within an hour's ride on my motorcycle. That was definitely one of the fun (and tricky) things about my job there: getting on my bike and riding across the open fields under the big sky, navigating sandy roads that could suddenly turn to jagged hard clay. Sometimes, especially on early morning rides, with the red, gold, and orange rays of the new sun bursting overhead, I might skirt the edge of a valley and look down to see it full of white fog, like a giant bowl of cotton soup. Often I would pull to a stop, shut off the engine, take off my helmet, and soak in the silence of the world around me. I would marvel at the fact of where I was, a tiny speck on the vast earth to be sure, but when I thought about where I had come from, where I had been a year earlier, never even comprehending an experience like this as an option in my life, it made me shudder with joy and incredulity.

Unfortunately, those wonderful bike rides led me to more awkward meetings with farmers, more sputtering attempts at explaining who I was and why I was there, over and over again. My language was getting better (the arrangement Pumbu and I had about not speaking English during the day was paying off), but as Pumbu had pointed out, the idea of digging a hole in the ground for the sole purpose of putting fish in there was strange and bizarre to the people I was living with. I was the first American to come live in this area of the country, and my job with this program was to get it up and running and break the ice; despite living directly on the equator, I definitely got a chilly reception at first. Everyone I met was respectful and polite, but no one had any interest in building ponds and raising Tilapia. I wasn't sure that if I were in their shoes, I would either.

———————•———————

One evening, after another fruitless day of holding seminars in a nearby village, I arrived back in Kitengo to find almost the entire population crowded in the main avenue, much like they had been when I had first arrived. I parked my bike at my house and found Pumbu in the middle of the crowd. Everyone was swaying and chanting in low tones, looking at a row of six chairs.

Sitting in the chairs was the family that lived diagonally across the avenue from me, an elderly couple, their daughter, and her three children, the oldest being a teenage girl. I didn't see the teenage girl. The straw-man dancers (who were called *munganji* dancers) rocked back and forth solemnly in the sand, a far cry from their usual wild gyrations. The matriarch of the family sat in the chair but kept raising her arms up to the sky and calling out names and words I didn't understand.

It was a funeral for the teenage girl. Sadly, just like Razz had pointed out to us, that morning she had been crossing the river in a canoe when she had drifted into a hippo lair and had been attacked, bitten in two. The further tragedy was that she had been with child, three months pregnant, and had been traveling to the village of her new husband, to start her own family there. Death was the binding force in the village; life was tenuous. A common question to ask when first meeting someone was: "How many children do you have left?" not "How many do you have?" Jackie, Vitesse's wife, had given birth to four children, but only two remained. That is why, I supposed, they didn't speak much about the fact that she was soon expecting her fifth.

The belief in the spirit world was very strong as well. Sometimes my landlord, Mutamba, would join us for dinner at Vitesse's house, and one night we got into a conversation about *ndoki*, or evil spirits. Mutamba had the reputation of being a powerful witch doctor, able to put curses on people, and had effectively been forced to retire by the chief of the village, only allowed to use his magic in extreme situations. I once asked him what was the worst curse he could put on someone. He said he could make someone's skin boil, their body turn white, and make them bleed to death from their ears and their eyes. Strange that about four years after I left, one of the world's first widespread Ebola epidemics broke out in that very area.

I was not spared from the world of magic either, as rumors ran rampant about who I really was and what I could really do. In one of our evening English sessions, sitting in the yard behind my house, Pumbu told me what many of the people in Kitengo believed about me. In the village, I didn't wear my contact lenses and instead wore a pair of glasses with transition lenses, the kind that changes from light to dark depending on where you are. Pumbu said the people thought they were magic glasses, that I could see into the future, or even better, watch my house at all times no matter where I was. That last part Pumbu said he didn't dispute, as he thought it a good idea to have people afraid to come mess with my things.

The other big rumor going around was that I could control the weather. A month after I got there, the rainy season began, and much like summertime in the southern United States, most every afternoon around three or four o'clock thunderstorms would roll in. I would often be down in a valley somewhere speaking (unsuccessfully) to farmers when the clouds would appear, the wind would pick up, and thunder would rumble in the air. We would stop what we were doing and walk back up the valley to the village, but the strange thing was we always made it to their houses before the rain came. So word spread that

I could control the storms and that whoever was with me would be protected and never get wet.

Pumbu and I had a good laugh about that one, but a couple of weeks later I went to visit the farm of a man called Kolombo, who lived deep in the forest near the river. It was about an hour hike on foot to get to his place, the roads not good enough for my motorcycle. He was actually my strongest lead, as he had sought me out and asked me to come see him and look at his land. The same thing happened on my visit: we were down on his farm when the clouds rolled in and a storm looked imminent. We quit, I escorted him back to his home, and then I continued the hour hike back to Kitengo, one of his brothers accompanying me to visit some friends he had living there. The two of us moved up and down mountains, through forests, with lightning flashing, wind swirling, but no rain. I arrived at my house and found Pumbu hanging out in the backyard with some of his buddies. I looked at him and his friends, pointed to the menacing sky, and smiled.

"Hey, Pumbu! Watch this. It's gonna rain right NOW!" I snapped my fingers, and on cue, the heavens opened up and torrents of water rushed to the earth. Pumbu and his friends froze a moment, stunned by my awesome display of power, before dashing for cover inside my house.

The funny thing was, a few weeks later I did, in fact, get caught in a rainstorm, but luckily I was by myself. No one was around to see it. The myth of my weather-mongering continued to live on.

As the fish pond–building business was not exactly happening those first few months, that meant I had a lot of spare time on my hands. I did a lot of reading. Our residence house in Kikwit had a large lending library full of books left behind by volunteers over the years, similar to the one at the training compound in Bukavu, and on the shelves, I'd found a thick college anthology titled *A History of Western Literature.*

It started with the Greeks and went up until the mid-twentieth century, so I opened to page one and began with *Oedipus Rex. Lysistrata, Medea,* and the rest soon followed. There was something vaguely nostalgic, maybe even Hemingway-esque, about sitting in my mud hut at night, reading by the light of a petrol lantern. I also started keeping a journal, jotting down thoughts and observations about the strange new world I was living in, thinking years later it would be useful to look back on my experience there as it was happening. It helped to create the sensation of stepping in and out of a bygone era—early twentieth century, full of pith helmets and adventure, very literary and dashing, even somewhat romantic (if you didn't think too much about the political subtext).

Dinners at Vitesse's house continued every night as he had requested and predicted that first time he knocked on my door. It was something I looked forward to at the end of every day. His wife Jackie would sometimes join us out in the yard after the kids went to bed. She would nick a cigarette from me and pour herself a mug of palm wine, collapsing into a chair after another day full of chopping and carrying firewood, gathering water, pounding manioc, tending the fields, washing clothes, cooking, and taking care of two kids (the amount of work the village women did each day was truly astounding. I was in awe).

She would often pepper me with questions about life in America, similar to my conversations with Ilunga. She especially wanted to know what it was like to be a woman there: What do they wear? What do they look like? How many kids do they have? How many husbands?

"What kind of work do the women do?" she asked me one night. "Do they have to cook?"

"Well, yes, most do. Or they go to restaurants."

"Do they chop firewood?"

"No, not usually."

"How do they cook then?"

I explained what a stove was and her eyes lit up.

"Do they have to carry water?"

I explained about sinks and faucets and she shook her head in disbelief.

"What other work do they do?"

"Um, pretty much whatever they want. Some are politicians, some are doctors—"

She slapped her knee in delight. "Really!" She poked Vitesse on his arm. "See, if we move to America, I could be a politician. Naya could grow up to be a doctor!"

Vitesse just smiled his sheepish grin. A song by Tshala Muana came on the radio. Jackie pulled Vitesse to his feet and they danced in the front yard. All my nights spent with them, I never once heard them say a cross word to each other, nor did I ever feel any tension between them. They might have been the most happily married couple on the face of the earth. Jackie seemed like the kind of person who was *born* happy. She almost always had a smile on her face.

———————•———————

Eventually, I just left my radio there on a full-time basis, as well as many of my cassettes, especially the mixed tapes of Zairian music. Sometimes, impromptu dance parties broke out at Vitesse's place, and I bet we could have started charging admission and turned his front yard into a nightclub.

Occasionally, I would play some of my favorite rock or pop songs, and once, in a moment of mad genius, I slipped in a song by the punk band Black Flag and taught them all the delicate art of slam dancing. I kind of created a monster, because they loved it, loved bouncing their bodies around off each other, especially the kids. Many times they would come up in the evening and ask me to "slamma-jamma," with them but often, my legs heavy from a day of hiking through the woods, I'd have to disappoint them and refuse.

Speaking of hiking, all the walking and physical activity of life in the village was getting me in killer shape. I was getting ripped. I always joked that I should write a book called *The Congolese Fitness Program* and make a million dollars. Step one: live in a mud hut in a small village in the middle of Zaire, Africa. Step two: walk down into and up from deep valleys every day, sometimes carrying heavy jugs of water in your hands, or freshly cut tree trunks balanced on your head, then use those tree trunks to build houses or gazebos or kitchens or chicken coops in your village. Step three: eat lots of palm grubs, salamanders, stewed caterpillars, fried crickets, snake, snake eggs, manioc leaves, rice and beans, squash seeds, *fufu*, various types of mysterious bushmeat, and every part you can imagine of a cow, chicken, goat, or pig, including stomach, brain, liver, and heart. It works. My fast-food diet from the States was long gone, and I had cut way back on smoking, having only a few in the evenings. I was in the best shape of my life.

Pumbu was invaluable. He was my confidant, my translator, my advisor, my teacher, my good friend. I raised his salary to ten thousand Zs a month. I didn't need it. He taught me many skills of village life: how to wash clothes using rocks, how to cook, how to frame a mud house.

Together we did several home-improvement projects to our compound. We built a stand-alone kitchen next to one side of the house. On the other side, we built a chicken coop, then purchased four hens and one unruly rooster. Soon, we had fresh eggs on a regular basis. We also built a gazebo, or *paillote*, in our backyard, kind of like they had in Bukavu, to hang out and relax in during those blistering-hot days.

Soon after that, we started work on building his new house on an empty plot about two doors down. In order for us to have the thick red mud to build the walls, it had to be brought up in buckets from the valley. The sand in the village was useless. So he organized a group of kids to run up and down the trails and dump the dirt near the house frame. Their payment? Shiny pages of photographs from my copies of *Newsweek International* magazine. They loved it, loved looking at the amazing images, the cars, the planes, the people, and the food. It was better than cash, as there was nothing to buy in the village anyway. They would take those pages and hang them up on the walls of their huts, using pieces of *fufu* to tack them in place. I guess it says something that the main food people ate for three meals a day could also be used like glue to decorate their huts and repair holes in cracked pans and pots.

The rest of my spare time was spent just hanging out with the people of Kitengo, getting to know some of the crazy characters. Besides my witch doctor-landlord, there was Kachamba, the local fix-it man who would spend time in the evenings screaming at the night sky. There was "Fangman" whom I'd met at the chief's house. He actually was a super-sweet guy and liked to come over and play chess with me. I just had to try not to look at his teeth. Allone, the teacher, and his wife were very gracious and often came over to my house to learn more English on their own. We even had a Crazy Cat Lady who lived by herself at the edge of the village but whose yard was always full of twenty to thirty feral felines (the actual number varied throughout the year—

depending on the food situation in the village). And out of all the kids, there was one in particular who spent a lot of time around us, a young boy of about ten named Lupu. He was a budding artist, and after one of my trips to the city, I gave him a notebook and a set of colored pencils I had bought for him. He filled that book with sketches of the people of the village, including a great one of me, wearing my magic glasses and sitting on my motorcycle, looking all powerful and commanding, the *mendele* from another world.

———————•———————

As I went through each day, I often wondered how the others in my program were getting along, especially Sheila and Gabriel. Couldn't just pick up a phone to call them because there were none. There was no postal system either. Letters had to be relayed from village to village by hand, so it was a very nice surprise when one day about three weeks before I was due to travel to Kikwit, a young girl walked into my backyard and handed me an envelope. I was actually sitting in my chair, plucking *chigoes*— sand fleas that had burrowed beneath my skin and laid eggs— out of my toes. As the egg sacks grew, the same amount of my flesh disappeared. I had to use a thorn from an acacia tree to dig them out which left caverns of missing tissue at the tips of my toes. Then I had to put on antibiotic cream from our standard-issue first aid kit and bandage them tightly. It was one of my least favorite things to do, so when the girl arrived with the letter, I gladly took a break, thanked her, and asked if she wanted money or magazine pages. She chose the pages.

The letter was from Sheila. It was dated two weeks prior:

Dear Michael,

I hope this letter finds you well and I hope it finds you at all. Not sure what the average delivery time is out here, but since I haven't come across any Federal Express offices, I'll have to take my chances that you get this sometime before the end of the century.

Well, you missed quite the adventure with Gabriel. It got pretty scary. By the time we got back to Kikwit his fever was close to 105. The hospital there is pretty sparse, more like a clinic, run by two Portuguese doctors, and they immediately dumped his body in ice baths to try to cool him down. He was crazy out of it, couldn't remember who Razz or I were, hallucinating and talking gibberish. For the first forty-eight hours, it was pretty touch-and-go; he couldn't keep anything down, no medicine, not even water. They had him hooked up to an IV and even gave him morphine to knock him out and force him to sleep. Eventually, they had to use the "nuclear option": massive doses of quinine to poison the parasites in his body.

I stayed with him the first three days but eventually had to go out to my post. Razz kept in touch and said Gabriel ended up in that hospital for close to two weeks. He finally got out to his post, and Razz said he's doing ok. I sent him a few letters but don't know if he ever read them. In fact, since I've been here in my village, I haven't heard a word from him… But I digress.

Anyway, how is your village? Mine is pretty nice. It's a forest village, so we are not getting blasted by the sun all day long. I'm taking over from a previous volunteer, so there are already a few fish farms out here. My job, I guess, is to keep those going and try to expand them and get more up and running. The people here have been great. The food, however… Well, I guess we can compare notes when I see you next in Kikwit. I hate to admit it, but I'm counting the days. My assistant speaks no English at all, which has been good for my Kikongo, but sometimes I just want to hang out and run my fucking sailor's mouth all night long and not have to worry about translation!

Are you wearing the hat I gave you? You better. I'm sure you are knocking them dead out there. Just remember how far you've come (how far we ALL have come) since those first strange days in Bukavu. I'm sure when this is all over, it will have forever changed our lives.

Stay safe and take lots of pictures!

Yours truly,
Sheila


I carefully folded the letter and slipped it back into the envelope. I was, in fact, wearing the hat she had bought me. I wore it every day. I took it off my head and looked at it. I twirled it on my finger, round and round.

# CHAPTER THIRTEEN

"**A**nother! Another! Another! Pour me another one! Let's get this party started!"

A girl named Caroline, a health volunteer from a town near the Angolan border, slammed two shot glasses on the dining room table. Stevie, a teacher in a village just outside the town of Gungu, poured a bottle of Johnnie Walker Red Whisky over the glasses, spilling as much on the surrounding wood as in the glasses. The two of them quickly tossed the drinks in their mouths.

The residence house was jam-packed; over forty volunteers from all over Bandundu had converged on our regional headquarters after three months out in the bush. For most of us, that had meant three months without electricity, three months without seeing another American, three months without speaking English, three months of grilling palm grubs over campfires, three months without like-minded companionship, and three months without cold water or beer. It was a nuclear explosion of pent-up energy in that house—*our* house, a huge two-story, split-level building with a wide green-grass yard. It was a real home made of brick, wood, and glass and with a large circular patio. It had a refrigerator, a real stove, and electric lights and stereo systems and rooms full of bunk beds. Guest cottages lined the backyard, and it was all tucked away in a nice leafy neighborhood, the clean, lush suburbs surrounding the old frontier town of Kikwit. When we got there, we were like sailors on shore leave. For the next seven days, for most of us, all talk of peace, love, and cross-cultural understanding would fly out the window; we just wanted to party and have a goddamn good time.

After I read that letter from Sheila, I too had begun counting the days until it was time to leave my village and travel there. I was ready for the break. It had been a three-hour motorcycle ride from my house, back over the river, back down that empty, desolate stretch of highway, to this sparkling, welcoming oasis. Pulling up to the corrugated steel gates and beeping my horn for Kutanga, our sentry, to open the doors, I was shivering in anticipation. Then, seeing that giant, beautiful yard and the big house with its cheery red paint, and all the other parked motorcycles lining the edge of the tall stone fence (with shards of broken glass embedded on top so no one could climb on or over it), I felt a deep wave of happiness and relaxation wash over me.

Sheila was the first one to run out the house and greet me, nearly tackling me with a big hug the second I climbed off my bike.

"Soooo good to see you! You look great!" she said and buried

142

her head in my shoulders. "You look so tan. You look fit! Lost weight?"

"A bit, yeah. You look great too." I noticed her strawberry-blonde hair had grown out, now nearly touching her shoulders. "How long you been here?"

"Just pulled in this morning." She hooked her arm in mine and led me to the house. "Feels good to be here, huh?"

"Yes. Most definitely. My village is great, but—"

"Say no more. I understand. We *all* feel that way. Welcome home."

Music was blasting from the stereo as I walked inside: "Love Removal Machine" by The Cult. I saw two people chasing each other around the room with pairs of scissors. I saw half a dozen half-sleeping bodies piled on top of each other on the long sectional sofa.

"Put your stuff away and come out on the patio for a drink. I want to hear all about your adventures. I think there are still some free beds in the back room, or you can grab one of the guest cottages. That's where I am."

"Sure thing. Let me check my mailbox."

Sheila looked at me, her gray eyes beaming, and she gave me a kiss on the cheek. "So good to see you. Really, really good."

I went to a wall of wooden cubbyholes where each volunteer had a slot, their names written on masking tape below each one. Most of the slots were full of fat letters and beige boxes, care packages sent from home. The only things in mine were the last three issues of *Newsweek International*, which we all had complimentary subscriptions to, so, in effect, it was empty. I was disappointed, to be sure, but not entirely surprised.

In the back of the large house, past Razz's bedroom (he lived there full-time now, having graduated from a mud hut in a village), were several rooms with rows of steel-framed bunk beds. I threw my backpack down on an empty striped mattress to stake my claim and headed back to the patio.

The swirl of activity continued inside and out. There was a side staircase leading to the roof, and four people were up there, lying on towels, sunning themselves. On the wide circular patio, several volunteers sat in chairs, taking turns giving each other haircuts, while others lounged in soft, cushy recliners and sofas, thumbing through their letters and packages. In the yard, a group of six was playing three-on-three volleyball. I was just about to sit down on a sofa next to Sheila when I heard a beeping from outside the steel gate. Kutanga pulled open the doors and Gabriel came riding in on his motorcycle.

"Well, look who it is!" I said and turned to Sheila, expecting her to be as excited as I was. She just chewed her bottom lip and stared blankly out at the yard.

I hopped off the side of the patio and walked briskly through the grass over to the motorcycles parked along the wall. As Gabriel pulled his tall body off the bike and removed his helmet, I grasped his hand, gave him a hearty shake up and down, then wrapped my other arm around his shoulder and gave him a quick hug. "What's up, brother? Great to see you!"

At first, he didn't say anything, and his eyes avoided mine. I noticed his face was much thinner, slightly more sunken than when I last had seen him.

"You're alive!" I continued.

"Yep," he said, rather softly. "Good to see you too." He had created two saddlebags for his motorcycle out of old flour sacks, white cotton fabric printed with blue letters of the company name Midema Flour (they were ubiquitous, and people used them to make everything from shirts, to pajamas, to purses). He pulled some clothes out of them and looked at the patio. Sheila stood near the edge, staring out at us. Neither made any gesture to each other.

"So, Sheila sent me a letter, told me all about what happened to you with the malaria," I said. "That's crazy. But if anyone could get through something like that, I knew you could."

"Yeah," he said. "It was something all right."

"Well, come on in the house," I said. "The party has already started."

We walked up the small hill to the main door, and as we got to the top step, Sheila appeared, giving us a half smile.

"Hey, stranger," she said. "Been a long time. You don't write. You don't call. You don't send smoke signals."

"Yeah, sorry about that," he said and looked at the ground. "Been busy, you know, trying to make up for lost time." He hesitated a moment before leaning down and giving her a quick kiss on the cheek. "It's nice to see you."

"Mm," she replied.

"Well, let me go put my stuff away," he said.

Sheila shook her head once from side to side. I followed Gabriel like a puppy over to the mailboxes. His was full with a couple of letters and a small package. "I didn't have anything in mine," I said and leaned against the wall. "Kind of bummed."

Gabriel didn't respond. There was definitely a sense of distance about him, in his eyes that seemed a darker shade of blue. His body language, from where sparks used to fly, was quiet; it now seemed a protective shell had taken its place. I remember all that clearly. That was the first time I sensed something had begun to change within him.

Sheila was standing across the room watching us, with her arms folded over her chest. They looked at each other, and Gabriel silently went by himself toward the rear of the house to claim a bunk. Sheila closed her eyes for a second, then drifted back out to the patio. I was left alone in the middle, standing next to my empty mailbox.

———————•———————

About thirty minutes later, all three of us were sitting outside. Gabriel was in a chair, reading a letter. Sheila and I sat on one of the sofas, sipping from bottles of Fanta orange soda. Razz and a couple of other volunteers, including Caroline and Stevie, were hanging out as well. A plate of cheese sandwiches sat on the table between us. "Waiting in Vain" by Bob Marley drifted from the stereo inside.

"Hey, what's a fax machine?" Razz asked as he looked up

from an issue of *Newsweek International*.

"What's sat?" Caroline responded, slightly slurring her words.

"A fax machine. It says here in the magazine that sales of fax machines have exploded in the States. What's a fax machine? Does anyone know?"

We all shook our heads or shrugged our shoulders.

"Really? No one?" he said. "Wow, what other stuff are we missing out on back home... holy shit! There's a *Batman* movie coming out this year?"

A skinny brown cat leaped onto the table and tried to gnaw at one of the sandwiches. Stevie leaned forward and swatted it away. "Goddammit, there's that stray cat again! It keeps getting into our food." The cat tried once more to get on the table. Stevie stood up, stumbling a bit as he did, and lunged at it until it scrambled off the patio.

"We should get a parachute and send the damn thing to Borneo," Razz said.

"We shoulds eat it," Caroline said.

Stevie slapped his knee. "We should! We should catch it and eat it! Come on, sister!"

Caroline jumped to her feet, and the two ran into the yard, chasing the cat against the far wall. Gabriel looked up from his letter. He watched as the two stumbled drunkenly through the thick grass, zigging back and forth after the cat.

"They're not really going to eat the cat, are they?" he asked, speaking for the first time in nearly half an hour.

"Might," Razz said. "Wouldn't be the first time."

Sheila cleared her throat. "So, Gabriel, how's your village?"

He continued to look out at the yard. "It's fine."

"So, have you got a hundred farmers lined up?" I said, trying to be cheery. "Got dozens of ponds in the works?"

"No. Nothing yet."

"Hang in there, Gabe," Razz said, still reading. "It'll happen for you."

"I'm sure it will." He turned around in the chair as Stevie and Caroline finally cornered the cat near the front gate and grabbed it. They came hopping back across the yard, Caroline with the cat in her hands. The animal squalled and hissed.

"We're going to eat the ca-at!" they sang. "We're going to eat the ca-at!" They held it out in front of Gabriel. "How do you like your kitty?" Caroline asked. "Stewed, fried, or barbecued?"

"You're not really going to do this?" he asked.

"Hell yeah!" Stevie said. "This thing's always getting into our food."

"Because it's *hungry*," Gabriel said.

Razz put down his magazine. "Guys," he said and looked at Caroline and Stevie. Razz shook his head no.

"All right," Caroline said and sighed out. She dropped the cat to the ground where again it scurried away. "Don't blame us next time it eats your breakfast."

"Come on, let's get another drink," Stevie said, and the two of them went inside the house.

We sat there in silence for a couple more minutes. Gabriel

went back to reading his letter, and then he suddenly stood up and left the patio. Sheila rolled her eyes. Razz again looked up from his magazine and over at me. I shrugged my shoulders. A minute later, Gabriel emerged from the front door, carrying all his clothes in his hands as he walked over to the motorcycles. He quickly began to stuff everything back in his saddlebags. Sheila motioned to me. I jumped off into the bushes and went over to him.

"Hey, what are you doing? Are you leaving?"

"Yeah," he said as he fastened the top of each of his saddlebags.

"But you just got here. We're all planning to hang out this week. There's a big party tonight."

"Sounds great. Maybe next time."

"Is it about the cat? I'm sure they were just joking."

"Whatever, it's fine. I just, you know, haven't done anything yet. Need to get back out there. Get some things going... sorry, nothing personal." He looked at the patio. "Tell Sheila... Tell her I promise I'll write to her. Ok? Take care, man. You look great, by the way. You look fit and healthy. Keep it up."

He put on his helmet, slammed his foot on the kick-starter, and rode down the hill out the front gate.

Sheila came up next to me as we looked toward the now-closed gate. "What did he say?" she asked.

"Nothing really," I said and reached into my pocket for a cigarette. "He said to tell you he'd try to write."

"Mm," she said, then walked back up the hill inside the house.

# CHAPTER FOURTEEN

That evening, a large group of people gathered at our residence house for a party. Besides Razz and the forty plus of us Bandundu-region volunteers, dozens of community leaders from Kikwit were there as well. Several local Zairian government officials that we worked with as counterparts attended, including regional officers of the Agriculture and Economic Development ministries who helped to set up and advise our programs. The Portuguese doctors that ran the local hospital came along with Belgian, Indian, and Zairian shop owners from downtown Kikwit.

Different people took turns as DJ, cueing up cassette tapes on their Walkmans, then playing them on the main stereo, shifting back and forth between American and African tunes. The night air was typically hot and thick with humidity, but we didn't care that much, our insides lubricated by very cold bottles of Primus beer or fruit soda. Our own private generators kicked into overdrive once the city electricity was shut off (also supplied by giant gas generators that usually only ran about twelve hours a day).

The front gates opened, and a slender, dark-skinned man wearing a shiny short-sleeved shirt walked through. Sheila saw him, screamed, jumped off the porch, and ran across the lawn. "Aaahhh! Ilunga!" She gave him a big hug and led him over to me.

"Mr. Michael, so good to see you again," Ilunga said and gave me a high five and a quick embrace. "You look well, very healthy."

"Everyone keeps saying that," I said.

Sheila had her arm around Ilunga's shoulder. "Because it's true!" Her eyes were a bit watery and her face flushed as the beer had started to take effect.

"How's your language? Did you remember everything I taught you?"

"Of course," I said. "We would have been lost here without you."

"And Mr. Gabriel? Is he here?"

Sheila waved her hand. "Ah, he's off in the bush. He'd rather be playing with a shovel than hanging out with us."

"Well, he did get a late start," I said, trying to defend him.

"Pishposh," said Sheila. She led Ilunga over to a tub of iced beer. "So tell me about everyone back in Bukavu? Do they miss us…"

The party continued onward as a great success. It was such a stark contrast to our lives out in the village. Both were good; I had found immediate acceptance, if not complete understanding, by all the villagers in Kitengo, and those evenings I spent at Vitesse's house, sitting in his yard, listening to the faraway radio station, with the enormous night sky above our heads, unspoiled by any electric light within hundreds of miles, are still some of my favorite memories; but that house in Kikwit was something special as well. I know I've already called it an oasis, but it truly was a shimmering island full of warmth and camaraderie, our own private, lush landing spot in a very barren region of the world. It served its purpose well, to give us respite and a place to recharge ourselves, get refocused and energized to return to our often arduous work in the field.

Razz was completely bombed. He kept going around asking everyone if they knew what a fax machine was. A few couples had peeled off from the main group and were on the roof, necking like teenagers in a parking lot. Even the brown cat was having a good time; I saw him in the bushes at the base of the patio, and he was happily chewing on a mouse he had caught.

I was standing at the far edge smoking a cigarette when Ilunga came up to me.

"She looks sad," he said.

"Huh?"

He pointed across the patio to where Sheila sat on one of the steps by herself, her face kind of blank, her shoulders drooped, nearly touching her knees.

"You should go speak with her," he said. He reached over, taking the rest of my cigarette from my fingers, and put it in his mouth. With his other hand, he patted me on the back. "Go on."

As I walked across the patio toward her, Sheila's expression and body didn't change, frozen like a statue. It wasn't until I sat down on the step next to her that she came out of whatever deep thoughts she had been lost in. She looked over at me and barely smiled. "Hey," she said in a soft voice.

"You ok? You seem like you were kind of out of it for a bit."

"Yeah, fine. You know…"

We sat a moment in silence. "Look," I said. "You know how he is. He's very driven. Very focused. Sometimes I wish I could be more like that."

She sighed and looked up at the night sky. "No, you're good the way you are," she said and took a sip of her beer. "It's fine, really. We'd kind of been drifting apart for a while, before he got sick. It stings a bit, but I guess it was just a fling we had… God, listen to me. So gloomy. On this beautiful night. At this great party. With good friends." She turned her face toward mine.

"Thanks," I said. "I do my best."

"You do great."

The wildly popular Zairian song "Keteke" by Jean Papy Ramazani came on the stereo, and a cheer went up from the crowd dancing in the middle of the patio. She grabbed my hand and stood up, pulling me with her. "I love this song. Come dance with me."

We dove into the middle of the crowd and began moving to the fast beat. It was a *soukous* song, with pulsing horns and jangling guitars, a very popular style that featured lots of chanting and call-and-response. Almost everyone at the party was crammed onto the patio, and Sheila and I danced around each other, throwing our hands up over our heads, shouting "Hey, hey, hey! Whoa, whoa, whoa!" spinning, swaying, and each time her face turned round and round, her expression changed; it started as all smiles, having fun to the music, but bit by bit something else began swirling around us. I felt it, she felt it, and each time she passed by my face, her eyes kept looking at me in a different way, as if they were seeing me for the first time, studying me, opening wide...

———————•———————

Late night now and the party was nearly over. Most people had left, passed out, or gone to bed. Sheila and I sat on one of the sofas on the patio. She had her legs curled on the seat, her hands folded between her knees, and her head lay on the top of the back cushion. The song "Under the Milky Way" by The Church played at a low volume on the stereo.

"...I'm serious," I continued. "Two snakes in one day! It was there sitting in my bed. Not sure what I would have done if Pumbu hadn't been there."

"He sounds great," Sheila said.

"Pumbu? Yeah, he's awesome. I really lucked out having him come work with me."

"I saw a spitting cobra once," Sheila said and yawned. "It was pretty freaky."

"You look sleepy."

She half closed her eyes and nodded. "Yes, I think I'll call it a night."

"Me too." I stood up, and she stuck out her hand, waiting for me to help pull her up.

"Will you walk with me to the cottage?" she asked.

"Um, sure"

We climbed down off the patio and into the yard. A nice breeze moved through the palm trees surrounding the lawn. Sheila wrapped her arms across her chest and lifted her face up to catch some of the wind. "Mmm, that feels nice... It's weird sometimes, isn't it? Where we are. That we are actually here, doing what we're doing. You ever feel that way?"

"Yeah, at least once a day it hits me. I look around and just can't believe it."

"Me too," she said softly.

I looked down at her, at the curve of her neck, at the small mole behind her right ear, at the slope of her shoulder, and I thought: *Don't do it. Swooping in on your friend's girl. Even if they are broken up, it's too soon. Don't do it.*

We reached the door of one of the half-dozen guest cottages in the backyard. "Ok, I guess I'll see you tom—"

Before I could finish, Sheila reached up and grabbed the back of my neck, jerking my head down to her mouth, and she kissed me deeply and hard, pressing her body against mine. With her other hand, she quickly opened the door and pulled me into the room, panting and grinding her waist into my thigh. After a moment, we broke apart. I stood in front of the bed and she took a couple of steps backward. We were both breathing heavily as we looked at each other.

"Should we be doing this?" I asked.

Sheila stared at me, taking several more deep breaths. "Note to self," she whispered. "Fuck his brains out." She then ran and jumped on me. I tried to gallantly catch her, but she knocked me off my feet, causing both of us to fall backward onto the bed so hard the wooden frame immediately broke apart, sending the mattress crashing to the concrete floor. We didn't stop, not for one second; she rolled on top of me, ripping off her own blouse, then she tore off my shirt as well.

# CHAPTER FIFTEEN

Early morning. Pale blue light dripped through the window of the cottage. I rose from the bed, stepping over the shattered bits of the frame, and wrapped a towel around my waist. I walked outside onto the lawn, the grass wet and thick with morning dew, sticking to my ankles and between my toes. I went to the back of the main house where the showers and toilets were to relieve my bladder. We had to use the "bucket flush" method in the house, by filling a pail of water from the tub and pouring it in the bowl to wash away the old. I heard a few other early risers rumbling through the great house and, when I went back to the lawn, saw a couple of folks sitting on the patio, plastic mugs of coffee in hand, watching the new sky crawl to life.

I stood in the doorway of the cottage. It looked like a tornado had ripped through there, with the shattered furniture, clothes everywhere; we had even managed to knock over a table lamp, leaving a pile of broken glass in the corner of the room.

I watched as she lay in bed, her strawberry-blonde hair spread out against the pillow. She was gorgeous, and I had certainly never *not* thought that, but it wasn't like these past months I had been secretly pining for her, waiting for my chance. Yesterday afternoon, we were one thing, now we were something completely different.

She raised her head slightly. "What are you doing?" she whispered, her voice slightly hoarse. "Come back to bed. We aren't on village time."

Each step I took, slight twinges of guilt shot through my body, but once I was back on the mattress lying down next to her, they quickly disappeared. We stayed wrapped around each other, drifting in and out of sleep for a few more hours, while through the concrete walls, snippets of the outside world waking up and getting active—motorcycle engines revving, trucks lumbering down the nearby roads, laughter and music from the patio— seeped into the room. Around 10 a.m. she rolled over, half-awake and placed her chin on my chest.

"Hey," she said. She reached up and kissed me lightly on the lips, then put her head back down near my shoulder. "Wow, what a mess we made."

"Yes, we did."

"It was worth it," she said, and looked into my eyes. "Wasn't it?"

I hesitated a moment. "Yes, of course."

"You're worried about Gabriel."

"A bit, yes."

"You mean the 'guy code' and all that? Honestly, I really don't think he'll care." She put her head back on my chest and stared at the wall. Her fingernail skated across my rib cage, then stopped. "Maybe you're right. Maybe it was a mistake." She kicked the sheets free from her legs and started to get out of bed.

I cupped my hand on her shoulder and pulled her back down. At that moment, I didn't want her to ever stop resting her head on my chest, didn't want to ever stop seeing her lying next to me. I leaned over and kissed her, to try to reassure her. "No, you're right. This wasn't a mistake. Please stay."

Sheila searched my face looking, I supposed, for sincerity. She nodded and returned beside me. A few quiet minutes passed before she stretched her legs along mine. "Hey, I've got an idea. Let's take a shower."

"Here? Not sure if we can get away with that."

"No, I know a place about ten minutes outside the city. Put on your swimsuit and grab a towel. Then we can ride into town and get some food. I'm starving."

We got dressed and went outside, over to where our bikes were parked along the wall. A few people saw us coming out of the cottage together, and we caught a few knowing winks and smiles. We drove our motorcycles out the front gate, through the winding neighborhood, then back out on the main highway that headed west toward Kinshasa.

About ten kilometers away, Sheila led us off on a path through a small patch of woods. We parked the bikes, then hiked about five minutes until we came to a small waterfall, about five meters high, pouring from a wall of rocks into a small lagoon. No one was around, the wall of trees a natural barrier, and we peeled off our clothes down to our swimsuits, the cold water first taking our breath away. Soon, we were standing beneath the outflow and splashing around the reservoir, the blue sky towering above us.

We lounged like turtles on a pair of flat rocks, the sun warming our bodies. "Ahh, this is amazing, right?" she said.

"Perfect," I said. "How did you find out about it?"

"One of the other volunteers, a girl named Chris, showed it to me the day before I went out to my village."

"Ahh, the village. Four more days, and it'll be time to get back out there. This week here will spoil me, to be sure."

"I know, but it's kind of nice to have both experiences, extreme as they might be."

I slid off the rock into the waist-deep water and squatted down so it covered my shoulders. "What do you want for lunch? I'll cook."

Sheila slipped in the water next to me. "You cook?"

"Yeah, I love it. My mom was a chef. She taught me a lot."

"Was?"

"Yes. She died a couple of years ago. My sophomore year. Breast cancer."

"I'm sorry... dad?"

"He passed when I was six."

"Jesus."

"It's ok."

Sheila shook her head. "God, all my friends have such terrible stories about growing up. Gabriel has some horrible stories. He

162

had a really, really fucked-up childhood. I always feel so guilty because I've never had anything bad happen to me. My parents are great, I love them. My sister is my best friend. My grandparents are all alive. The worst thing that ever happened to me was I broke my toe once in sixth grade."

"You shouldn't feel guilty. Not at all."

"It's just, you know, sometimes when people tell me things like that, I don't know what to say. I can't say: 'I understand' because I don't. Sometimes I wish some horrible tragedy would strike me—"

"You should never, ever wish that," I said. "Really, be proud of what you have, and hold on to it as long as possible."

She nodded and looked at the water then back at me. "No brothers or sisters?"

"Nope. Just me."

She took a few steps through the water, placed her hands on both sides of my face. "Not today, baby," she said. "Not today." She circled her legs around my waist, her thighs pressing into my hips, and I wrapped my arms around her, lifting and holding her wet body tightly against mine.

———————•———————

Around noon, we drove our bikes into downtown Kikwit. It looked like exactly what it had once been: a frontier stop, an old colonial trading post from all the rubber plantations (the name "Bandundu" meant rubber tree), like a set from an Old West mining town, the main streets lined with straight rows of one- or two-story buildings made from wood or cinder block, with rusty tin roofs. Around the old district, newer buildings had been constructed including a community sports center that had open-air basketball and volleyball courts and a café with large umbrellas emblazoned with the logo of the soft drink Orangina, but the bulk of the shops and activity were centered on the streets that backed up against the wide black Kwilu River.

There was a nice, brightly lit deli run by a Portuguese family that had special cuts of meat and various types of food imported from Europe. There was a green wooden sign hanging above the counter, hand-painted in white letters in five different languages (French, Kikongo, Portuguese, English, and for some reason, German) that said: "HERE: Suck Pigs." A pleasant-looking Zairian girl that didn't look above sixteen-years-old was behind the register and cheerfully filled two bags with our order. We bought half a dozen eggs, sliced ham, a block of parmesan cheese, some tomatoes, green onions, a sweet potato, and a pineapple. I saw a tin of salted almonds on the shelf and had an idea.

"Ooh, how about I make some almond fudge?" I said to Sheila.

"Chocolate! You do know the way to a girl's heart."

I bought the tin of almonds, a can of Nestlé Quik chocolate powder, a hunk of margarine, and a can of condensed milk. Sheila and I divvied up the groceries between us, and we carried the bags on our laps as we rode back to the residence house.

We got lucky and had the kitchen to ourselves. Most of the

others had finished lunch and were lounging around outside, some playing a game of Wiffle ball in the yard with a big red plastic bat. Sheila and I got to work and chopped the tomatoes and green onions into small bits, then took a carving knife and peeled off long curly shards of the parmesan cheese. I whisked the eggs together in the bowl and, on one burner of the stove, took a cast-iron pan and began cooking our omelets. I chopped up the ham, potato, and pineapple and, on the other burner, started grilling them into a kind of hash.

"This sure beats palm grubs and fried crickets," I said.

"Absolutely," said Sheila. "Have you had termites yet? Do they eat them live or cooked where you are?"

I flashed back in my mind to that meeting with the chief on my second day. I shuddered a bit. "Both," I said. "But I draw the line at eating them alive. No way."

"Actually, let's stop talking about it," she said. "I don't want to ruin our appetite."

"Agreed."

We devoured the dish in half the time it took to make it. The eggs were fluffy and fragrant, the pineapple/potato hash salty and sweet. Sheila didn't speak much but did a lot of groaning and moaning—always a good sign of success. I then set about baking the fudge, combining the Quik powder, condensed milk, and margarine in a saucepan and bringing it to a boil, then dropping in the almonds and spooning the mixture into a glass baking dish, covering it with a towel, and setting it aside to cool. Thirty minutes later, we had nice thick chunks of fudge. We ate half the pan ourselves, then went to the patio and passed around the rest of it to a very surprised and appreciative group. Razz had three pieces all by himself.

---

It was late that afternoon, maybe around four o'clock, when Sheila and I were sitting at the dining room table. We had just finished a game of chess (which she won, of course), and she was showing me some of the photos from her village. She sat next to me, one arm around my back, and her chin resting on my shoulder as she explained each picture. That was when I looked up and saw Gabriel standing next to the wall of mailboxes.

"Gabriel? When did you come back?" I asked.

"I—forgot to drop off a package for my sister."

Sheila took her arm from around me and scooted her chair over an inch or two. Gabriel stared back and forth at both of us. "Wow. That was fast."

"Gabriel…" Sheila began.

"No, it's fine," he said softly. "I'm not staying. Just dropping off this package." He put a small brown box in the outgoing mail bin by the cubbyholes. "Take care."

He turned and quickly walked out the door to the yard. I sat a moment at the table, my face flushed, my jaw tightening. "God damn it," I said and stood up to follow him.

"Michael, wait, just let him go."

By the time I got to the yard, he had already turned his

motorcycle around and was heading out the front gate. I hopped on mine, no shoes or helmet, cranked the kick-starter and gunned the engine down the hill out onto the road. I followed him through the neighborhood streets, sometimes pulling up even with him, yelling at him to pull over, but he ignored me. Finally, we came to one of the main intersections in town. There was a small roadside market across the street, only about a dozen crooked stalls. Gabriel steered his bike off the road into the empty space next to a woman selling manioc. He took off his helmet but left the cycle running as I followed and came to a stop next to him.

It took me a moment to figure out what to say. "Gabriel, I'm sorry. It just kind of happened. Last night. It's not something we've been planning or doing behind your back."

He waited for a moment to respond. "It's fine, Mike, really," he said in a calm voice. "I blew her off. I hadn't spoken to her in a couple of months."

I looked carefully at his expression, trying to decipher if what he was saying was how he truly felt, or if he was just trying to save face.

He looked at me for the first time. "Seriously. It's ok. She's a great girl. She really is. I'm just not interested in anything like that right now." He turned his head to his left. Over our shoulders, two young boys, shirtless and barefoot, were digging with their hands through a dusty, smoldering trash heap. "I didn't come here for a two-year paid vacation. I didn't come here just to party and get laid. I came here to do something. To make a difference."

"I know," I said.

"It's nothing against you or Sheila. Ok?"

"Ok."

"Good. Look our next break is in July. I *promise* we'll hang out then. Catch up. All right?"

"Sure. Sounds good."

He held out his hand and I shook it. He put on his helmet and began to drive away…

Many people who have serious accidents or are involved in near-death experiences report that time seems to slow down just at the moment of impact. Like in the movies, when the camera goes into slow motion, and you see the person slowly mouthing the words *no* or *stop*, maybe even the voice is stretched out in a warped fashion to heighten the effect.

Well, I didn't have time to say no or stop, but I can still see Gabriel slowly driving away, his head turned, looking back at me as if to give me one last bit of reassurance that everything truly was fine, everything was really ok, right before he pulled into the street in front of a large cargo truck. Then everything sped up, horrifically so, the sickening smack and thud of metal against bone, the screaming, the screeching of the truck's brakes as it tried too late to stop, the sound of the metal of the motorcycle scraping against the road, sparks flying all around, as the truck pushed it and Gabriel's body, crunching over on top of both of them, then spitting them out like a faulty part, discarded and spinning to a final stop in the middle of the road.

I ran out to him, his body pinned beneath the bike, his whole lower left side smashed and covered in grease and blood, the white shards of his leg bone jutting out from his thigh and hip. He was quiet, but I saw him moving, trying to push the bike off of himself, and I ran and lifted it, dropping it to the side. I took off his helmet so he could better breathe. His face was frozen in stunned silence. I slipped my hands under his head, cushioning it from the asphalt of the road.

"Hang in there, hang in there," I whispered.

That was when I heard the first thrown rock. It slammed against the hood of the truck. The driver was still inside, sitting motionless with both hands gripping the steering wheel, looking stunned. A crowd surged along the side of the road, pouring out of the market stalls, and someone ran up and smashed the front windshield with a stick. Others quickly surrounded the truck, yelling, throwing more stones, and they began to rock it side to side, lifting the tires off the ground. A swirl of angry arms reached into the front seat and clawed at the driver, trying to pull him out. He fought back, screaming at them in French to leave him alone and that he was sorry, so sorry.

I had no choice but to pull Gabriel out of the street and away from the mob, over to the other side. He screamed in pain as I dragged his leg across the asphalt. Out of the corner of my eye, I saw Sheila riding to the intersection on her motorcycle. I furiously waved at her. "Go back! Go back! Get Razz! Get his truck!"

She immediately turned her bike around. Gabriel looked

across the road at the crowd that had descended on the driver. "No," he whispered. "Don't let them kill him. Please, Michael, don't let them kill him."

But there was nothing I could have done. They pulled the driver out the front windshield, over the hood, his arm tearing across a sharp spike in the front grill, down to the pavement where he disappeared beneath the crowd, a swarm of people beating and kicking him until his skin was nearly stripped from his body.

# CHAPTER SIXTEEN

Torn. Shattered. Shredded. Those are the words that always come to mind when I think of what happened that day on the side of the road. Gabriel's shattered leg, his motorcycle shredded in pieces across the street. The windshield of the truck shattered, the driver's lifeless body torn and shredded by dozens of furious hands. Sheila had been quick: only about five or six minutes passed before I saw Razz's truck screeching around the corner of the intersection (I know because I kept constantly checking my watch). I had dragged Gabriel underneath a papaya tree on the other side of the road, moving him against the highest threshold of pain I thought he could tolerate. Three level-headed good-Samaritan Zairian men had seen what happened and stood in front of us creating a human wall, shielding us from the insanity of the deadly mob that had erupted on such a beautiful, sunny day.

Razz told us he had sent a message ahead to the hospital, so when we pulled in front of the dusty, low-slung building, the Portuguese doctor on duty and two Zairian nurses were standing outside waiting for us. All of us, including myself and Sheila, helped to carefully slide and roll Gabriel's bloody, broken body from the back of Razz's truck onto a stiff wooden board then onto a gurney. The nurses wheeled it inside straight to their single operating room, a sparse blue-tiled space with a small tray of tools, a sink, a light, and an IV bag.

For Gabriel, the initial shock of the accident continued to wear off and more pain set in, terrifying pain, for while we stood outside the doors to the room we could hear him screaming over and over again. It was a sound one should really never hear, especially coming from the mouth of someone you love. Sheila was crushed, crying heavily as she slumped to the floor, her body pressed against a cracked plaster wall. Razz peered in through the windows of the door, tears filling his eyes as well. For all his gonzo, wild-man attitude, it was always clear to everyone Razz took his job very seriously, that he cared ferociously about all of us as if we were his own children.

"Come on, buddy," he whispered. "You're the big man. We'll get you through this."

Blood covered my fingers and smeared the end of each cigarette I lit while I paced around the dimly lit corridor. A wall clock across from the door could barely be seen, but it seemed each loud click of the second hand fell in rhythm with Gabriel's grunting and yelling, a symphony of despair until suddenly everything from within the operating room fell quiet. Suddenly there was no sound at all, and that brought Sheila, Razz, and I running to the door. I pushed it open:

*Was it? Was he? What had happened? What?*

The doctor looked up at us and briefly pulled down his mask with his bloody glove. "Morphine," he said. "He'll be out for a while."

I saw Gabriel's chest moving up and down under the green sheet. One of the nurses adjusted his head on a pillow as his eyes fluttered but remained shut.

---

**N**ight had fallen now. The three of us continued to sit in the hallway. As Sheila had mentioned in her letter to me, the place was really more like a rural clinic than a hospital, so we weren't surprised when the doctor came out and shook his head.

"There's not much more I can do here," he said. "We're not really equipped for something this serious. I'll give him some more morphine for the pain and antibiotics to prevent infection. I also wrapped his left hip and leg best I could to keep it stable and from fracturing further. But he will need surgery. Sooner the better."

"I sent a shortwave message to our headquarters in Kinshasa," said Razz. "They are sending out our medical officer, Doc Peters. He'll be here in the morning. He'll probably take him back to the US Embassy hospital, let them decide what to do."

"That's best. We'll keep an eye on him, make sure he is not in pain, watch his temperature."

"Can we stay here with him tonight?" Sheila asked.

"If you wish. We have some extra cots we can pull out for you."

Razz and I followed a young orderly to a supply closet and helped him to pull out three rusted foldaway frames and three straw-filled mattresses. While we were setting them up in rows along the hall, one of the nurses opened the doors to the operating room and pushed out the gurney, rolling Gabriel past us. He turned his head and opened one eye, looking right at me.

"Mike," he said.

"He's awake?" I asked the nurse.

"For now," she said.

We followed as she brought him to an empty patient room at the far end of the corridor. Once she had connected him to a new IV, we went in and stood by Gabriel's bed. He was semi-conscious, still heavily doped up on the morphine. He half-opened both eyes and waved for me to come closer. I leaned near his mouth.

"Did they kill him? The driver, Michael, did they kill him?" he whispered.

"Gabriel, don't worry about things like that," I said.

He grabbed my arm with what little strength he had at that moment. "Did they?"

I knew the answer, of course, but I couldn't tell him. "I don't know," I said. "I don't think so."

"Good," he said, and closed his eyes. "That's good," he said one more time then fell back asleep.

---

We had a fitful night on those cots, none of us really dozing off for more than a couple of hours. The nurses went in and out of Gabriel's room on a regular basis, and we could hear him start to moan and writhe each time the morphine began to wear off. A few times Sheila reached over to my cot to clasp my hand in hers.

Just past daybreak, Doc Peters walked down the hallway. We climbed to our feet to greet him.

"How was the drive?" Razz asked.

"Roads get worse each time," Doc said. "But I'm here. How is he?"

Razz tilted his head from side to side "Stable, but lots of dope."

We followed as Doc entered the room. Gabriel lay on his back, staring at the ceiling. Doc looked at the clipboard chart hanging on the end of the bedframe then took a penlight out of his shirt pocket and flashed it into each of Gabriel's eyes. He checked Gabriel's temperature, and checked Gabriel's reflexes on each leg and foot. Doc peeled back the bandages on the left leg. "Tissue looks good. No infection yet. Pupils dilate. Right leg normal to stimulus. Left leg unresponsive."

"So what do you think will happen?" Razz asked.

Doc sighed out. "Damn motorcycles. I've been trying to get them banned... Well, he's going to have to have his femur reconstructed. I don't think the embassy hospital in Kinshasa can handle it. Probably have to med-evac him to South Africa or maybe back to the States."

"No," Gabriel moaned. "Don't want to go back to the States."

Razz put his hand on Gabriel's forehead. "We'll have to see, buddy. See what the doctors say."

"Will he be able to come back?" Sheila asked.

"I don't know," said Doc. "Too early to tell."

"Have to come back. Haven't done anything yet," Gabriel said, slurring his speech.

"Shhh, listen to me: you still got time," Razz said. "Lots of time."

Two nurses entered the room followed by the Portuguese doctor. His eyes were bloodshot, looking like he had had a similarly fitful night of sleep as the rest of us. He reached out and shook hands with Doc Peters. "Jon," he said.

"Miguel," Doc said.

"I did the best I could."

"I know," Doc said. "You did fine. Thank you. I'll take it from here." Doc nodded to one of the nurses on duty. "Ok, let's get him ready for the ride back to Kin." He took a couple of vials of morphine from the bedside table and put them in his other shirt pocket.

The nurses tightened and rewrapped Gabriel's bandages. All of us followed as they rolled the gurney down the dark, unlit hallway, out the front door into another strangely out of place, beautiful blue morning. We strapped Gabriel down carefully in the back of Doc's full-sized Land Rover.

"I'll check in with you each day over the radio," Doc said to Razz.

"The next group of trainees doesn't come until next October, so we got plenty of time to decide if we need to replace him. Let this play out as long as you can," Razz said.

"Will do." Doc turned to Sheila and me. "Michael, Sheila, nice to see you again. Wish it was under better circumstances."

Sheila hooked her arm in mine. "So do we."

Doc climbed in the front seat and turned the car out the dirt parking lot. He waved goodbye one final time, then disappeared down the asphalt road.

Razz wiped tears from his eyes and placed his hand on my shoulder.

———————•———————

The accident certainly cast a pall over the rest of our time in Kikwit. No more big parties. We had several meetings to discuss the progress of our projects. We spent one whole day taking apart and cleaning our motorcycles. On the day before our break was scheduled to end, Razz told all of us Gabriel had been sent to a hospital in Cape Town to have surgery on his leg and hip. Still no decision if, or when, he would be back.

In retrospect, I'm surprised Gabriel's accident didn't drive a quick wedge through my fledgling relationship with Sheila. Instead, it brought us much closer together. By the end of that week, we both knew it was no fling, no random short-term hookup. We spent each night together in the guest cottage, and on our last morning, before we were due to travel back to our villages, we went again to the waterfall on the outskirts of town.

"I don't want to say goodbye," she said. We both leaned against the warm flat rocks in the lagoon. "I mean, I'm excited to get back to work, but I don't want to wait three months to see you again."

"Neither do I."

Sheila thought a moment. "Maybe we could both plan to come back here in a month to 'buy supplies,'" she said, using her fingers to create air quotes.

I exhaled. "Sounds good, but Razz will see right through that."

"He won't care. As long as it's short. He knows we're out there working hard. He knows we're not slackers."

I looked at her perfectly shaped face, her wet hair pulled behind her ears. "Ok, one month. Back here. 'Supply shopping.'"

She put her head against my chest. "I should have never said that last time we were here. I should have never said I wanted something bad to happen."

I put my arm around her waist and gave her body a quick shake. "Stop it. I was the one who followed him. I was the one who got him to stop at that market by the road. I was the one he was distracted by when he drove into the street."

"Think he'll come back?"

"Yes, definitely," I said. "He'll come back and blow all of us away."

We floated around in the water for another half hour, then dried off and went back to the house. We packed, said goodbye, and each rode our motorcycles out of town. Sheila turned south, I continued east. The city quickly disappeared, and soon I was back out on that long, empty stretch of highway. I would miss her for certain, but as she said, I was also ready to get back to my village, ready to get back to work. At the very least, it would help take my mind off what had happened to Gabriel.

# CHAPTER SEVENTEEN

I pulled into Kitengo late afternoon. As usual, all the kids in the village dropped whatever they were doing and ran alongside me yelling *"Mendele! Mendele!"* I made the final sharp turn down the main avenue and pulled to a stop in front of my house. The children clamored and pressed their bodies against my fence.

Pumbu came walking around from the backyard and greeted me. "Mr. Michael, so good to see you," he said in Kikongo and shook my hand. "How was your break?"

I climbed off the cycle and removed my helmet. After a week of speaking English nonstop, I was surprised how easy (and comforting) it was to slip back into Kikongo. "Good to see you too," I said. "The break was good. It was also not good. A lot to talk about."

"Would you like coffee?"

"Yes. That would be fantastic."

While in Kikwit, I had some saddlebags made like Gabriel had, and I filled them with food from the Portuguese deli. I had a bag of rolls that I thought would last about a week, canned vegetables, canned tuna, mustard packets, tins of sardines, dried fruit, and I brought the Nestlé Quik to make fudge. I put everything away in our pantry and settled in the chair in the salon. Pumbu brought two mugs of coffee and joined me.

"Are we going to Vitesse's tonight for dinner?" I asked.

"I don't think so. He had to travel to Gungu, to the magistrate's office."

I was disappointed. I had been thinking about it on the long drive down the highway, looking forward to relaxing under the stars with a good cup of palm wine and listening to *The Marlboro Hit Parade*. "Really? What happened?"

"He had palm oil stolen from him. From down in the forest. Two barrels. Thieves came in a truck in the middle of the night."

"Oh no, that's terrible."

"Yes. He went to report it. But I'm sure nothing will come of it. They will fill out a form, and then just stick it in a drawer."

I had been to Vitesse's palm oil press in the forest and watched him and his cousin Foster. It was backbreaking, hot, sweaty work. They had to climb the palm trees and cut down the stalks of palm nuts, boil them to soften them and peel away the skin, and then they had a large press they had made out of bamboo, where they turned it to mash the palm nuts and squeeze out the thick orange buttery oil. Then they had to filter it and capture it in large steel drums. From there, they had to transport it to a wholesale market, where each drum would fetch between twenty and twenty-five thousand Zaires. Vitesse was afraid of the river, so his cousin Foster would be the one to float the oil down in a canoe. Each barrel took a long month's work to complete.

Pumbu filled me in on the other gossip in the village: several births, thankfully no deaths. I then told him about what happened to Gabriel, and he said he would pray for him. Pumbu was very religious, he read a French version of the Bible daily, and after he finished building his house and started his new family, he wanted to build a small church there in Kitengo.

We finished our coffee, and I stood up and looked out the window of our front door. The sun was fading, and most everyone had returned from the valley and was getting ready to cook dinner and settle in for the night. I thought about my work then, the job I had been sent there to do, to teach people how to build ponds and raise fish, and the fact that nothing had happened so far.

"Pumbu, what am I doing wrong?"

"What do you mean, Mr. Michael?"

"I've been here over three months now, and nothing is happening. No one is interested in what I'm trying to do. They smile and are polite, but they ignore me."

Pumbu climbed out of the chair and came over to stand next to me. He switched to speaking in English.

"They are not ignoring you, I can assure you that," he said. "You are all they talk about. You are a celebrity here. But you have to understand, life here in Zaire is very different from America. And life in the village is very different from the city. Time is different. You are doing the right things. You are meeting people and getting to know them, but most importantly, they are getting to know *you*. They first must trust you before they can understand you. And they are. They will. You have to let them come to you. You cannot force it. Then once one person comes to you, I promise, others will soon follow."

I looked at him and smiled. "Thanks."

"Can I ask you a favor?"

"Of course, anything."

"My fiancée, Neva, wants to come here next week to visit me. Is it ok if she stays in my room with me? We will be respectful, I promise."

"Sure, of course. I can't wait to meet her. How's the house coming?"

"Good. A bit slow in the rainy season. Hopefully, in a couple of months, it will be done."

"Well, please take as much time as you need. On a purely selfish level, I like having you here, especially when I find pythons waiting for me in my bed at night."

Pumbu laughed. "Yes, but they are tasty, no?"

"They are pretty good. Speaking of which, I'll cook tonight since we aren't going to Vitesse's. Have you ever had fudge...?"

After dinner, I heated up a pot of water and took a bucket bath in my "shower" room. I checked my bed—no snakes—and after I extinguished the petrol lantern, I just lay in the darkness, thinking about Sheila, remembering the way her skin smelled like Ivory soap, the way her body felt when it was wrapped around mine. Then I thought about Gabriel, far away in South

Africa, and I could envision him in some physical therapy room, pushing himself, learning how to walk with his new leg and hip, not giving up, spending every ounce of energy he had to get whole and healthy and to get back here as soon as he could.

———————————•———————————

The next morning, after a breakfast of *fufu* and stewed caterpillars given to us by Mutamba and his wife, I pulled a chair into my backyard and opened up my giant anthology of Western literature. I was up to the mid-1800s now, and started reading Edgar Allan Poe's short story "The Gold Bug." A nice breeze swished through the dry savannah grass, and the steady pounding of mortar and pestles filled the air and vibrated through the sand at my feet. It was a typically beautiful and relaxing morning in the village, far from car horns or diesel fumes. I had no appointments or presentations planned that day, so after lunch, I was going to help Pumbu with his house.

I had just gotten to the second page in the story when Vitesse came slowly walking in my yard. He had his head down and his hands in his pockets as he shuffled his bare feet through the sand. Jackie followed him.

"Vitesse, Jackie," I said. "I'm so sorry. Pumbu told me what happened."

He just grunted and nodded his head.

"Did you get any help at the magistrate's office?"

He shook his head no and kept pacing back and forth in front of me. I offered him a cigarette and he took it. After a few puffs, he stopped and looked down at me, staring at me as if he was trying to decide something.

"Yes? Is there anything I can do to help you?" I asked.

He took one last drag of the cigarette, stubbed it out in the dirt. Jackie gently put her hand on his shoulder. "Go on, now," she said.

Vitesse stood up straight like a soldier snapping to attention. He cleared his throat.

"I want you to show me how to grow fish."

# CHAPTER EIGHTEEN

I followed Vitesse to the bottom of the valley, across the stream, to where he had his land. We each carried a shovel in our hands. He showed me the tire tracks in the dirt the thieves had left, next to a large pile of empty palm nut husks.

"I don't want to do that work anymore," he said. "I'm tired of it."

"Ok, well, the first thing is to check out what kind of soil you have." I dug a hole about half a meter down, then reached in and grabbed a hunk of dirt and pressed it into a ball in my palm. I dropped the ball of dirt to the grass and most of it held together. "Perfect," I said and explained to him that he wanted a good mixture of clay and sand. Too much sand and the pond wouldn't hold water; too much clay and it would be too hard to dig and shape. We then walked around the edge of his property, and I saw a spot where a bend in the creek rose at a slightly higher angle. I explained to him we could dig a canal and divert some of the water to fill up the pond.

"But where do the fish come from?" he asked.

I took out the flip chart from my backpack and showed him how, the first time only, I would put baby fish in the pond. I would get them from another farmer's pond or from a hatchery not too far from us near the town of Lutshima. I explained it would probably take about a month or two to build the pond, then six months to "grow" the fish. After that, it would be his responsibility to continue to restock his own pond at the end of each harvest.

"Are you sure you want to do this?" I asked. "It's a lot of work at the beginning, but then once you have it, it's pretty easy to take care of."

"Yes, yes," he said, not hesitating. "My cousin will help us. He's tired of palm oil as well. I want to do this."

"Ok," I said. "Let's measure it."

There was a pile of dried vines next to his palm oil press, and I used the walking stick Gabriel had made for me to measure out a rectangle ten-by-twenty meters. We pinched the vines along the way with twigs to give us the outline of his first pond. We stood in the center of the rectangle and raised our shovels.

I looked at Vitesse. "I promise you. You won't regret this."

We hit the ground with the steel blades at the same time, slicing through the grass to the red dirt below.

———————•———————

By the end of that first day, we had dug a small square of about one-by-two meters. That was pretty much the pace we kept up during the first week. His cousin Foster was away visiting family in another village and wouldn't join us until sometime later, so during those initial days of building his pond, it was just me and Vitesse walking every day to the bottom of the valley, toiling and sweating under the intense Bandundu sun. We took frequent breaks, and we brought lots of snacks and water with us. Lunchtime we spent in the shade of his thatched day shelter next to his now-abandoned palm oil press. We talked a lot about many things. He told me lots of stories about the history of that area including Pierre Mulele's short-lived but violent rebellion in the 1960s that nearly wiped out the entire village, but there was one particular conversation we had that I will never, until the day I die, ever, ever forget.

We were sitting in the shelter, and Vitesse took out a folded banana leaf from his raffia day bag.

"You hungry?" he asked, holding up the leaf.

"Sure," I said, thinking it was probably some peanuts or fried plantains. He peeled it open and I jumped back in my seat. Inside was a whole smoked bat—wings, fur, head, ears—everything. He grabbed it in his hands and snapped it in half like a cob of corn. He gave me the top half with the face looking back at me, and Vitesse wasted no time chowing down on his portion. I pulled off a small sliver of meat, trying to avoid getting a chunk of fuzzy hair and put it my mouth. Immediately, I began to gag; it was absolutely (and to this day) the worst thing I had ever tasted. It was bitter and metallic, like what I imagined it would be like sucking on a dirty penny. I immediately spit it out on the ground.

Vitesse laughed. "No good?"

I swished water in my mouth and spit it out and tried to keep from vomiting. "No. I'm sorry. That is not for me. We don't eat that where I come from."

Vitesse shrugged his shoulder and took my half from me and quickly devoured it. I took some dried pineapple from my backpack, trying to kill that hellish bitterness with some sweet and sour.

"So where do you come from again?" he asked. "What's the name of your village?"

I spit a few more times on the ground. "Columbia," I said. "Columbia, South Carolina."

"Where is that?" he said and licked his fingers.

"It's in the south. The southern part of the United States."

"Where is that?"

"Where? America?"

"Yes."

"America is part of North America."

"Where is that?"

"Well, you have the United States and Canada and Mexico. That makes up North America."

He poured some palm wine from a gourd and gave me a cup. "Yes, but where is that from here? How would I go there?"

I took a sip of the wine, and that finally did the trick, finally killed the taste of bat. "Ok, let me show you," I said. I took a stick and began to draw a rudimentary outline of Africa in the dirt. "You see, this is Africa. This is the continent where you live. And here"—I drew a simple outline of Zaire—"here is Zaire. And this is Bandundu. And there is Kikwit, and this is where we are, here in Kitengo. Now, if you take a plane and you fly over Africa, and across the Atlantic Ocean, then on that side you have North and South America, and the United States is in North America, and South Carolina is down here in this part, and my village is Columbia, right here in the middle of the state."

"Mm. But where does it all end?" he asked, very matter-of-factly.

"What do you mean where does it all end?"

"Everything. The world. Where does it end?"

The proverbial lightning bolt. The clap of thunder and sizzle of electricity out of a clear blue sky that strikes you and jolts you and changes you forever; that's what that moment was, though in reality it was more of a slower build, a dawning realization about just what Vitesse was saying.

"Um, it doesn't end," I said, almost whispering. "The world doesn't end."

"Mm," he said as if I had just mentioned it might rain.

"No, seriously, it doesn't end. The world is round."

Vitesse smiled at me politely and folded up the bat bones in the banana leaf.

I had a nectarine in my backpack, and I pulled it out and held it in front of us. "The Earth is like this," I said. "It's like a ball. It's round. It doesn't end. It just keeps going in circles."

Again, he smiled and nodded his head.

I had been living in the village for over four months now, but it wasn't until that moment that I truly understood where I really was. Most of the people who lived there, like Vitesse, had never left that area. Many of them had never even traveled to Kikwit, seen a town with electricity, used a phone or seen a TV. A radio or flashlight was about the highest extent of technology they had ever experienced. Their whole world, from birth to death, from waking to sleeping every single day, was that village, that valley, their farmland, and nothing else.

I could have told him the world was a triangle and Vitesse still would have nodded and smiled politely at me and accepted whatever I said. But there was something beautiful in that revelation: I was experiencing life at its most pure, most basic. There was a liberation of sorts in that simplicity, of not caring about "What should I do with my life? What should I *be?* How do I matter in this world?" No anxiety about whether the US or the USSR were going to one day blow half the planet to bits with nuclear weapons. No caring about what kind of car to drive, or which credit cards to get, or whether my health insurance will pay my bills. At the same time, of course, it was an incredibly harsh existence, but mostly from my perspective. For Vitesse and most of the residents of Kitengo, it was all they knew. It was what it was and that was that.

After I used the nectarine to explain why we have night and day, we went back to work, digging, digging, sweat dripping in our eyes until late afternoon when the clouds rolled in and a storm looked imminent. We stopped work and walked back to the village, back to Vitesse's house, and as usual, we got there just before the rain decided to fall. My magic powers saved us yet again.

---

Toward the end of May, we had finished the main part of the pond, had dug the depth to one meter, and had sloped the pond banks at a 3:1 ratio—all the things Gabriel had taught me.

Foster had now joined us and the construction was speeding along. I estimated we had another two weeks or so of work left to do. We had to plant grass on the pond banks, build a compost pile, create a drainpipe out of bamboo with a mesh cover, and then fill the pond and put leaves in the compost bin to "cook" the water, which meant growing a nice brownish-green algae bloom for the baby fish to feed on, before we were ready to stock it. Again, all these things Gabriel had drilled into my head at our sessions in Bukavu.

A funny thing began to happen, however, as the pond inched closer to being finished and the other villagers of Kitengo could now see with their own eyes what it was the crazy *mendele* was doing. They began to stop by on a regular basis while we worked, asking lots of questions. "Mr. Judas Priest"—the farmer I had first spoken to all those weeks ago (he wore that T-shirt almost every day)—became especially interested, and finally, one day as Vitesse and I were setting the drainpipe in place, he reached in, helping me climb out of the bottom of the pond, and said to me:

"I want one of these as well."

So there you had it: customer number two was in the books.

# Chapter Nineteen

**W**e decided to take a short break on building the pond as I was due to meet Sheila back in Kikwit for our "supply shopping" trip. It wasn't really a total lie as I needed quite a few things, and I was hoping if we saw Razz, he could give us an update on Gabriel. I created a list of what folks in my village needed/wanted: new sandals for Pumbu; some vitamins for Vitesse's wife, Jackie, (she was six months pregnant now); some fabric for Mutamba's wife; batteries, cigarettes, notebooks, pens. I had to keep it somewhat on the down low, as I obviously didn't have enough space on my motorcycle to carry back items for the whole village. I felt a bit bad about that; I wished I could be Kitengo's version of Santa Claus, but reality was what I had to follow.

When I arrived at the house in Kikwit, it was a welcome sight to see Kutanga, our sentry, pull back those gates for me to drive my motorcycle up the hill. I saw Sheila's bike against the stone wall and parked next to hers.

"Honey, I'm home!" I shouted.

Sheila came running out into the yard before I had even

turned off the engine. "Darling!" she said and nearly tackled me to the ground. "So good to see you!" She ripped off my helmet and covered me in kisses. "You won't believe it, but I think we have the whole place to ourselves. Razz is out visiting other posts. It's just you, me, and Kutanga."

"Really? That is good news. I wonder what we should do first?"

"Mmm," she said. "I wonder." She hooked her arm in mine, as she always loved to do. We went straight inside the guest cottage that we had now named The Sheila, and took our reunion a few steps further.

In the evening, we walked to the night market, which was down a sandy road behind our house. We bought several roasted chicken breasts—grilled over open coals with hot peppers and limes—some roasted corn, peanuts, fresh mangoes, and half a dozen bottles of beer. We invited Kutanga to have dinner with us in the house, and then afterward, Sheila and I spooned together on the patio sofa, drinking beer and listening to music, the Zairian chanteuse M'Bilia Bel, while we stared at the night sky.

"Mmm, I don't feel guilty about this at all," she said.

"Neither do I. I've got two farmers now, by the way, one pond almost finished."

"Get out! That's awesome. And to think all those months ago, you wanted to quit and go home."

"Seems like years ago. But, thanks to you and Gabriel, here I am."

"Heard any news about him?" she asked as she pressed her

head against my shoulder.

"No. I was actually hoping to catch Razz while we were here, see what he knew."

"I never did get a chance to speak with him. About what happened with us."

"You will," I said, once again trying to sound confident about something that I had no idea about.

"Hey, we should plan a vacation together, a real one," Sheila said. "We have a lot of days saved up. Maybe in November, to celebrate our one year anniversary of arriving here."

"We should."

"We should go to the beach."

"Zaire has a beach?" I asked, seeing that mostly landlocked map in my mind, except for the very tiny sliver of the country that touched the Atlantic Ocean.

"A small one," said Sheila. "But it's supposed to be really nice. I was talking to one of the other girls here, and she said a bunch of them went last year and loved it. We can take a bus to Kin., visit Zongo Falls, hire a car to Matadi, then we can get on a ferryboat down the Congo River—"

"The Zaire River"

"Whatever. Then we take that riverboat from Matadi, down to the coast. It actually stops briefly in Angola. At the beach near Muanda, they said there is a beautiful old Portuguese mission. Costs only about five bucks a night to sleep there."

"Yeah, I think Robert got stationed near Matadi. Remember him from training? We can see him on the way."

"Perfect."

"Let's do it, then."

"Let's."

The next couple of days we spent shopping in downtown Kikwit, hanging out at the rec center café, cooking in the big kitchen. We fell into a deeper and deeper rhythm with each other, both physically and emotionally. It was fun "playing house," and we both saw it as a glimpse of a possible future. Eventually, however, we had to head back to our villages, but we weren't too sad about it, as we were only five weeks away from our next break in early July. And beyond that, we now had our vacation to look forward to, though at the time, of course, we had no idea how that innocently planned trip would forever alter so many lives.

———•———

Back in the village, Vitesse and I finished all our final preparations on his pond and were now just about ready to stock it. In addition, I had started building Mr. Judas Priest's pond (his name was Bakombe, by the way), and the farmer named Kolombo—the one who lived deep in the forest, about an hour's hike from my house—sent word with one of his brothers that he was ready to start building one as well. Not much time anymore for reading my anthology of Western literature, so I remained stuck in the mid-1800s with that book.

It was the second week of June now, and Vitesse and I were

just arriving back at the village from a long day down in the valley when I saw Razz's truck come barreling down the avenue and stop outside my house. As I walked up to greet him, he just stayed in the driver's seat and stared at me with a cold, angry gaze.

"Hey," I said.

"Heard you were at the house a couple of weeks ago."

"Um, yeah. Had to get some supplies."

"Mm," Razz said, still staring at me. "I heard Sheila was there too."

"Yeah, kind of a coinci—"

"You think I don't know what's going on?" Razz snapped at me.

I could feel my heart start to race and my lips quiver. "Look, I-I'm sorry, I—"

Suddenly Razz broke into a big smile. "Ahhh! I really got you! Oh, you should've seen the look on your face."

"Goddamn it, Razz!"

He opened the truck door. "Man, I'm just fucking with you. I don't care about stuff like that. Good for the two of you."

"Really? We were actually kind of worried about that."

"I trust you guys to do what needs to be done. Hell, I trust all of you with my life. I ain't one to micromanage. Just busting your balls a bit!"

"Gee, thanks. Why are you here, by the way?"

He pulled back the tarp on the truck to reveal a drum of gasoline. "Thought you'd probably be low on fuel by now."

"Perfect. Yes, I'm almost out. Good call."

"That's why they pay me the big bucks. Is Pumbu around? We'll need his help to get this thing off."

Pumbu was down working on his house, so I gave one of the kids that was hanging around a magazine page in exchange for going to get him. The three of us rolled the barrel off the truck and into my pantry, and then we transferred what was left from the old drum into the new and put it on Razz's truck. It was getting late by then, the sun nearly gone.

"Mind if I crash here tonight?" Razz asked.

"Sure," I said. "But Pumbu is still sleeping in the front room."

"Nah, I'll sleep in the truck. Got a bag and pillow. Do it all the time. Plus..." He reached into the driver's seat and pulled out two bottles of Johnnie Walker Red Whisky. "I brought you guys a present."

"Awesome. We usually eat dinner at one of my farmer's houses. We'll head down there in a bit. Hey, any word about Gabriel?"

"Yes," Razz said. "He's comin' back."

"No shit? I knew it. When?"

"In a couple of weeks. Should be here for our July break. Doc said he's been in Kin. the past couple of weeks, doing PT at the embassy. Says he's looking good, bugging him every day about wanting to get back here."

"Of course," I said. "I wouldn't expect any less."

We had a big meal at Vitesse's house, stewed chicken, *fufu*, and grilled pineapple. Afterward, we took our usual spot in his yard and turned on the radio. Razz cracked open one of the bottles of whisky and poured cups for each of us. Even Vitesse's wife took a small sip, saying it was good luck for the baby.

"Wow, this is nice, here," Razz said. "You come here every night?"

"Yes," I said, "Vitesse and his family have been very gracious to me. Since day one."

Vitesse nodded. "It is our honor."

"And you said you got three farmers working on ponds now?" Razz asked.

"Yes. Vitesse here was the first one. We're ready to stock his pond."

"Damn, Michael. You're killing it," Razz said and lit a cigarette. "Three farmers in your first, what, five or six months? It took me almost a year to get my first pond up and running." Razz turned to Pumbu. "Damn, Pumbu, what's this boy doing? Does he have some kind of voodoo? Some *ndoki*?"

Vitesse and Pumbu laughed. "No, Mr. Razz," Pumbu said. "Mr. Michael is working hard, and the people here really like him."

"I'm sure you've had a lot to do with that," Razz said.

Pumbu sheepishly smiled and half closed his eyes. "I do my best, sir."

"He does awesome," I said. "I'd be lost without him."

Razz took the bottle and poured another round. "So you say you're ready to stock the pond? Where are you going to get the babies?"

"I was going to go to Lutshima. To the hatchery there. Drive there this week."

"Yep, except the roads down there are a mess. Rains have torn them up. I was just there last week. Better to go by the river. Get a canoe. There's a farm near Pembe you can get fingerlings from. Actually a bit closer. Hey, why don't we go tomorrow? The both of us. I know a guy who's the best pilot on the river. He knows how to keep away from the hippos."

"Ok, sure." I turned to Vitesse. "You ready to start growing the fish?"

"Yes," he said. "Very much."

We hung out for another hour or so. Jackie joined us after the kids went to bed, and when Vitesse told her we were ready to start with the fish, she clapped excitedly. Vitesse asked me to put in a cassette of Koffi Olomide in my radio, a slow, crooning song, and then he asked Jackie to dance with him. They giggled like two teenagers on a first date. Razz, Pumbu, and I watched in silence as the two of them held each other and swayed to the music, shuffling in the sandy yard beneath that huge nighttime sky.

———————•———————

Razz and I left the village just past sunrise, driving in his truck to a spot on the river just south of where I lived. We parked at the bottom of a slick red-dirt hill next to a wooden shed. Behind the shed was a small dock with three long hand-dug canoes bobbing in the water. Razz whistled loudly, and a few minutes later, a tall elderly man with a short gray beard came out of the forest. Razz gave him a thousand Zs and explained where we were going and what we needed to do. I took two red plastic five-liter canisters from Razz's truck, and we climbed aboard the widest of the canoes, sitting down as our pilot used a long pole to push us away from the shore and out into the middle of the river.

It was a stunning journey. An otherworldly thin mist clung tenuously to the water's surface. It was very quiet in the early morning, only the occasional sharp calls of hornbills sounded from deep within the treetops. We were the only ones on the river at that hour, and again it was one of those moments, that sensation of having this strange, exotic world all to yourself while at the same time being humbled by the enormity of it, feeling like such a small part of a much greater whole.

It took only an hour to reach the shores of Pembe, and from there it was about a twenty-minute hike to a three-pond farm Razz had helped to set up when he first came to the country. I paid the farmer two thousand Zs for two hundred Tilapia fingerlings I would take back to Vitesse. After that, it would be my job to teach Vitesse how to keep it going on his own, and how eventually, once I was long gone, he could teach other farmers to set their ponds up as well.

I divided up the baby fish, one hundred in each of the red plastic cans, and filled each three-quarters full with water. Razz and I stopped at a small roadside café, a hut really, and each had a cup of sweet coffee and an egg sandwich on a roll.

The trip back was upstream and took almost two hours, but again it was relaxing, and again for most of the journey we were the only boat on that stretch of the river. The sloshing of the water in the canisters, the calls of the forest birds, and our pilot humming some unknown tune were the only sounds we heard. I started to think I should *only* travel by canoe, hippos and crocs be damned.

We arrived back to Vitesse's pond, and he, his wife, their children, his cousin Foster, Pumbu, and the chief of the village himself were waiting for us. I could see the curiosity and excitement quivering in their faces, expecting some great colorful moment, like a ribbon cutting or fireworks or *munganji* dancers, so it was kind of a letdown for them when Razz and I each took a plastic jug, waded into the middle of the pond, and simply unscrewed the top to let the baby fish swim free into their new home.

"That's it?" Vitesse asked.

"Yes, sorry," I said. "Nothing much exciting to see at this point. But just wait, six months from now, you will have a pond full of fish. When we pull them up in a net and you see them, that will be exciting, that will be fun."

Vitesse cocked his head to one side and shrugged his shoulders. The chief of the village held out a bowl of live termites for me. I respectfully passed.

# CHAPTER TWENTY

In early July, a large group of us huddled in the darkness of the great house, whispering and giggling, hunched behind chairs and sofas, waiting, waiting. Finally, we heard a truck horn beep, and Kutanga opened the front gates so Razz could drive up in the yard. From the large front window, I could see him get out of the truck, then from the driver's side, another figure emerged, tall, long legs, and now with long hair down to his shoulders.

Gabriel looked up at the dark house and walked across the lawn, a slight limp in his left leg. Razz tried to help him up the steps, but Gabriel politely pushed him off. Then as soon as the front door opened, we flung on the lights and leaped from our hiding places, shouting "Surprise!" Razz smiled and Gabriel froze in the doorway.

A big hand-painted banner (a bedsheet) hung from the ceiling that said: "Welcome Back, Gabriel! Man of Steel!" Everyone pushed forward and surrounded him, touching him, hugging him. Sheila and I held back until the first wave passed and the crowd parted. Gabriel looked across the room at us, and he smiled, a big smile, a welcome smile, a smile that set us at ease.

Sheila, tears rolling from her eyes, walked over and gave him a huge hug. "I'm so glad you're back. I'm so glad you are safe."

"Thanks." He waved me over. "Mike," he said and put his arm around my shoulder, drawing me to his other side. The three of us held each other in a tight circle, like a broken egg put back together. Someone cranked up the stereo, the rolling piano lines and ska rhythms of "I Confess" by The English Beat. When we separated, I saw that Gabriel's eyes were red and watery. He looked around the house and took a deep breath. "Wow," he said. "Feels good to be home."

We soon lost him to others in the house, everyone wanting to talk to him, to touch him, and to welcome him back and wish him luck. Sheila hooked her arm in mine as we watched all the adulation and joy unfold.

"He looks good," she said.

"He looks great," I said and sighed out with a very deep sense of relief.

———•———

The party continued for a few hours, a fairly mellow affair by our usual standards, as folks mingled in and out of the house chatting and catching up. Everyone could be heard talking about all the progress they were making with their programs, how great things were going, when Razz walked over to where Sheila and I were standing on the patio and motioned up to the roof. I looked up and saw Gabriel sitting by himself in the semidarkness, staring out at the sky. A big, fat, blazing full moon hung above the dark tree line. Sheila put her hand on my shoulder. I knew what she meant. I quietly nodded and headed toward the side staircase.

"How's it going?" I said as I climbed across the loosely tiled roof and sat down next to him. "You're missing your own party."

He smiled. He took a few deep breaths and looked up at the purple sky. "No, it's fine. Just, you know, a little overwhelming. Just need to take a deep breath and let things soak in."

It was beautiful up there on the roof. I had never been up there at night. The wide circular patio glowed below us like a lazy sun. "Sure, I understand, I guess… Actually, I don't think any of us can really understand what you've been through."

"It is what it is," Gabriel said.

"Hey, look, you're back. A lot of people, most people, wouldn't be."

"Well… You know the old saying: whatever doesn't kill you makes you stronger."

"Is that how you feel? Stronger?"

"Yes," he said and looked straight into my eyes. "This is not going to stop me. I'm not going to quit, you know. I'm not going to fail."

"I know you won't."

"And I'm not going back to the States either. They kept trying to send me there, and I refused. There's nothing for me there. I'm going to make things work. First here, then maybe somewhere else."

"Yes, I'm sure you'll do great things, but…"

"But what?" he asked.

"Well, I mean you *have* been through a lot. Maybe take it easy a bit at first. Ease back into things."

"Man, I've already wasted so much time. It'll soon be a year we've been here, and I haven't done anything."

"I know, I know. I'm not saying don't work hard, but just, let things unfold the way they're supposed to."

"I'm sorry, Mike. I don't believe in destiny or fate or that certain things are meant to happen certain ways. I believe you have to make things happen for yourself."

I took out a cigarette. "Ok," I said. "Ok."

Gabriel looked at me and smiled and put his hand on my shoulder. "Thanks. I know you're trying to help." We both looked down at the patio where we could see Sheila looking up at us. "You guys make a nice couple, by the way," he said.

"Thanks."

"I mean it. I don't want you two to worry about any of that stuff. It's all good with me. Make sure she knows that."

"I'll tell her. You want to come back down?"

"In a minute," he said. "I'll be down in a minute. Just want to continue to decompress a bit."

I nodded and climbed back down the stairs and went over to Sheila on the patio.

"Is he all right?" she asked.

"Um, yeah he's fine."

"Mm," she said and went inside the house to get a soda.

---

That night, as Sheila and I lay in the cottage, I looked at my watch and it said 2 a.m. I heard a motorcycle engine roar to life, and I went to the window and pulled back the curtains. I saw Gabriel steer his new bike down the hill and out the front gates, disappearing into the darkness of the surrounding streets.

# CHAPTER TWENTY-ONE

The fish pond–building business was booming. By late September, I had half a dozen farmers working on ponds in various states of construction in four different villages. I was on the road every day, walking up and down deep valleys, through steaming forests, digging holes, planting grass, fixing drainage pipes.

I had one guy who, with his daughter, had walked over fifty kilometers to my house asking me to help him come start a fish farm. He even offered his daughter as my wife. I politely declined, of course, but explained to him I would gladly help him start a fish project and he didn't have to give me a thing.

Pumbu helped me keep track of all my appointments, as well as what stage each farmer's pond was in, in a large green ledger. Vitesse's pond was going great, and people could now see the second generation of fish flashing and swimming in the water. We had his first harvest planned for mid-December.

It was all starting to take its toll on me, however, and one morning in early October, I woke up with a sharp burning in my stomach, like someone was stubbing out lit cigars in my gut. I was sweaty and nauseous and couldn't even keep down water. Pumbu suggested I travel to Totshi, a Belgian mission about forty-five minutes from our village. They had a school there, a generator, and a small infirmary with basic medical supplies.

It was a tough motorcycle ride, the sky and ground blurring and quivering as I steered down the thick dirt roads, but when I arrived at the long sandstone complex, with its arched buildings and wide green manicured lawns, it kind of reminded me of our training compound back in Bukavu.

Sister Rose, a Belgian woman in her late sixties, ran the place and welcomed me with open arms. I described the symptoms to her, and she was immediately certain I had amoebic dysentery. She had one of the other nuns, a younger woman with translucent green eyes named Sister Jeanette, prepare a room for me.

My fever was now above 102 and I could barely stand. Rose started me on a regimen of Flagyl to treat the parasites, and had Jeanette prepare an IV bag to keep my fluids balanced. Those initial couple of days were a blur of sweating, vomiting, spinning in the bed, clutching my stomach. It was the first time since those early moments in the country that I really, really wanted to go home. The past few weeks in the village I had been having the strangest recurring dream: I kept dreaming about being back in the States and finding water fountains, shiny metal boxes like you find on the wall of any school or office building, and the simplest act of being able to walk right up, stick your mouth over the faucet, and get clean, ice-cold, beautiful water anytime you wanted.

Sister Rose and the rest of the folks at Totshi took good care of me. If one had to get violently ill in the middle of nowhere, that was a good place to be. It was like something out of a movie, with its beautiful chapel, church bells ringing throughout the day, and the schoolyard with classrooms full of kids in perfectly clean white shirts and blue pants or skirts. My room was like a five-star hotel, with a huge, lush king-size bed, feather pillows, flowered curtains, breakfast brought in every morning on trays with a little vase full of flowers.

I was there for over a week before I was finally able to start eating and drinking normally again. The evening before I was to leave and go back to the village, Sister Rose and Sister Jeanette invited me to hang out at their kitchen table. Rose brought in a tray of cold bottles of beer, frosted glasses, and plates of assorted Belgian chocolates.

"Wow," I said. "I need to get sick more often."

They laughed. "So tell us more about your project. You raise fish?" Rose asked.

I channeled my inner Gabriel, speaking almost word for word many of the things he had taught me in Bukavu. It actually filled me with confidence to really know what I was talking about. I realized I had crossed a line; I was no longer a trainee struggling to figure it all out. I was now a professional (and successful) freshwater fisheries extension agent.

"Sounds fantastic," Sister Jeanette said. "Maybe we should

get one here as well. Rose?"

"Love it!" Rose said. "Yes let's start a fish farm. Will you help us?"

"Of course," I said. "But only if there will be more cold beer and chocolate whenever I visit."

"That," Rose said, "is something we can definitely arrange."

As night fell, we continued to sit in the cool fluorescence of their kitchen. Just outside the walls, I could hear the steady hum of their generator. The conversation switched to the weather, then to books, then to movies, specifically American movies. They said they were both fans of the Indiana Jones films and couldn't wait to get a videotape of the new one, *Indiana Jones and the Last Crusade*. I didn't even know it existed. We chatted until close to midnight. I certainly have many great memories seared into my brain from my time in Zaire, but sitting around drinking very cold beer and shooting the breeze with a group of funny, witty (and kind of sexy) Belgian nuns in the middle of nowhere has to rank near the top.

———————•———————

**I** had a lot of work to return to, and as soon as I pulled up to my house I had planned to sit down with Pumbu and go over my schedule for the next few weeks. I found him in the backyard cleaning out our chicken coop.

"Mr. Michael, so good to see you back and healthy. Come with me."

"What? Not now. I want to go over our schedule for the next couple of weeks."

"It can wait," he said. "I want to show you something."

I followed him down to Vitesse's house. We passed the giant, tangled mango tree in the middle of the village, and I began to worry as we approached his yard. "Is everything ok?" I asked.

"Everything is fine," Pumbu said. "Please, follow me inside."

We entered their hut without knocking, and there in the corner of the room, dark except for a single candle on their scratched wooden table, sat Jackie in a chair, nursing a very new baby. Vitesse sat next to her and looked up at me, grinning between each of his pointy ears.

I tiptoed over like most people do when they see a baby. "Is it a boy or girl?" I asked.

"A boy," Vitesse said.

The baby finished drinking, and Jackie wiped his mouth, then motioned for me to come closer. She held him out and I took him, his little legs and arms shaking and twitching. I sat down at their table, marveling at the new life I held in my hands. "What's his name?" I asked.

Vitesse kept grinning and looked at me. "Michael."

I felt my jaw pry itself open. "What?" I asked.

"His name is Michael," Jackie said. "After you."

I looked up at Pumbu and he just smiled. I felt a very thick knot growing in my throat. "I—I don't know what to say."

"Say hello," Vitesse said.

I looked at the baby boy's face, his slitted eyes barely open.

"Hello, Michael," I said.

Vitesse and Jackie laughed and held each other's hands. Baby Michael yawned and went back to sleep.

---

Ok, that memory is probably top of the list.

Anyway, I had a lot of work to do before the second week in November, when I was to go meet Sheila in Kikwit and head west toward the coastline for our vacation. I made the long sixty-minute hike through the sweaty, bug-infested forest to Kolombo's farm three times in one week to check on his progress and give him a list of things to do while I was away. I did the same kinds of visits with my other farmers in the surrounding villages, driving there on my motorcycle several times to make sure they were in good shape and knew what to work on to keep things moving forward in my absence. I went over in detail with Pumbu what to do in case problems arose, and created a troubleshooting guide that he could use as a proxy.

It wasn't until later that I realized November fourth was the day I was down in our valley working with Bakombe (Mr. Judas Priest), digging an irrigation canal from the creek, when I heard a sharp whistle. I looked up to see Sheila standing on the downslope of a bright-green hillside, just above Bakombe's nearly finished pond. She held her yellow motorcycle helmet in one hand and, with the other, waved at me to come over.

"Is that your wife?" Bakombe asked.

"No," I said.

"Mistress?"

"Kind of."

"That's good," he said. "She's pretty."

I was shirtless and covered in mud and sweat as I walked over to see Sheila. "Hey! What a nice surprise. I thought we weren't meeting until next week?"

She leaned over and kissed me on the lips. I avoided touching her with my dirty arms. "I know," she said. "But I needed to see you."

I saw her face was flushed, and I watched her breathing getting quick and shallow. "Sure," I said. What's wrong? Is everything ok?"

"No. It's not. I need to speak with you."

My first thought was: *is she pregnant?* If so, I wouldn't have been unhappy. "Of course. We can go back to my house. What is it?"

She placed her palms on her cheeks as if trying to calm down. "It's about Gabriel."

# Part Three: Matadi

# CHAPTER TWENTY-TWO

**W**e sat in the main room of my hut, which Pumbu and I called the salon. It was late in the afternoon, and I opened the front and rear doors to let a crisp breeze blow straight through and fill the space between my mud walls. Pumbu entered carrying two orange plastic mugs of coffee and handed one to Sheila and one to me. As he began to leave, I stopped him.

"Pumbu, please stay," I said. "I want you to hear this."

He settled in a sling-back wooden chair near the side wall. Sheila's hand shook slightly as she brought the cup of coffee to her lips.

"He's not right," she said. "I had heard he got sick again, got malaria again, so I decided to go see him in his village. It's only about a thirty-minute moto ride from mine." She half laughed and shook her head. "Can you fucking believe it? I didn't realize. All this time and we were only half an hour apart... But, you know, I never had a chance to speak with him directly about how things ended with us. And about what's now going on with you and me." She looked at Pumbu and batted her eyelids. "Sorry

221

about my language."

"It's ok," Pumbu said, calm as ever.

"So what do you mean he's 'not right'?" I asked.

"Do you remember that night in the dining hall? During training? When we were practicing our final presentations?"

"Yes."

"It was like that," she said. "But much worse."

I lit a cigarette, sucked it deep into my lungs, took a sip of coffee, and glanced at Pumbu before turning my attention back to Sheila.

"He's lost a lot of weight," she continued. "And he's building two ponds in the valley near his village. *By himself.* I tried to talk to him, but he mostly ignored me. I guess I'm not his favorite person."

"He doesn't think that about you," I said. "He told me so."

"Maybe. Maybe he was just in that weird zone of his, but he kept muttering about his 'vision' and about how he was 'going to show everyone.' How once they saw what he could do, it would be beautiful. They would all come running to him, and then they would see what he was truly capable of."

I let a sharp sigh blast through my lips. "What do you think, Pumbu?"

He took a moment to carefully study his response before speaking. "Well, I have never met him. But I have seen things like this before. As I spoke to you previously, a lot of Westerners, people from Europe and America, they come here and they just push too hard. They fight against the rhythm of life here instead of trying to join it. Sometimes it destroys them. Sometimes they break. There was someone from your organization, several years ago when I first started, a young man from Texas, I think. They had to come and take him out of his village. He had hurt someone and then hurt himself. He cut off one of his own hands with a machete."

Sheila scrunched her face half in disgust, half in fear. "I don't think Gabriel would do anything like that. Do you, Michael?"

"No. I don't think so... I don't know..." In my mind, I did a quick scan of images of him, memories I had, mostly from when we were in training, that powerful energy he always had pouring out of his skin. Maybe it had turned on him, but I still couldn't see him ever doing something that extreme. At least, not on purpose. "No," I finally declared. "No way."

"He has been through so much since he got here. I know it's worn him down," Sheila said. Tears began forming in the corner of her eyes. "I tried, I just didn't know what to say to him."

I put my hand on her leg and gave it a gentle squeeze. "It's ok," I said. "Look at me."

She raised her face and stared into my eyes.

"It's ok," I said again.

She quietly nodded.

I sat back in my chair. I looked out the open front door. Streaks of purple and gold burst across the fading sky. Another evening was descending on the village, and people were moving about in their yards, preparing for the final meal of the day, chopping and cooking over charcoal and wood fires. Kids were chasing each other down the main avenue. Stray goats and chickens nosed in the dirt, looking for snacks. If Norman Rockwell had ever come to Kitengo, he would have loved it, capturing it in bucolic, swirling paintings. But wherever you go and whomever you meet, (I was beginning to understand) there were always many things, unknown and unseen, rumbling and roiling just beneath the smooth, clean surface.

"I'll go see him," I said. "Tomorrow."

"What are you going to say?" Sheila asked.

"I'm going to get him to come with us, on our trip. We can start it a few days early."

Sheila hesitated. "Ok, but—"

"I know he'll refuse, at first. But I'll get him to come. Then, when we stop in Kinshasa on our way to the coast, I'll go to HQ and see Doc Peters and tell him what's going on. Have him come speak to Gabriel."

"You're going to trick him? He'll never forgive you."

"If he's getting as bad as you say he is, I don't care. At the very least, if nothing comes of it, we still get him to take a break. To step away from all this for a bit. To relax. Maybe that's all he needs. Pumbu?"

He nodded his head and reached for the pack of cigarettes on the table. "Yes, I think that is a good idea. As you said, either way, maybe something good will come of it. He is your friend. I'm sure he will understand you are trying to help him."

Sheila took a sip of her coffee. "Ok. Yes, let's do that. I think the beach might be good for him. Get some perspective on things." She stood up and went to her backpack in the corner of the room and pulled out a light-blue button-up sweater. "It's getting a bit chilly in here." She wrapped it around her shoulders and stood next to my chair. She reached down and took my hand, locking her fingers around mine.

Pumbu quietly took his cigarette, walked out the back of the house, shut the rear door and left us alone. The wind tunnel was cut in half, and I closed the front door with a whoosh, the wood slamming into the frame, completing the task.

Sheila sat on my lap and pressed her warm forehead against my cheek. "Can I stay here tonight?" she asked.

"Of course," I said.

"Will people here say things?"

"They won't care. If needed, I'll have Pumbu give a press conference to spin things."

Sheila chuckled and brushed her lips on top of mine, gently letting them touch and stick together. She continued moving her lips across my face, just barely caressing my cheeks. I breathed in the scent of her skin, always so fresh and clean like the purest of Ivory soap. She flicked her tongue in and out of my ear and wrapped her legs tighter around my waist pressing her hips into me. "I'm so tired of being alone," she whispered.

"Not tonight, baby," I said. "Not tonight."

# CHAPTER TWENTY-THREE

Sheila left in the morning soon after breakfast. She had some work to do back in her village, but we made plans to meet in Kikwit the following day. I too had a few appointments with farmers that I needed to keep, so it wasn't until midafternoon that I packed clothes for the trip to the coast, gave final instructions to Pumbu, and left Kitengo for Gabriel's village. As I drove my motorcycle along the sandy road, the edge of the valley on my left, the wide savannah grassland on my right, I didn't know that it would be nearly a month before I would return, a lot longer than planned. And I certainly didn't know at that moment how much and how deeply life for myself, those closest to me, and those I had yet to meet would irrevocably change.

I had a rough idea where Gabriel's village was, about ninety minutes northwest of mine, but I did have to stop a few times in a few different places to ask directions. When I finally got on the right path and made the final turn down the main avenue, past a wooden sign nailed to a papaya tree that stated the name of the village as Kitombe, it was as if someone had photocopied my village and dropped its doppelganger here. The layout was nearly identical, as was the terrain, even the sounds and smells.

I pulled my cycle to a stop in the center of the main row of huts, and I saw a girl of about eleven or twelve standing in front of one of the tree-branch fences. She wore a dusty red smock, had a closely shaved head, and big saucer cup–shaped brown eyes. I waved her over to me, and she carefully shuffled her bare feet through the sand. I climbed off the bike, put my helmet on the handlebar, and squatted down in front of her so my face was even with hers.

"Hey, sweetie," I said to her in Kikongo. "What's your name?"

"Mevanda," she whispered.

"Hello, Mevanda. It's very nice to meet you. My name is Michael. I came here to see Mr. Gabriel. Do you know where his house is?"

Her big eyes grew bigger and she silently nodded. I stood up, and she put her tiny hand in mine, leading me down the avenue to the last row of houses. We stopped at the final hut, a small thatched-roof house about half the size of mine. I saw Gabriel's motorcycle parked out front next to his drum of gasoline. There was no fence and the front door was half-open.

I called his name a few times without a response, then went inside. The first thing I noticed was that it looked like no one lived there. It was nearly empty. The front room had a small wooden table and chair. There was nothing on the table: no books or anything. There was also nothing on the mud walls. Over time,

Pumbu and I had done a lot to my house to make it more attractive, more like a comfortable home. I had bought some carvings and masks from local artists and hung them around my salon, and some bright, multicolored African fabric to give the place a cheerier feel. I also had several drawings that the young boy Lupu had done for me, including the one of me sitting on my motorcycle. My table at home was full of books and magazines, journals, and ledgers. There was none of that there.

I poked my head in his bedroom, and it was similar. Just his plain bed and a basket in the corner where he kept his clothes, dirty or clean, bunched in a heap. The third room was where he kept his bucket bath. A single bar of soap sat on the windowsill. Nothing else. It was all downright gloomy.

Mevanda was waiting for me near the main avenue, watching me carefully with those big eyes.

"Hey," I said. "Do you know where Mr. Gabriel is right now?"

Again she nodded and slipped her hand into mine. We walked halfway back to where I had left my cycle, then turned on a narrow footpath that cut through a field of waist-high grass. After about ten minutes, we came to the edge of their valley. She pulled me forward several meters along the rim to a small outcropping jutting from the side. We walked to the edge and she pointed down.

About thirty or so meters below, I could see two rectangular holes, two half-dug fish ponds sitting diagonally to each other. Light was starting to fade as evening approached, and I could also see, dotting the rims of each of those ponds, about two-dozen petrol lanterns, little balls of yellow, glowing light, creating a sparkling outline. Within one of those glowing rectangles, I saw a tall, now very thin young white man with long hair and no shirt. He was limping around with a shovel in his hand, tossing dirt on the side of the pond, then jumping up and down to tamp it down with his feet. I felt a slight wave of panic come over me, that old fluttering in the chest and the thickness in my throat. I balled my hand into a fist and squeezed it hard several times.

Mevanda looked up at me, a wide-eyed expression of fear and worry in her face. "He doesn't sleep," she simply said.

That felt like a punch in the gut. I placed my hand on her shoulder, half to comfort her, half to steady myself. "Thank you, sweetie," I whispered. "If you need to go back home now, you can."

She turned the way we had come and disappeared into the tall grass. I stood there at the edge for a few more minutes, looking below, watching Gabriel move around as the light continued to dim all around us. I cupped my hands to my mouth, took several deep breaths, then began my descent down into the valley.

———————•———————

He didn't pay any attention to me as I approached. I walked carefully up to the ponds as if I were nearing a crouching dog, not sure if it was just resting or ready to pounce. He wore muddy cargo shorts that looked like they hadn't been washed in weeks, and as he limped around, I could see part of the long red scar that ran along the outside of his upper left thigh. The sky above us had turned deep red as well. He sliced the ground with his shovel, threw the dirt on the pond bank, then stomped on it, favoring his left leg, sometimes teetering just a bit.

"Gabriel," I finally said in a soft, neutral voice.

He didn't look up or over at me. Slice the ground. Throw the dirt. Stomp on the dirt. Repeat.

"Gabriel," I said a bit louder.

"Hi, Mike," he said, his back to me as he sliced the ground yet again.

"Good to see you."

"Yes, good to see you too," he said, still not looking at me.

"So… You've got two ponds almost done. That's great."

"Lot of work still to do. Lot of work." Stomp, stomp, stomp.

"Why don't you take a break? Talk to me a bit. It's almost night anyway."

He quickly glanced at me for the first time, then pointed to the lamps. "I've got lights here," he said. "Lots of light. Lots of work to do."

I walked around so I stood in front of him, then climbed down into the bottom of the pond. "Hey," I said. "Take a break."

"Can't. Gotta show these folks what to do. They won't listen to me so I gotta show them. There's another shovel over there if you want to help."

I looked at the shovel at the far end but quickly dismissed it.

"Gabriel, you have to take care of yourself. That's the first thing. You can't do anything if you're run-down. Sheila said you got sick again."

He jumped up on the side of the sloping bank and turned the shovel around to its flat side, using it to pack the loose dirt. "Sheila, Sheila bo-belia, banana-fana fo-feila, fee fy mo-meila. Sheila!"

Fear and anger rose within me. Fast. "Gabriel, stop it. *Now*. Stop a moment and talk to me."

"Can't, Michael!" he said and started to jump up and down. He looked right at me, smiling, and spaced out each word to time them with his feet landing on the ground. "Gotta-show-these-folks-how-it's-done.  Give-a-man-a-fish-and-he-eats-for-a-day. Teach-a-man-to-fish-and-he-eats-FOREVER! Isn't that what we want, Michael? For them to eat forever?"

"Goddammit!" I yelled. "Stop! Stop this! Stop a fucking minute and talk to me!"

He suddenly jumped down to the pond bottom right in front of me, leaning over me, his deep-blue eyes only inches from mine, his face seemingly stretched to the breaking point. "Well, what the fuck else am I supposed to do, Michael?" he screamed. "What? Tell me! These people won't listen to me! I've been trying, but they just won't listen to me! They have to see how great this can be. It's gonna be amazing. It's gonna be majestic! But I have to show them. I have to do it all myself then they will see! Then they will finally get it! Then I can do what I came here to do. I'm not going to fail! I'M NOT GOING TO FAIL!" He spun around with the shovel in his hand, like an Olympic hammer toss, nearly striking my head, and threw it deep into the tree line, screaming as loud and as long as he could, a deep explosion of sound that had been building for God knows how many days or weeks.

Silence. Only the sound of his breathing as his chest heaved up and down. Only small, pencil-thin streaks of light were left in the darkening sky. The ring of petrol lanterns blanketed us in a flat yellow glow.

"Feel better?" I asked.

He didn't respond, just kept breathing hard, staring at the ground in front of his feet. I reached in my pocket, then lit a cigarette. He finally collapsed against the slope of the pond bank. I sat down next to him.

"Why won't they listen to me?" he asked, his voice quiet but plaintive.

I exhaled a thick plume of smoke. "They will," I said. "They will. It just takes time."

"But I've hardly been here."

"Exactly," I said. "You haven't. None of it your fault. You haven't done anything wrong. But you have to adjust your timeline. Your expectations. You gotta relax. You gotta take it easy. You're driving yourself nuts. And if that happens, then nothing will happen. Nothing good."

Gabriel reached up to the top of the pond and pulled down his backpack. He dug inside and took out a canvas-covered tin canteen. He took a long sip of water, then handed it to me, and I took a sip as well.

Gabriel shook his head back and forth. "I just don't understand," he said. "I don't understand the way things have happened. I never expected this. I never planned for this."

"Gabriel, when I came here, I had no idea what I was doing. You know that. I planned and expected nothing at all."

"So that's the right answer? That's the right way? Just drift through like a zombie and expect nothing? Leave it all to fate?"

"That's a bit harsh, my friend. I remind you, I didn't just drift through, thanks to you and Sheila. I remind you of all that time I spent with you in Bukavu, sitting together above that training pond like we are now."

"Yes."

"So now it's my turn to pull you through. I want you to listen carefully to what I'm about to say."

"Fine. Whatever."

I finished my cigarette and stubbed it out in the dirt. "You need to take a break. You need to walk away from here. You need to relax. Sheila and I have planned to go to the coast for a vacation. You need to come with us."

He shook his head back and forth several times. "No. No way. I've missed so much time already. I've got so much to—"

"Shut the fuck up and listen to me," I said. He looked at me, and for the first time, I felt like I was now the parent, he the child. "You *are* going to come with us. You *are* going to take a break. We are going to Kikwit tomorrow. Then we will take the bus to Kinshasa. We'll stay there a couple of days and visit Zongo Falls just outside the city. Then get a bus or hire a car to Matadi. We are going to meet Robert there. You remember him? From training? His post is near Matadi. Then we will take a riverboat down to the coast. There, we will stay in an old Portuguese mission for five bucks a night, and we will relax, eat seafood, and have fun. You have been going nonstop since you got here. You have gone straight from stateside training, to training here, to getting malaria, to having that horrible accident, to months of painful physical therapy, to coming here and getting sick again. You need a fucking break!"

He was listening. I could tell. I almost had him, but not quite. He shook his head again and started some BS excuse. "But—"

"Shut up, shut up, shut up," I said. "These ponds aren't going anywhere. Your village is not going anywhere. They will all still be here ten to twelve days from now when you get back. All this is not going to disappear. But if you don't chill out and get your shit together, you're going to disappear. You're either going to kill yourself, or you'll be dragged out of here in a goddamn straightjacket."

He froze, his body still, his dark-blue eyes staring straight ahead at nothing. I patiently waited. I could feel victory was very close. A wave of loud, buzzing cicadas rose in the dark trees behind us.

He nodded. "Ok," he said quietly. "Ok."

I exhaled. "Good." I put my hand on his shoulder, and he looked up at me almost like a confused puppy. "We all love you," I said. "Me, Sheila, Razz, everybody loves you. You are better than all of us put together. You've had some tough luck, but we are going to get you straightened out. We are going to get you on that golden path. I promise."

He clasped his hand around mine. "Thank you," he said. "Thank you."

I looked at the deep-black sky. "It's late," I said. "Should we stay here tonight, or do you want to ride to Kikwit?"

"Let's stay here and ride in the morning. I'm tired. I'm so fucking tired."

"Got it." I stood up and helped to pull him to his feet. We climbed out the bottom of the pond and went around blowing out all but one of the petrol lanterns. I carried the last glowing lamp in my hand as we hiked up the craggy dirt path, out of the valley and back to his village. We got back to his hut, and Gabriel went straight to his bed and collapsed without speaking. Within about sixty seconds, he was deep asleep. I stretched out a thin blanket on his dirt floor and lay down. I should have felt victory and fallen into a peaceful slumber myself, but I stared into the darkness of his room. Something still didn't feel right, like an itchy scab at the rear of my brain. I wanted to pick at it, but I would have had to split open my skull to do so.

# CHAPTER TWENTY-FOUR

Gabriel and I pulled into the yard of the Kikwit house the next morning just past 10 a.m. Sheila was already there and walked out the front door of the big home to greet us. She glanced at me, looking for a wordless update. I slightly raised my eyebrows as if to say *not sure*. She put her hand on Gabriel's arm, asking if he was ok, if he was feeling better. Gabriel half smirked and nodded yes, then went straight into the house, straight into one of the back bedrooms and collapsed on an empty bunk. Just like the night before, he was deep asleep in less than a minute. I shut the door to the room. Sheila and I went out to the patio.

"Razz isn't here," she said. "He's out on rounds, won't be back for a couple of days. I was going to send a radio message to HQ to let them know we were coming, but can't figure out how to work it."

"I'll take a look," I said. "But not sure I'd be much better."

"So what did you think when you got there?"

"Yeah, it was like you said. It wasn't easy getting him to come. His house—did you see the way he was living?"

"No."

"It was sad. He's isolated, alone in an empty hut. At the edge of the village. I think the people there are scared shitless of him. Still… I mean he's not completely far-gone. Maybe this will be what he needs."

"Hope so," she said and chewed her lip.

I looked back at the house. "He's probably gonna sleep all day. Wanna go to town to get some food and supplies?"

"Sure," she said, sounding completely unsure.

"I don't think he'll run away."

"Sounds like we're talking about a dog."

We went to the usual spots in town, a stop at the Portuguese deli where we got a half-dozen fresh-baked rolls, a large tomato, an avocado, two cans of tuna, a hunk of white cheddar cheese, six bottles of water, and two packs of shortbread cookies. We also stopped at the Zairian-owned pharmacy, a small room with high shelves and folding tables piled indiscriminately with various goods, in order to stock up on toothpaste, shampoo, razors, and the like. The rec center café was nearly empty in the middle of the afternoon when we arrived and had two very cold bottles of Orangina soda. Neither one of us spoke much, both deep in thought as we watched a breeze slip through papaya and banana leaves.

When we got back, Gabriel was still sleeping. I went with Sheila to the radio room to try to send a shortwave message to Doc Peters at HQ, to alert him to what was going on. There was a laminated instruction card, but we kept missing some crucial step, because each time we tried, we couldn't get through. After our twelfth failed attempt, we gave up and went to the kitchen to make tuna, cheese, avocado, and tomato sandwiches for our bus trip the next day, putting them in the fridge to keep fresh.

In the evening, we returned to the night market for roast chicken, plates of rice and red beans, and grilled corn. We took it back to the house, and I was able to briefly rouse Gabriel from his bone-deep sleep. He had dinner with us at the big table but didn't speak and went straight back to bed as soon as he was done. Sheila and I retired early to our special guest cottage. We skipped the sex, and after staring at the dark ceiling for a good half hour, we finally drifted away in each other's arms.

———————•———————

Taking a bus trip in a country like Zaire is quite the experience, but the route from Kikwit to Kinshasa was downright infamous. As Razz had told us when we first got to Bandundu, there was only one paved highway that cut through the center of the province, and the story went that the government transportation official who was in power at the time of its construction, took funds to build a standard ten-inch-deep asphalt road, but instead built a five-inch-thin road and pocketed the rest of the money. As such, the road didn't last long, soon being stripped by heavy use and heavy rains. Often large chunks were completely gone, leaving not only growing potholes, but sometimes full craters. The driving distance between the two cities was three hundred and fifty miles, and under normal conditions, even calculating in half a dozen bus stops on the way, the travel time should have been six to seven hours. However, trips routinely took twelve hours or more, sometimes as much as twenty-four, and sometimes, the journey was never completed at all. Breakdowns, accidents, and plunges off rickety bridges were not uncommon.

The bus depot in town was no more than a small cinder-block and tin-roof shack. When Sheila and I arrived the next morning, there was already a crowd of hundreds of people, many carrying large suitcases or burlap sacks, surrounding two half-rusted old buses. The Zairian woman at the ticket counter told us getting on one of those was a *cause perdue* (a lost cause) but if we paid an extra two hundred Zs each, we could get "guaranteed" tickets for the afternoon bus to Kinshasa leaving at four o'clock. We paid the extra fares and got three tickets, but from our experience chasing the airplane in Goma, we knew there was no such thing as guaranteed transportation in Zaire. So, after lunch, we left our motorcycles parked at the big house, took a taxi to town, and the three of us arrived an hour early. A good-sized crowd had already gathered, but when the driver saw us sitting on a low brick wall in the hot sun, he waved us over and let us board first. It wasn't that uncommon for working Zairians to grant small favors like that to us *mendeles*, and I always felt a bit guilty about it, wondering if it was still a leftover mindset from the days of colonialism.

We settled in the very back seat and popped open the window, as of course there was no AC. The top of the bus was weighted down and tied off with piles of luggage and sacks of food and clothing, so once it was full, at five thirty, a good hour and a half past its scheduled departure, it lurched forward, lumbering and sputtering along the highway. Not long after leaving the city limits, we came across our first road crater. The driver slowed to a crawl to navigate around it, moving deep into the sandy fields along the side of the road. We passed several spots like that, as well as several broken-down cargo trucks and Land Rovers, the passengers frantically waving us down to stop. The driver kept going. We also crossed a couple of very narrow and scary bridges, where we could look down and see the dead, rusting carcasses of former unlucky buses, pointing nose down in the water.

We didn't speak much during the trip, and Gabriel continued to sleep through most of it, his head pressed against the windowpane. Around 11 p.m., we came to a fuel depot that was roughly at the halfway point of the journey. The driver announced in French that we would take a thirty-minute break for food and bathrooms, and if we weren't back on the bus when it left, too bad.

It was the Congolese version of a truck stop, and it had about as little charm as you would think. It looked and smelled like a giant oil slick. Vendors crowded around the bus stop hawking dried fish, peanuts, mangoes and papayas, beer, clothes, cigarettes, and such. There were several "cafés," unscrupulous-looking roadside bars with slinky-looking people crawling in the doorways. Each had giant stereo speakers sitting on overturned empty beer crates, blasting Zairian music at full distortion.

Sheila, Gabriel, and I found an old wooden bench and sat down to eat the tuna sandwiches we had prepared the day before. In front of one of those ramshackle bars, two young kids, a boy and girl, about five or six years old, shimmied and shook their little bodies to the music, shuffling their bare feet, bumping their hips together.

Gabriel watched them, and then, for the first time in several months, I actually saw him smile.

# CHAPTER TWENTY-FIVE

**W**e arrived in Kinshasa at about six thirty on the morning of November eighth, thirteen hours after we had left Kikwit. It was a tough journey, but it was also a thrill to approach the big capital at sunrise, to see all the tall buildings and electric lights and wide, busy roads. Kinshasa came across to me as a surprisingly modern and well-kept city. The never-ending outskirts were typically sprawling and tenuous, but the city center was full of hotels, shops, restaurants, leafy neighborhoods, as well as vibrant, pulsating markets; and then, of course, there were all the famous nightclubs and music venues, districts full of row after row of places that filled up late at night and went until dawn, where you could see and hear all that beloved Zairian music, live and in person. A lot of my fawning impressions had to do, I'm sure, with how long we had been living in the sparse "boondocks" (as Razz called it), but the fact that you could find Chinese food, consistent air-conditioning, and one-hour photo shops really blew my mind.

We took a taxi from the bus station into one of those nice tree-lined neighborhoods where our residence house stood. It was a comfy and compact L-shaped white brick house, behind a tall white fence and next to a stone courtyard surrounded by thick bushes and flowers. It was nicknamed the Malade House, *malade* meaning sick in French, as it was where many of the people in our program stayed when they had to come to the capital to be treated for any serious illness or injury. About two blocks down to the left was the American embassy club with its tennis courts and swimming pool. About two blocks down to the right was a shopping center where we could find that diner that served burgers and shakes. Interestingly, about halfway that same direction was also a Playboy nightclub, complete with a tall sign of the famous black-and-white bunny logo. It was a circular building ringed with a red-carpet entranceway and velvet ropes. It was, we were told, where the well-heeled businessmen went looking for high-priced companionship. Intriguing in a voyeuristic way, but definitely out of my pay grade.

About four blocks straight ahead of the house was our headquarters, and that's where I went soon after I woke up from our morning nap. When we first arrived, Gabriel, as had been his recent pattern, went straight to one of the dozen bunk beds in the back rooms and collapsed on the mattress, instantly falling asleep. Sheila and I decided to partake of the endless supply of hot water and took a shower (separately—there were a few other people staying there), then dozed off in one of the bedrooms, having not gotten much sleep during that marathon bus ride. I woke before she did, and let her keep slumbering.

I knew there was one of those photo shops on the way, so I reached into our backpacks and took out half a dozen rolls of film we had brought to be processed. The weather seemed about twenty degrees cooler than in Bandundu, and despite the uncomfortable reason for my trying to see Doc Peters at HQ, it was a nice, pleasant, springlike walk down the streets. I dropped off the film and opted for the cheaper twenty-four-hour service to be picked up the next day, stopped at a newsstand to buy a copy of the latest *International Herald Tribune,* and bought a cold bottle of Fanta Lemon soda from a young boy selling drinks from a cooler.

Our headquarters was housed in a one-story low-slung, square complex with a courtyard in the center. All the doors to the offices faced the open space, and Doc Peters' exam room was in the corner, opposite from the director's office. His nurse—a stunningly beautiful Zairian woman named Dimena (there were rumors she was much more than his nurse and that Doc Peters' very Catholic wife back in the States refused to give him a divorce)—was there putting away medical supplies. She greeted me warmly and said the good doctor was currently traveling back from the east and would return the next morning. I hesitated when she asked if there was anything she could do to help me, then politely said no.

It was lunchtime, so most everyone else was out of their offices. Along one of the walls in the yard was a message board, and next to that were wall boxes with different forms. I filled out travel itineraries for the three of us (as was the rule for any trip lasting more than three days) and put them in the correct slot, then began my walk back to the residence house, taking an alternate route past an open-air jewelry and souvenir market, packed with long tables full of bright-green malachite and shiny copper.

I found Sheila sitting in a lounge chair in the courtyard, thumbing through a copy of *National Geographic* someone had left behind.

"So, what did he say?" she asked.

"He wasn't there. He'll be back in the morning. Is Gabriel up yet?"

"Yes, I think so. I think I heard him start a shower."

I sat down next to her. She put her palm on the side of my face.

"So, what should we do for the rest of the day?" I asked her.

She glanced at her watch. "It's only one. Zongo Falls is only one hundred and twenty klicks outside the city."

"English please," I said. I still struggled with the whole miles to kilometers conversion thing.

She scrunched up her face in light sarcasm. "About seventy miles, doofus. There are taxis and vans running there all day. We could go, hang out for a bit, get a late lunch, then be back by nightfall. I hear it's stunning. There's supposed to be a nice park and some good food stands."

Gabriel walked out to the courtyard, wearing (clean) cargo shorts, a plain white T-shirt, and his wet hair slicked back. "Hey," he simply said.

"How're you doing?" I asked. He seemed the most relaxed I'd seen him in ages.

"Good." He nodded. "I'm good. I'm hungry."

"We were thinking of going to the falls today," Sheila said. "I hear they have some good BBQ there."

"Yeah, that sounds great," Gabriel said. "I'm all-in."

There was a definite and very palpable lessening of tension in the air, both from him and between the three of us. Sheila glanced at me to acknowledge it, as if to say: *Finally. We may be getting somewhere.*

"Let's do it, then," I said. We quickly gathered our backpacks, some cash, and went out to the street to hail a taxi. There were several depots around town where you could get long-range taxis and semiprivate vans to travel outside the capital. We paid five hundred Zs each for one of the semiprivate rides, basically a cargo van where someone had screwed down parallel wooden benches in the back. We climbed aboard with half a dozen other folks, some of them obviously tourists heading to the falls, same as us.

———————•———————

Stunning is too mild a word for how beautiful Zongo Falls were. I'd never been to Niagara or Victoria Falls, so I didn't have much to compare it to, but it was just a drop-dead gorgeous and wonderful place to spend a cloudless, sunny day in the middle of Africa. A large section of the great Zaire (Congo) River below

Kinshasa narrowed into an unnavigable stretch that ran all the way down to Matadi. Boat travel was impossible because all that volume of water got squeezed into roaring falls and foaming, rocky cataracts. A nice park had been built next to Zongo and there were wide, lush picnic grounds with several thatched shelters. Large groups of Zairians, Indians, and white Europeans had fires going in stone pits, and the smell of charcoal and grilled meat drifted everywhere we went.

We climbed up to one of the popular viewing spots, the roar and whoosh of the water like a hundred freight trains rumbling past.

"Amazing," Gabriel said as he looked out over the water, the huge boulders, the green canopy of the surrounding forest. "Simply amazing." His whole body had started to change, his shoulders and long limbs relaxing and getting looser. Sheila reached over and squeezed my hand.

At the bottom of the falls, off to the side, there was a section where the water dropped at a gentler pace, flowing over rocks carved so perfectly into flat steps that they looked almost fake. There was a good-sized wading pool at the bottom as well. We walked around on the rocks, getting soaked by the cold but refreshing water, and on top of many of the boulders was a slimy mixture of mud and moss that was easy to clump in your hands and throw at someone. The three of us engaged in an epic battle, chasing each other and pelting our bodies with the stringy mess, Sheila screaming constantly each time Gabriel or I splattered her with the mud, and then we all jumped into the wading pool to clean off.

Gabriel leaned his head back and floated. "Oh my God, this feels fantastic."

"So beautiful here," Sheila said.

After a few minutes of silently enjoying the moment, Gabriel asked: "Hey, you guys wanna play Botticelli?"

He was referring to a game that was popular among many in our organization, especially when we had time to kill. It was kind of a souped-up version of Twenty Questions. "Sure," I said.

Gabriel shifted to an upright position, kneeling down so the water covered his shoulders. "Ok, I'll go first. The letter *B*."

"Did you paint *The Birth of Venus*?" Sheila asked.

Gabriel tilted his head. "Really? No, I'm not Botticelli."

"Are you president of the United States?" I asked.

"No, I'm not George Bush... Thank God."

Sheila went next: "Did someone make a movie about you?"

Gabriel shook his head. "No, I'm not Alexander Graham Bell."

"Do you wear a cape?" I asked.

Gabriel thought a moment. "Um... um... damn. Yes, I'm Batman. That was too easy."

"Ha!" I said. "By the way, there *is* a Batman movie. Came out this year in the States. Michael Keaton plays him."

"Michael Keaton as Batman?" Gabriel replied.

"I know, right? But apparently, it was a big hit."

"Also," Sheila said, "there was a movie in the sixties with the original Batman, Adam West. It was a comedy."

"Oh," Gabriel said. "Sorry. Been a while since I played this. A bit rusty."

"That's ok," I said. "We forgive you."

Suddenly Gabriel shot out of the water and loomed over us. "Bunch a know-it-alls!" He put his hands on our heads and dunked us under the water.

We splashed around for a bit, and for the first time in a long time, Sheila and I stopped constantly watching Gabriel and worrying about him. Instead, the three of us just *were*. It was nice, and it harkened back to that day in training when we tumbled around in Lake Kivu, a day that seemed like ten years in the past.

Eventually, we went to one of the many food stands and got a couple of skewers of grilled freshwater prawns and grilled pork, slathered in a spicy red-pepper sauce known as *pili pili*. It tasted great when washed down with bottles of ice-cold, super-sweet bright-red grenadine soda. We hiked around for a couple more hours, then came across a group of Zairian teenagers tossing a Frisbee. They asked us to join them, and we got up a spirited game of Frisbee football.

We arrived back to the residence house about 8 p.m. and lounged around before deciding to get a late-night dinner at a Mediterranean-Middle Eastern restaurant not too far away. It was a very nice and popular place with a wide patio. We took a table under a trellis woven with ivy and sparkling white lights, and we ordered a couple of platters of light appetizers—spanakopita, Greek salad, grilled veggie kebabs, and hummus (my first time eating it—I was instantly addicted).

Briefly, we considered going down to one of the entertainment districts, but we were so relaxed and chilled that the thought of getting jostled around by rowdy, sweaty crowds of people was not appealing. So instead, we went back to the house and hung out in the living room where, on the bookshelf, there were several board games. We cracked open the box to Trivial Pursuit, and after an hour of chasing each other around the board, Sheila won by nailing her final question, which was: who shot the Archduke of Austria, Franz Ferdinand, in 1914, thus igniting World War I? The answer was Gavrilo Princip.

Just past midnight, I collapsed onto the bottom of one of the bunk beds (Sheila took the top spot) and quickly began to fall asleep. But before I did, I went over everything in my head, all that had transpired since we got off that bus early in the morning, and decidedly declared that it had been one of the best days ever in my life.

# CHAPTER TWENTY-SIX

The next morning, I heard someone stirring around in the kitchen. The other volunteers who had been there when we arrived had left, Sheila was still lying in the bunk above me, so that meant Gabriel had gotten up ahead of us. I could hear him whistling. Sheila rolled over and dropped down to her feet, then climbed in my bed and briefly spooned with me.

"Is that Gabriel?" she mumbled.

"I think so."

She kissed me, then got up and shuffled to the bathroom. I pulled myself off my mattress and stretched, my elbows popping.

We both walked into the kitchen to find Gabriel had laid out a full breakfast for all three of us. There were egg sandwiches on soft rolls, large paper cups of coffee, and sliced mangoes.

"Oh my God, Gabriel," said Sheila. "This is so great, thanks! Where did you get it?"

"There's a construction lot down the street. Couple of guys there with tables of food set up to sell to the workers."

We sat in the dining room and I took a sip of the coffee. It was typically very light and sweet, more like hot chocolate, and the rolls had streaks of yellow mustard between the layers of fried eggs.

"This is fantastic," I said between large bites. "Thanks, man."

"So," Gabriel said, his face bright and smiling. "We're heading to Matadi today?"

Sheila reached under the table and put her hand on my leg. In a couple of hours, our trickery, our other reason, our *real* reason for inviting him with us, would become apparent. "Um, yeah," I said. "Sheila and I have a few errands to run, pick up some photos and such, then I guess we'll leave in the afternoon."

"Great!" he said. "I might go for a jog while you're out. I forgot how nice it is around here. Still need to get strength back in my leg. Can't wait for the beach. Should be fun."

"Yeah. Supposed to be great," I said.

Gabriel took a couple sips of coffee, then cleared his throat. "Actually, I um… I have something I want to say to both of you."

"Sure. You can tell us anything," Sheila said.

"I just… wanted to thank you. Both of you for bringing me with you."

Sheila dug her nails into my leg.

Gabriel continued: "I know you guys had planned this trip for yourselves, but this has been really good. You were right, Michael. I really needed something like this. I think this will be a big help."

I could see water filling the corners of Sheila's eyes. She

reached out her other hand and put it on top of Gabriel's. "Of course, sweetie," she said. "We just want to make sure you're healthy. That's the important thing."

"Yeah, I understand…You guys mean a lot to me."

I wasn't much of the crying type, but I started to get a bit misty. "Thanks," I simply said.

Gabriel stood up and collected the used plates. "Anyway, can't wait to get on the road. It'll be fun to see Robert again."

Sheila and I went to the back bedroom, had a quick, hushed conversation, deciding that we should still go speak with Doc Peters, then took turns taking wonderfully hot showers. When we came back out to the front of the house, Gabriel had already gone.

---

Nurse Dimena greeted both of us in the exam room at our headquarters. "Oh, I'm so sorry," she said in French. "The doctor's return has been delayed. A volunteer got hurt. Another motorcycle accident. My, how the doctor hates those things. He now won't be back for another two to three days."

Sheila and I looked at each other, trying to figure out what to do next. "That's too bad," I said.

"Is there not anything I can do to help you?"

"Um… No, it's fine," I said.

"Do you want to leave a note for the doctor?" she asked. "I can put it on his desk."

"No, it's not urgent."

Dimena looked back and forth between us, her sultry curved eyes trying to create a diagnosis of the real reason for our visit. She made it clear she had figured out our relationship and lightly put her hand on Sheila's forearm. "Darling, are you with child?"

That flustered Sheila. "What? Oh no. No. No, I'm not."

"We have birth control here if you need some. Both of you."

Sheila nervously laughed. "Thanks, I… I have that taken care of."

I held up my hand. "Me too." I didn't. I don't want to go into details, but when we first started, Sheila did, in fact, say she was ok in that area.

Dimena settled her voluptuous body into her desk chair. "Ok, darlings. Should I tell the doctor you were inquiring about him?"

I smiled a little bit too hard. "It's ok, we'll catch up with him at a later date."

Sheila and I walked out to the courtyard, stood at the opposite end next to a garden fountain in the shape of a stone elephant. "So what should we do?" she asked. "Should we wait here the next few days?"

I thought a moment. "He seems better, don't you think? He really seems better."

"Yes, definitely." She too searched her brain for some reasoning. "Are we overreacting?"

"No, but maybe this will really do the trick. Maybe Gabriel just needed to step away and get some perspective."

"Robert's probably there in Matadi waiting for us," she said.

"It's too late for us to get a message to him."

She was right about that. Kinshasa was basically the only place in Zaire with a phone system, and it barely worked there. Outside the capital, forget it. "Look," I said. "We have to pass through here again on our way back. So if we go and he starts acting funny again, we can try to catch Doc when we return."

Sheila looked into my eyes, then nodded. "Ok, yeah. That's true... Let's go then. Let's go today. To the beach. Hope Gabriel keeps smiling."

As we turned to leave, we ran into Director Cole crossing the courtyard, dressed impeccably as always in a three-piece suit and red polka-dot tie, his bushy, Groucho Marx face lighting up in a smile when he saw us. He took a second to recall our names. "Sheila," he said. "And Michael?"

"Yes, that's right," I said.

"Great to see you both! What are you doing here?"

"Oh, we just stopped by to see Doc Peters," I said.

Director Cole tilted his head back. "Yes, I think he's still near the eastern border." He then peered at both of us, showing true concern. "Is everything all right?"

Once again, like the day before when I first spoke to Nurse Dimena, I hesitated. Right there at that moment I could have told Director Cole about what had been going on with Gabriel, about our concerns, and asked his advice. But I didn't. "Yes, fine," I said. "Just needed more malaria meds, that's all."

"Ok, you guys on vacation?"

"Yes," Sheila said. "We're heading to the coast."

"Ahh, I love it there. Small beach, but beautiful. Great seafood, grilled right by the water."

"Yes, we're looking forward to it," I said. "We filled out travel itineraries."

"Great!" said Director Cole. "Well, have a safe trip." He took a couple of steps toward his office, then stopped and turned toward us again. "By the way, Razz can't stop raving about the job you're both doing out there. Especially you, Michael. He says what you're doing at your post is phenomenal."

"Thanks," I said. "We're working hard. It seems to be going well."

Director Cole smiled. "Well, we are just so fortunate to have both of you as part of our organization. I appreciate so much all you have done. Keep up the great work." He patted me on the shoulder, then continued into his office. Such a genuinely pleasant man, he was.

As we walked through the corridor leading to the street, Sheila took her hand and popped me on the back of my head. "Phenomenal! Jeesh!"

I grinned. "And don't you forget it."

———————•———————

That afternoon we hired another semiprivate van, and Gabriel, Sheila and I arrived in Matadi, Zaire, around 4 p.m. It was November ninth. A few months prior, Robert had sent a letter to us with the address of a Swiss mission on the outskirts of town that rented private rooms with private showers for about eight bucks a night in local money. After a short taxi ride from the city center, we entered a rectangular compound surrounding a sandy courtyard. One of the buildings appeared to be a nursery/day care where about three dozen Zairian children ran around a small playground scattered with kids toys like green tricycles and pink plastic dollhouses. The main building was painted a fading light blue with a brick floor and a short hallway leading to a small chapel. A young desk clerk gave us registration cards to fill out, then led us out back to a long line of red-painted wooden doors.

That's where we found Robert, sitting in a chair outside one of the rooms, reading a worn out copy of *Atlas Shrugged*. His bowl haircut had been replaced by an angular crew cut, and he looked beefier than when we last saw him, like he had been working out. We all exchanged hugs and high fives. He advised us to settle in our rooms and take a nice break, as the "action" in town didn't get rolling until sundown. When Robert realized that Sheila and I were taking a room together, not Sheila and Gabriel, I saw an expression of surprise and intrigue crawl across his flat, rather birdlike face.

Once inside our cozy room with a queen bed, dresser, and desk, Sheila lay down to take a nap while I went into the shower. I exulted in the hot water running over my body (my third hot shower in three days—I was living large). As I rubbed shampoo in my hair and soap all over my limbs, I evaluated where we were and what we had done since I found Gabriel in his village and convinced him to come with us. *It was working*, I said to myself as the water flowed. *This is actually working. Gabriel is getting better. We are having a great trip. The falls were fantastic. Kinshasa was fantastic. And it's only going to get better from here. The beach is going to be amazing...*

*And Gabriel is going to be just fine.*

# CHAPTER TWENTY-SEVEN

To this day, I'm still not exactly sure what happened during those three hours of downtime after we arrived at the mission, but when we all gathered together again just ahead of 8 p.m., ready to go to town for dinner, Gabriel had changed. If Gabriel of the day before at Zongo Falls and that morning at breakfast had been the old Gabriel—the blazing, charismatic one from training—the one I saw outside those red wooden doors was a retreat to the recent Gabriel, the one with a hard, distant look in his eyes and a tense body ready to snap like a pencil. I don't know if Robert had said some smart aleck comment about Sheila and me now being together that set him off, or if it was just the roulette wheel of jumbled emotions and ideas spinning in Gabriel's head once again landing on black; but whatever the cause, our dear friend had slipped back into a disconcerting negative energy drain that worried us. Sheila noticed it as well and whispered in my ear.

I pulled Gabriel aside. "Hey, how are you feeling? You all right?"

He wouldn't look directly at me. "Sure. Why?"

"It's just—you know, it's been a long three days. Lots of traveling. If you're tired, we can just hang here for the night. There's a market across the street. We can get food there."

His face was stoic and businesslike as if he were listening to a stock report. "No, I'm fine. Really," he said. "We're here. New city. Let's go check out the town." He patted me on the back and rejoined Robert and Sheila.

So we were back to that again, that watching and analyzing each gesture for clues: *he's ok, he's not ok, he's ok...*

We took a taxi to the main part of town, getting out at the top of a hill. We could see down into the city center, and to our left was the great Zaire River, restored to its normal width. From that point, it would flow down to the coast and out into the Atlantic Ocean. There was a long harbor full of boats of all sizes that had traveled up from the sea, and there were tall cranes, as well as stacks of multicolored, rusting shipping containers lining several loading docks. Brown hills rose all around us with mostly brown buildings and houses pushed into the side. Palm trees lined the streets, but they too seemed brown, not the usual vibrant green. The streets were packed with people moving in a hurry, scampering in all directions. There was an unhinged energy in that town, and in fact, everything seemed to be teetering, on the brink; that was the strong feeling I had as the four of us began to walk down that steep hill. It felt like the whole world was tilting on its side.

We passed by a large mural of the Big Man—Mobutu—

looking down on all of us in his leopard-skin hat. Robert started telling us about this "scintillating town," as he called it, and about five minutes after he started speaking, I began to feel we had made a big mistake.

"Yes, my village is only about thirty minutes from here," Robert said. "I come here almost every week. Been thinking of renting a house here actually. Fascinating place. Not for the fainthearted, though. Matadi is a port city, all sorts of stuff moving in and out of those docks. You've got diamond smugglers here, counterfeit cash, drugs, weapons, gangsters—you name it."

"Sounds like a wonderful place," I said, my sarcasm unmistakable.

"Yes, it's kind of like a black Casablanca," Robert said.

I saw Gabriel's face tighten up at that ridiculous remark. Sheila looked at me and narrowed her eyes.

"Where are we going?" I asked.

"*Les Paillotes*," Robert said. "That'll be our first stop, just up the hill there." He pointed to our right past a jam-packed open-air market. "It's a slick place. Where all the bigwigs hang out. Good steaks and hot waitresses," he said, poking Gabriel in the side and laughing at his own words. "Lots of yummy chocolate cupcakes!"

None of us laughed with him. "Wait...What?" Sheila snapped. "Did you just call African women 'chocolate cupcakes'? Gross!"

Robert rolled his eyes. "Ok, I'm sorry. I meant to say, beautiful *ladies."*

He led us up a narrow, winding street, in front of a snooker hall packed with teenage Zairians. Two boys hissed and whistled at Sheila as we passed. We heard screaming and shouting from a tin shack on our right, and then a plump man and a tall woman in the middle of a violent argument ran out into the street in front of us, the woman slashing her arms in rapid circles as she tried to dig her nails in the man's face.

At the top of the hill, floodlights shot beams of white light into the darkening sky. There we came to a sprawling restaurant and nightclub. The building was covered by a series of tall thatched roofs. The outside walls were covered in fresh paint, the orange-and-brown pattern of the Okapi (similar to my cigarettes). Loud Zairian music poured out over the top of the walls (clear music, not distorted like often heard at downscale bars). Very well-dressed people, most of them African, some of them white, shouted and laughed and moved in and out of the arched front entranceway. Above the door, bright-yellow neon letters spelled out: LES PAILLOTES. BIENVENU!

As soon as we entered the foyer, a short Zairian man wearing a dark-blue *abacost*, with a bottle of beer in one hand, bounced off one wall and stumbled toward us, his arm knocking into Gabriel. He dropped the bottle, which shattered at Gabriel's feet.

The man clung to Gabriel's shoulder, his lips and eyes watery. *"Je regrette, mon ami. Je regrette,"* he slurred.

Gabriel clenched his jaw and pried the man's hands from his body, stepping to the side so the drunken sot could continue his teetering walk out into the street.

All the men who worked at the club wore leopard-patterned vests with white shirts buttoned all the way to their necks. All the waitresses, however, wore long colorful African-print skirts and very tight, low-cut T-shirts. One of those young girls, with long braids and large gold hoop earrings, smiled at Robert in recognition.

"Jakinda, good to see you. I brought friends. Table for four, please," Robert said, speaking to her in French.

"Of course, Mr. Robert," she said. "Do you need menus?"

Robert pointed to his head. "No, dear. Got it all up here."

She waved us forward, and we followed her into the main part of the club, which was a wide open-air restaurant, about the size of two basketball courts laid side-by-side. There were small reflecting pools in each corner that threw shimmering waves of light up on the tall back walls. Staircases led to an upper balcony. There were two dance floors with colored lights glaring down on them, and three curved wooden bars were packed with customers. Each dining table was covered by its own thatched roof. Robert's comment about "black Casablanca" was crude, but I could see the comparison. It had an elegant but lawless feel to it, and I could imagine all the illegal deal-making that was probably going on right at that minute.

We settled at a table near the back wall.

"Gabriel, you drinking tonight?" Robert asked. Gabriel shook his head no.

Our waitress, Jakinda, leaned closer to hear Robert over the loud music. He put his hand on her lower back, just above her rear. "Ok, honey. A basket of *cossa cossa* (spicy prawns) to start, then four plates of steak and fries, a Fanta for my tall friend over there, and three very cold bottles of Primus for the rest of us. Keep those beers coming until I tell you." She nodded, and he patted her ass before she walked away.

Sheila scowled. Gabriel stared. I reached for a cigarette.

It's often said there is nothing like living in another country to find out who you really are, that the life of an expat brings one's true self to the surface. Sitting there in that club, watching Robert continue to grope our waitress when she returned with our drinks, it suddenly occurred to me that none of us really knew him. I didn't even know where he was from in the States. We only had hung out with him a couple of times during training, and he had always been a bit of a wiseass but in a jovial kind of way. I now began to think Robert's once amusing cynicism had started to morph into something much darker and uglier.

"So let me get this straight," he said, looking the three of us over. "Sheila, you and Michael are together now? Not you and Gabriel?"

I watched Gabriel continue to glower at Robert. Sheila's eyes froze as well. "Yes, Robert," she said. "How very observant of you."

"Well, I guess in a place like this, alliances do tend to shift quite a bit. That's why I prefer shorter-term liaisons."

"Like our waitress?" Gabriel asked. "Your little 'chocolate

cupcake'?"

"Now, Gabriel, a gentleman never kisses and tells… But I'm not a gentleman. So, yes. Why, you interested? I could set that up for you. I don't mind crossing swords!"

"All right, Robert," I said.

"What? Just a joke. Wow, I don't remember you guys being so uptight."

Jakinda and another waitress brought our plates of food. I stubbed out my cigarette.

———————•———————

Throughout the meal, we had the great pleasure of listening to Robert talk nonstop, going on and on about how great a job he was doing at his post.

"It's easy, you know," he said, through forkfuls of steak. "I took over from another volunteer, so everything was pretty much set up once I got there. I just travel around a few days a week, check on my farmers, give them a few pointers, help with their harvests, but really, when you look at it, what we're doing here, noble as it may be, doesn't really make much of a difference in the grand scheme of things. Might as well try to push back the ocean with a broom."

I could see Gabriel getting wound up but trying to tamp it down within himself.

"But," Robert continued, "all that free time, gives me plenty of room to pursue other, shall I say, more amorous adventures.

Whew, these women around here, they're something else. There was this teacher I hooked up with a few months ago, she was a tigress…"

He went on for several more minutes, giving us the rundown on all his hookups, and every one of the women were "monsters," "beasts," "lionesses," and the like. I watched Sheila's face fill deeply and more unmistakably with disgust. When a busboy came and took away our used plates (Gabriel had barely touched his food), Robert looked up at the balcony behind us. And that's when we first saw her: The Girl in the Yellow Dress.

"Well, look at that," Robert grinned, like a thief eyeing a half-opened safe.

Two girls stood on the balcony just above us, staring at our table. I would have been shocked if they were older than sixteen or seventeen. The one in the yellow dress looked like a taller version of the girl Mevanda I had met when I went to Gabriel's village. She had a closely shaved head, big wide eyes, and her yellow sundress seemed too big on her slender frame. She had pinkish makeup on her face, which looked unnatural and out of place, and her companion, a bit plumper than her, wearing an emerald-green dress, was similarly made-up and wore dangling silver earrings that I guessed were probably clip-ons. The yellow-dress girl kept staring at Gabriel, and her friend kept whispering something in her ear. Initially, they didn't come across to me as "young professionals," but rather like two high-school girls, awkwardly standing against the wall at the Big School Dance, waiting for some boy they have a crush on to pull them to the floor.

"Wow," Robert said. "That one cutie can't take her eyes off you, Gabriel. I bet you could get it for free."

Sheila exploded. "Goddamn it, Robert! What the fuck is wrong with you? Were you always this much of a pig?"

Gabriel joined in: "Why is everything so nasty with you?"

"Nasty?" Robert said, mocking the way Gabriel had said it. "Come on now, you guys can't be serious? Two girls looking like that? In a place like this? You know, I don't live in some Kumbaya Fantasy Land. I see the world the way it really is." He turned to Gabriel. "Maybe that's why you haven't done anything yet at your post," he said. "Why you're flaming out." It was then I imagined the conversation they might have had back at the mission, while Sheila and I were resting. "Maybe it's because you're chasing something that isn't real."

That stabbed Gabriel right in the chest. I could see the invisible blood pouring out of the wound, and I watched him breathe deeply, in and out, grimacing through the pain. He looked up at the two girls, then pushed his chair back and stood up. "I'll show you," he said to Robert. Gabriel climbed the stairs to the balcony, the yellow-dress girl's eyes growing wider with surprise as he neared her. The two girls giggled nervously as Gabriel stuck out his hand and introduced himself.

Robert shook his head. "Always such the crusader." He motioned to one of the waitresses for another beer.

I lit a cigarette and planted my eyes on the balcony as Gabriel sat down next to the two girls. It was too loud with the music to hear what he was saying. He was smiling, a bit of a forced smile, and the girls kept giggling, sometimes nodding in response. This went on for several minutes. Sheila reached under the table and took my hand and squeezed it. Robert occasionally glanced up at Gabriel but seemed more interested in scoping out the dance floor for new targets. I could see Gabriel's mouth and body getting more and more animated, more and more focused and adamant about what he was saying. The girls' giggling faces turned into blank stares. Two long dance songs finished playing before Gabriel finally rose to his feet, again shaking their hands. The yellow-dress girl looked stunned and sad to see him leave. She yanked Gabriel's arm once, trying to get him to stay. He put his hand on her shoulder and said one final thing, getting her to nod silently in agreement.

He came back to the table and collapsed in his chair. Robert glared at him. "Well?"

Gabriel tried to avoid eye contact with all of us, looking up at the thatched roof. "They are whores," he said quietly.

"See," Robert said. "And let me guess: You tried to talk them out of it, passionately going over and over how bad it was, how dangerous it was, how they could do so much more with their lives, how there are people who could help them, and they could be whatever they wanted to be! And in the end, they just went lower on their price."

"Goddamn it!" Gabriel said and jumped to his feet, lunging at Robert, knocking our table and bottles of soda and beer to the ground, smashing them into bits. Robert jumped to the side, just missing Gabriel's fist. I sprang up and got in between the two of them, holding my arms out to keep them apart. Robert grinned while Gabriel stood with his tall body shaking and trembling. Several customers at nearby tables and a few of the waitresses and busboys turned to look at us, having seen and heard the commotion.

Sheila stood up, tossing her napkin on the table. "It's time to go," she said. "Let's just go back to the mission. Call it a night."

"So early?" Robert said. "You guys are really going to leave me on my own in this *dangerous* little town?"

"I think you can handle it," I said. "Or come back to the mission. Do whatever you want. We're heading to the beach tomorrow morning. We can't stop you, but maybe best if you didn't accompany us."

"I'm deeply hurt," he said without any sense of sincerity. He pulled out a wad of Zairian cash and dropped it on the table. "Here, at least let me pay for our meal."

"Fine," I said.

"You're welcome," he said.

The four of us started walking to the front entrance when, behind me, above the loud music, I heard a girl's voice scream "No!" I turned to see the yellow-dress girl sprinting across the dance floor. Before I realized what was happening, she leaped onto Gabriel's back and wrapped her arm around his neck, yelling in French: "Don't go! Don't go! I'll love you. I'll be your good girl!"

Gabriel spun her around, and her legs knocked bottles off a

nearby table. A woman sitting at the table screamed. Dozens of heads stopped what they were doing and turned in our direction. Gabriel tried to pry her arms from his neck, but she just slid down and grabbed his waist, continuing to shout: "I'll love you! I'll be your good girl!" He tried to walk backward, but that just caused her bare shins to scrape across the concrete floor.

Robert and I reached in and helped to finally peel her off Gabriel's body, her arms slashing in circles, trying to break free from us. I saw a large Zairian man, probably one of the club's bouncers, closing in on us. Sheila stepped in front to block him, telling him: "It's ok, it's ok. We are leaving. We are leaving right away." Robert and I pushed the yellow-dress girl along with us as we hurried through the entranceway, back out onto the street. The big bouncer followed and stood in the doorway, staring at us, making it clear we were not *bienvenu,* as the yellow neon sign above him said.

Her friend in the green dress came outside but kept her distance, back near the wall of the club. The yellow-dress girl finally started to calm down, and Robert and I released her. We could see small trickles of blood running from the scrapes on her legs. Gabriel pulled her to the side and knelt down in front of her. Sheila handed him a dark-blue bandana from her bag, and he began to wipe away the blood. The girl put her fingers in her mouth as her chest heaved up and down. Finally, Gabriel looked up into her face and began to speak to her in French.

"Hey," he said softly. "Your name is Pauline, right?" She nodded. "Pauline, please. Please listen to me. Please stop doing what you are doing. It's not safe. It's dangerous, ok?" Again she nodded. "You and your cousin"—he motioned to the green-dress girl against the wall—"there are lots of things you can do besides this. These kind of men, they will lie to you, they will promise you all sorts of things, nice clothes and jewelry, but they don't really care. They'll eventually get tired of you then get rid of you. Here," he said and reached into his pocket, pulling out a large wad of cash. "Here, take this. You and your cousin. You said you have a place to stay, right? Go home to that tonight. Please, just go home, just for tonight, and think about things. Maybe in the morning you will see what I mean."

She nodded and slowly took the money. Gabriel smiled at her. She gave him a long, tight hug, and then she went over to the wall where her cousin was standing. As they started to walk down the hill, Pauline gave one last look at Gabriel before disappearing from the glow of the electric lights. Gabriel stood and continued to stare after her, even when she was no longer visible, that hard, distant look growing in his eyes.

Sheila took him by the arm. "Come on," she said. "Let's go back to the mission."

Gabriel ignored her, still looking into the darkness of the hill below.

"Come on," she said again.

This time, Gabriel shrugged her off, pulled his arm away from hers. "No," he simply said.

"No what?" I asked.

"No. I don't want to go back to the mission yet. I want to see more of the town."

"What? Gabriel, no!" Sheila said.

"Why not? You guys are always saying I need to loosen up more, have more fun. Well, let's have some fun." He turned to Robert. "Robert, you want to show me the sights?"

Robert's eyes grew wide in disbelief. "Sure. Lots of places we can go."

Gabriel jumped over and put his long arms around Robert's shoulders. "Perfect! I'm gonna go out and get some beers with my good friend Robert here."

"There you go!" Robert shouted. "That's the spirit!"

"Gabriel, come on. That's enough," I said.

"You guys can go back. I'll see you in the morning." He turned and signaled for a cab up the road.

Sheila pulled at me, moving us away from the two of them. "Michael, come on, let him be."

"What? No. I'm not going to leave him out all night with Robert. Not the way he's been acting."

"He's a big boy. He's made his decision. He's not your child. He's not our child. There's only so much we can do. Come on, please. This was supposed to be *our* vacation. It's all getting fucked-up."

"Sheila, I'm *not* going to leave him. Not now. Not tonight. Please, come with me. I need you with me."

She stared into my face, her own so conflicted and trembling. The taxi stopped in front of the club, and Robert opened one of the doors. "Hey!" he shouted. "You two lovebirds coming or not?"

Sheila looked back and forth between me and the taxi. Finally, she dropped her shoulders and nodded yes.

"Great!" Robert shouted. Gabriel, Sheila, and I climbed in the backseat. Robert climbed in the front, then stuck his hand out the window and pounded on the roof.

"Let's go!" he yelled. The taxi spun a wheel and pulled away.

# CHAPTER TWENTY-EIGHT

Shoulda, woulda, coulda.

Robert dragged us all over town, each place we stopped becoming progressively less nice and seedier. Several times Sheila and I tried to get Gabriel to leave, but he refused. He had always told me he didn't like the taste of alcohol, which was why he didn't usually drink, but that night he kept tossing back beers, and suddenly, at least for a little while, he was Robert's best buddy. They were laughing and slapping each other's backs, telling stories from college, and once when Sheila threatened to leave on her own, I used that to get her to stay: "Hey, at least he's having a good time. He's laughing, he's blowing off steam, maybe this is just what he needed. Let's try to have fun too."

We didn't. Near midnight, we ended up in one of the most down and dirty watering holes I've ever been in. The Hotel Metropol (the oldest hotel in Zaire, Robert told us) was a tall, long brown brick building not far from the loading docks. In the back of the hotel was a bar, no sign, no outside light. Inside, it was nearly pitch-black except for the deep-purple glow of black lights ringing the walls. Even the music was harsh—hard rock and heavy metal songs instead of the usual Zairian dance songs or American pop. Hulking shadows of bodies packed in the place, mostly sailors and dockworkers, Robert said.

We took a sofa near the back wall, and Robert wasted no time in waving over a couple of high-heeled girls in very tight miniskirts. He "gave" one of them to Gabriel, but by the time we got there, I could see the initial euphoric stage of drinking had worn off Gabriel, and that heavy, bottomless tug that happens when the organs have been saturated with booze started to settle in. Gabriel ignored the girl, so Robert soon had two companions, one on each side, and it wasn't long before his hands started sliding up their legs. Sheila was mortified to the point of being comatose. I had had enough as well and told Gabriel we were leaving, with or without him. He nodded that he was finally ready to call it a night, but before we stood to leave, his face froze, and he stared across the room.

"No," he said.

At the far end of the room, leaning against a mirrored wall, was Pauline, The Girl in the Yellow Dress. A thin brown-skinned man leaned close to her, stroking her cheek. Gabriel leaped to his feet, nearly knocking over the table in front of us.

Robert looked up from his two women to see Gabriel crossing the room toward the girl. "Oh, no. He's not at it again, is he?"

Gabriel marched up, pushed the man aside and grabbed Pauline by the wrist. The man shouted at Gabriel, but Gabriel quickly turned around and stuck a threatening finger in his face.

As Gabriel was about twice his size, the man backed off. Gabriel turned his attention to Pauline and began speaking quickly and sharply to her. At first, she smiled, happy to see him again, but then it faded. She shook her head side to side, and then Gabriel grabbed her by the arm and led her out the front door.

I didn't actually see or hear anything that went on between them, but I could imagine it as if I had X-ray vision that could cut through those walls. I could envision him animated and insistent, probably looming over her, probably kind of scaring her as he pleaded with her, once again, to listen to him and stop what she was doing. I could see him taking more money out of his pocket and giving it to her. I could see her nodding once again, walking down the road, and disappearing into the dark city.

"Michael," Sheila said. "I can't take any more of this."

"You're right," I said. "It's time to go."

I tried to get Robert's attention, but at first, he ignored me. Gabriel then came back inside, alone.

"How much did she get you for this time, chief?" Robert said.

"Shut up, Robert!" he said. He turned to me. "Let's go."

"Finally," Sheila said.

"Robert!" I shouted. "We're leaving."

He rolled his eyes. "Ugh. All right. If you insist. You probably don't know how to get back to the mission, do you?"

"No. I have no idea where we really are," I said.

"Fine. I guess I'll come back here another night. On my own." He kissed each of the girls, one on the cheek, the other on the lips, then shuffled out the front door with the rest of us.

We walked around to the front of the building, near the street. It was empty. Completely empty. No cars moving at all. Robert looked at his watch. "Oh, yeah. Past midnight. Most taxis stop running at midnight."

"What?" Sheila yelled. "How the fuck do we get back to the mission?"

"Walk to a main road and try to hitch," Robert said.

"What do you usually do when you go out here?" I asked.

"I usually stay out until the taxis start running again in the morning."

"Great! This is just great!" Sheila said.

Suddenly from behind us came this deep, booming voice. "You guys need a ride?"

We turned to see a large Zairian man standing in the street, lighting a cigarette. He had very dark skin, almost invisible in the night air. He stepped toward us, moving under a streetlamp, and we could see he wore a tight brown *abacost*, his arm muscles bulging through the sleeves, and he had a big barrel-shaped chest. He looked like a football player. Half a dozen gold and silver rings covered his fingers. "You guys Americans?" he said in clear English, with only a slight African accent.

"Yeah," I said.

"I love Americans!" he said, a big white smile splitting his face. "I went to school at Boston College. Go Eagles! I loved it there, though a bit too cold for my tastes." He stepped toward me and stuck out his hand. "My name is Jamal. Jamal M'Bollo."

"Michael," I said, still surprised and not sure what was going on.

Robert stepped up and shook his hand as well. "I'm Robert," he said. "And behind me are Gabriel and Sheila."

"Very nice to meet you. I have a Land Rover, parked right down here," he said, pointing down a hill. "Where are you guys staying?"

"The Swiss mission," Robert said.

"Oh yes," Jamal said. "That is too far to walk. And at this hour, you won't find a taxi. So typical of my country, I'm afraid. Makes no sense, does it? Well, I can give you guys a lift. Give me a chance to practice my English. I just have to stop by the docks for a moment to check on one of my boats. You guys can come aboard if you want."

"Sure," Robert said. "That would be awesome." Sheila groaned and Robert turned to her. "What? He's offering to give us a ride. Least we can do is look at his boat."

"Fine," she said.

"Great," Jamal said. "My car is just down here. Follow me."

As we walked down the hill, Jamal M'Bollo explained he had been at the bar celebrating the birthday of one of the crew members that worked on his boat. Then he asked what we did, what we were doing in his country. Robert tried to explain about our organization and about the fish project we were working on.

"Oh, you mean like you guys are missionaries?" Jamal asked.

"No," Gabriel said, his eyes watery and his speech now slurring. "We are not missionaries. It's an aid organization. We volunteer to come here."

"You don't get paid?" Jamal asked.

"A little," I said. "But not much."

We arrived at his Land Rover parked along the curb, a shiny silver four-door. "Seriously? You don't get paid?" he repeated. "Tell me more..."

---

It was a straight shot down from the Metropol, so it took less than ten minutes for us to arrive at the dock. We passed a couple more dark and nefarious-looking bars along the way, then arrived at a chain-link fence with a large gate. Standing guard by the gate was a soldier in an olive jumpsuit with a rifle slung over his shoulder. The ground leading up to the fence was strewn with piles of broken concrete, like something had been recently torn down but not cleaned up.

As the soldier unlocked the hitch to let us in, I looked across the dock at two blazing, very bright work lights atop two poles. When Jamal had said he needed to check on his boat, I had imagined a fishing trawler or maybe a ferryboat; but beneath those work lights was a huge cargo ship, the size of a tanker, the deck and cabin lit up as well.

"Holy crap," Robert said as we climbed out the car. "That's *your* boat?"

Jamal smiled and held out his arms. "Yes, sir," he said. "I own several boats, but this is the one I'm most proud of. It's the largest boat to ever travel on the Zaire River."

"Fantastic," Robert said.

"Come aboard," he said and waved us forward. At the bottom of the stairs leading to the deck was another soldier with another rifle slung over his shoulder. As we passed him and started to climb the stairs, he fell in line behind us, following us. Gabriel looked over his shoulder at him.

Jamal waved his hand. "Don't mind him. He follows me everywhere. That's his job."

He gave us a quick tour of the boat, the cabin, living quarters, deck, etc. Painted on the outside of the top compartment was another Mobutu mural, the Big Man looking down on us as we crawled all over the ship. We heard a loud, repeated metallic scraping sound as we came to the edge of two large storage silos. We looked down to the bottom of one of them, and two Zairian men, wearing cut-off shorts, no shirts or shoes, were using flat metal shovels to scoop up spilled rice and were shaking it into burlap bags.

"We bring in all sorts of things from all over the world. This was a shipment of rice from Vietnam," Jamal said. He looked down and shook his head. "Look at these people. They should have finished this hours ago. Too slow."

Gabriel leaned over the railing to the silos and stared at the two men. The constant scraping against the floor, almost like nails on a chalkboard, continued over and over. Gabriel's watery eyes didn't blink. "How much do you pay them?" he asked.

"Pardon?" Jamal asked.

"How much do you pay 'these people'? A dollar a day?

Maybe two?"

"Here we go," Robert said.

"Gabriel, not now," I said.

He turned to face Jamal. "No, I want to know. 'These people' are your people."

"Do I *look* like them?" Jamal asked. "They are not my people."

"So you just screw them over, pay them slave wages?"

"Gabriel!" Sheila snapped. "Stop it. This is not the right place."

He stood straight and faced all of us, his body tensing up. "Where is the right place? Tell me that."

Jamal, his face half-surprised, half-irritated, took a step toward Gabriel. The soldier behind us took a step closer as well. "Listen, my friend, I pay money to hundreds of people. I give work to hundreds of people. I own half a dozen boats. I own a dozen shops, here in Matadi and along the road to Kinshasa, and I fill those shops with things people want, things people need. I help many more people than you missionaries do with your little buckets of fish."

"We're not missionaries!" Gabriel shouted.

"I agree with him," Robert said, motioning to Jamal.

Gabriel spun to face Robert. "Fuck you, Robert, you fucking pig! You belong with this fat cat, sticking your dick in whores and wearing gold rings on your greedy hands."

"Gabriel, shut up!" I said.

Jamal looked at me, completely stunned. "What is going on with him? I give you guys a ride and tour of my boat, and I get insulted?" He looked at Gabriel. "You're lucky you're not leaving here with a broken leg."

Gabriel leaned in close to Jamal's face. "I've already got one, thanks."

I stepped in between them. "Enough!" I yelled at Gabriel and turned to Jamal. "I'm so sorry, he's not been feeling well lately. He had too much to drink." I grabbed Gabriel by the shirt and pushed him back.

The soldier pulled the rifle from his shoulder and held it in his hands. Jamal held out his arm to keep him away. Gabriel looked up at the mural of President Mobutu, then suddenly spun out of my grasp and jumped up on the railing, balancing his feet on top and throwing his arms over his head. "Mobutu is a thief!" he shouted. "Down with Mobutu! Down with the president! He killed Lumumba! Kill the president! Kill Mobutu!"

The soldier pointed his rifle at Gabriel and began shouting at him in a mixture of French and Lingala. I reached up and grabbed Gabriel by the belt loop and used all my strength to yank his tall body down, throwing him on the deck. I jumped on top of him and grabbed his face with my hands. "Shut up! Shut the fuck up! You're going to get us killed. If you don't shut the fuck up, I'll take you out myself!" He started to speak, but I covered his mouth with my palm.

Sheila stepped up to Jamal. "Please, please don't hurt him," she pleaded. "We'll go. We'll find another ride."

"It's ok," Jamal said, almost whispering. He stared at Gabriel as one would stare at a horrible traffic accident. "It's obvious your friend is very troubled. I'm sorry to see it. Do not worry, I will still take you. It's too dangerous to walk this time of night."

"Thank you so much," Robert said. He looked at Gabriel and shook his head. "He's a nice guy, but very emotional."

I helped Gabriel to his feet, and Sheila came to his other side, wrapping her arm around his waist. He was quiet now and sullen as we followed Jamal and Robert across the deck and down the stairs. The soldier closely followed, then took his previous spot on the loading dock, watching carefully as we climbed back into Jamal's Land Rover. Robert sat in front, the rest of us slid in back with Gabriel pressed against the window behind the driver.

We slowly drove through the open gate in silence. We began to turn up the hill when Gabriel, looking out the window, suddenly said: "No. Goddamn it! NO!"

He opened the door and jumped out as the car was moving. I looked and saw Pauline, The Girl in the Yellow Dress, leaning against the fence. She was smiling as the front gate soldier pressed his legs against hers. Gabriel rolled on the ground, then leaped to his feet, sprinting across the pavement toward them.

"Stop! Stop the car!" I screamed.

Jamal slammed on the brakes. I was the first to jump out, trying to catch up to Gabriel, but he arrived at the fence first. He grabbed the soldier, yanking him away from Pauline, and he kicked him in the shins, then slammed him to the ground. He rushed to the fence and clamped his big hands on Pauline's shoulders. She did not smile when she saw Gabriel. She screamed.

Gabriel shook her, pressing her body into the fence, the chain link whipping back and forth. "What are you doing!" he shouted. "I told you not to do this! Listen to me! WHY WON'T YOU LISTEN TO ME!"

She screamed once again, and then I reached them, grabbed him by the neck and pulled him off. He immediately started swinging his fists and kicking his legs, his hands landing hard on my cheek and his foot in my groin. I buckled over and dropped to one knee. I heard Sheila screaming as Robert and Jamal ran up to him. Gabriel picked up a piece of jagged concrete off the ground and swung his hand, slashing both men across the face. They staggered backward. I tried once more to tackle him, but met the same fate, the concrete slab cutting my forehead. Blood ran into my eyes as I saw the other soldier, the one from the boat, sprinting through the gate, rifle in his hands. He jumped and slammed into Gabriel, knocking him to the ground and both went tumbling. The soldier ended up on top of Gabriel, then jammed the rifle under Gabriel's neck, trying to press his head down on the ground. Gabriel gripped the rifle with both hands, trying to pry it off, both men pulling and struggling until *POW!*— I could see that word like a comic book explode in the sky the moment the rifle went off. Sheila shouted, and I and everyone else ducked low, covering our heads, the sound of the gunshot bouncing and echoing off the docks.

Then silence. Then nothing.

Then we turned to see Pauline plastered against the fence, her eyes bulging from her face, crying, breathing rapidly in and out, as a bloody circle at the top of her left shoulder grew bigger and wetter, a bright-red stain spreading fast on her bright-yellow dress.

Gabriel rolled over and saw her. He reached out his hand, his fingers stretching as far as they could. "No… no, no, no."

The soldier raised the butt of the rifle above his head, ready to smash Gabriel's face when Jamal ran over and stopped him. "Easy! Easy!" Jamal said. "Leave him be!"

The soldier stopped. The other soldier, the one Gabriel first attacked, rose to his feet. Jamal shouted at him in Lingala and in French, but I could clearly hear the words *police* and *ambulance*. The soldier pulled a walkie-talkie from his belt and began to speak rapidly into the microphone.

Gabriel lay still on the ground, frozen, unmoving, making it easy for them to take rope from the back of Jamal's car and bind his hands behind his back. I later found out that there was a rescue station just up the hill and around the corner, which was why less than five minutes passed before a jeep covered with old white paint and a fading red cross pulled to a stop in front of the gate. Two workers rolled a stretcher to the fence, strapped Pauline in tight and covered her shaking body up to her neck with a white sheet. Soon after, a police cruiser, an old Crown Victoria sedan, arrived. Two cops in chin-strap helmets lifted Gabriel from the ground and pushed him into the backseat. Gabriel didn't say a word.

Sheila, Robert, Jamal, and I leaned against Jamal's shiny silver Land Rover. My hand trembled as I lit a cigarette and watched the police car rise to the top of the hill and disappear. Then the white jeep followed, moving away from the dock, no flashing lights, no sirens, silently gliding past the orb of electric lights, disappearing into the dark, empty streets.

Jamal put a handkerchief to his bleeding forehead. "Boy," he said. "You missionaries sure have a funny way of doing things."

None of us said another word.

# PART FOUR: KINSHASA AND BEYOND

# CHAPTER TWENTY-NINE

**D**oc Peters stopped writing and put down his pen. He rubbed both hands over his now bloodshot eyes. The ashtray in front of me was overflowing with cigarette butts. The TVs above the American embassy bar in Kinshasa were still broadcasting live reports from East Berlin. Later, when I read about the crumbling of the wall, I calculated that just about the same time the residents of East Germany had begun to storm Checkpoint Charlie, tearing off chunks of concrete, four thousand miles away Gabriel Moss from Virginia Beach, Virginia, was also breaking apart, spinning out of control on the docks of Matadi, Zaire.

*The world tilting on its side.*

Doc stared at me and Sheila. "I wish I would have been here," he said.

"I wish we would have waited," I replied.

I pulled out the last cigarette from my pack. A customer sat at the bar and asked that one of the TVs be changed to a different channel. The bartender flipped the dial to MTV. Two men in yellow and black short-pants suits danced across the screen to the song "She Drives Me Crazy" by Fine Young Cannibals. It drove me crazy. It was annoying.

"Can I get a drink?" I asked.

"Yes," Doc said. "I need one too. Sheila?" Sheila shook her head no. Doc caught the attention of the bartender and ordered two Johnnie Walkers on the rocks.

"So what happens next?" Sheila asked.

Doc looked down at all the notes he had made in his file. "I need to type these up then have you two sign them, verifying what you said."

"I mean with Gabriel," she said.

The bartender set two whiskey glasses on the table. Doc took a long sip. "I'm going to recommend to Director Cole that he be medically separated."

"You're going to psych-evac him?" I asked. "That's going to go on his permanent record."

"It's better than being administratively separated, which we very well could do seeing as he broke about half a dozen rules and got a girl shot in the process."

"It was an accident," I said.

"Yes, caused by his behavior. Look, there is clearly something going on with him. From what you both have just told me, about everything that happened this past year, he has gotten worse and will continue to do so if he doesn't get help. This way, if we medically separate him, he will get his full benefits and we will pay for his treatment for up to a year."

"Back home?"

"Of course. He can't stay here after what happened."

I sucked on my cigarette and felt a wave of heat rising within me. "Send me home instead. Say I did it. I'll take the blame."

"Michael, no," Sheila said.

"He's wanted this his whole life. Leaving here will crush him. He has nothing to go home to. I owe him. He covered for me before."

"What are you talking about?" Sheila asked.

"In training. You remember when that little girl fell in the river and almost drowned? That was me, not Gabriel. I was the one who knocked her in. He took the blame for me."

"I didn't know."

Doc shook his head. "Michael, that's very noble of you, but we have witnesses to what happened. Do you know who that guy Jamal is? He's one of the Big Man's cousins. He's in the inner circle. The only way we were able to get Gabriel out is that he refused to press charges. He said he knew Gabriel was sick and needed help."

So many images and emotions were swirling in my head, flashing like heat lightning on a summer night. I pressed my palm under my chin and pressed upward, mashing my teeth together. I saw Gabriel lying on the ground, the soldier raising his rifle before Jamal stopped him. "Yeah... He was actually a pretty nice guy, considering. He kept things from getting even worse."

"Gabriel's lucky he's not in jail... or dead. You all are."

Sheila's hands were trembling. "Where's the girl?" she asked.

"We've got her," Doc said. "She's at the embassy hospital. She got out of surgery last night. She'll live, but the bullet damaged nerves. She'll probably never have full use of her arm again."

Sheila covered her face and started to gasp and cry. "Oh my God. Oh my God…We're so sorry."

Doc took a moment to respond. "I know."

I reached out to Sheila, and she buried her head in my shoulder, her body shaking up and down.

"We'll take care of her," Doc continued. "We have several good foster families we work with here in Kinshasa. We'll pay all her medical bills. We'll pay for her to go to school if she wants, a good private school. We'll do all we can."

Silence fell between us. Only the sound of the competing TVs above the bar and the gradual lessening of Sheila's sobs. Eventually, she sat upright and took my whiskey glass, finishing the last of my drink. I stubbed out my final cigarette. "So what do you think is wrong with him?" I asked.

Doc sighed out. "I'm not sure. I'm not a psychiatrist. Might be early stages of bipolar disorder."

"Bi-what?"

"Bipolar," he said. "It's the term being used now for what was once called manic-depressive."

"Oh."

"It's not uncommon for it to first show up at this age. It might have been lying dormant, then from the stress of all that happened to him here, it finally started to affect him. But again, I'm not sure. He had nothing in his past medical records to indicate it. Maybe he just pushed himself too hard and broke."

"He told me his mother and sister had mental problems," Sheila said. "And his father—"

"Yes, I know about his father," Doc said.

"So can you cure him?" I asked.

"Cure? No. If it is bipolar, it's a chronic condition, but there are medications and techniques that help regulate it, control it. Many people are able to live relatively normal lives. I'm going back with him. I have some, um, things to deal with in the States." I thought of his nondivorcing wife. "I'll make sure he gets in a good clinic. And I'll keep in touch, continue to monitor his treatment from here best I can."

"When are you leaving?" I asked.

"Tomorrow."

"Tomorrow!" I suddenly felt nauseous. Too fast. Everything was happening much too fast. "Can I see him? Can I talk to him before you go?"

Doc thought a moment. "Ok. He's resting at my place. You can see him there."

I looked at Sheila, her eyes still ringed with water. "No, Michael. I'm sorry. I can't. You know I'm not good with things like that."

I put her hand in mine. "I know. It's ok."

Doc shut his file, put the pen back in his shirt pocket. "One more thing to discuss. Razz spoke with Director Cole, and wants you, Michael, to take over Gabriel's post, incorporate it into yours, finish the work he started."

"What? I—I—I can't think about that right now."

"Ok, I understand. You and Razz can discuss it later when you go back." Doc looked back and forth between Sheila and me. "You guys tried. I know you tried to do the right thing, to help him. I'm sorry it came to this."

We didn't respond. Doc stood up. "I'm heading to my house now if you want to go."

I looked at Sheila and she quietly nodded. I kissed her on the cheek, the salty residue from her tears stinging my lips. "I'll meet you back at the house."

I stood up and followed Doc out of the café, pushing open the glass double doors, leaving the air-conditioned room. We walked past the tennis courts and swimming pool, through the tall white fence, and finally stepped out into the hot, dusty streets of Kinshasa. I paused a moment, trying to brace myself for what was to come.

# CHAPTER THIRTY

**I** remember the sharp pain in my stomach I felt as I walked up to the hospital to visit my mother for the final time. I remember it was a beautiful fall day, crisp air, no clouds in the sky. Sitting in the room, looking at her lying unconscious in the bed, the hiss of the ventilator, the smell of hydrogen peroxide, I tried to think of all the good memories we had before cancer had appeared and spread quickly throughout her body. It was difficult. Eventually, you get to that place—weeks, months, years later—when the bad ending fades away, replaced by images of smiles, echoes of a hug or warm cheek pressed against your own, but that day all I could do was look out the window across the street where a Hess gas station stood. It had a green-and-white sign that spun slowly at the top of a post. I watched it for hours, the turning rhythm seemingly in tune with the oxygen pump beside my mother's bed, the autumnal sunlight flashing and glistening off the tall letters.

It was a similar feeling I had in my stomach as I walked up to Doc Peters' home. It was a two-story townhouse, painted pale yellow, standing behind a black iron fence. A small courtyard was full of bright tropical flowers. We entered and saw Dimena sitting on a sofa in the front room, drinking a cup of tea.

"Hello, Michael," she said softly.

Doc crossed the floor and leaned down to kiss her on the cheek. "Did he eat or drink anything?"

"No," she said. "I tried, but no."

Doc pointed down a hallway. "He's down there, in the guest room."

The walls of the hallway were decorated with large African masks as well as photos of a younger Doc Peters in various places around the world: Thailand, Brazil, Australia. I came to the last door and pressed my palm to the wood before rolling my fingers into a fist and knocking.

"Gabriel?"

No answer.

I knocked again. "Gabriel? It's Michael."

Again no answer. I looked back down the hallway where Doc and Dimena stood, their arms wrapped around each other. He nodded for me to go in.

I slowly entered the room and saw Gabriel lying on his back on the bed, staring at the ceiling. A wooden fan turned above him.

"Hey, Mike," he said, not looking at me.

I pulled a chair from a desk beside the bed and sat down. "Hey. How are you?"

He paused before answering. "They're sending me home."

"Yeah. I know."

He continued to look at the ceiling. "I think I've always known there was something wrong with me," he said very simply and calmly. "I've always kind of felt it, something not quite right inside. I guess I always tried to ignore it. Outrun it. Stay busy so it couldn't catch me. I guess there's only so long you can do that."

"Gabriel, Doc Peters said he's going to make sure you are taken care of. Find out what's going on and figure out how to treat it. He said lots of people can live... you know, can be ok."

"That's why you and Sheila brought me with you, wasn't it?"

"That was one reason, yes. We hoped to get you to see Doc, but... I'm so sorry, Gabriel. I'm just so goddamn sorry." I felt my mouth getting dry and my chest fluttering.

"It's ok. I know you guys meant well. I appreciate everything you tried to do. I mean it. I just... I just..." And then it all came rushing out, all that deep, searing pain, the death of dreams. He clutched both arms around his stomach, rolled to his side, and brought his knees to his chest in a fetal position. At first no sound came out, his mouth spread wide, those ten thousand daggers that were tearing at the inside of his gut, too strong, too powerful, taking away his breath and voice; but then he let loose a deep wailing noise, loud and mournful, all that heartbreak and soul-crushing bitterness bursting forth. "Oh... God... What did I do...? What did I do?"

I reached out to put my hand on him, and he grabbed my arm, yanking it like a drowning man grasping for a rope. He crawled along the bed toward me, and with my other hand, I began to stroke his head in slow circles. "It's ok. It's good," I whispered. "Let it all out."

"I... I... I tried," he said.

"I know you did," I said. "You tried so hard. More than the rest of us."

He went on for several minutes, everything pouring out of his body until there was nothing left, and as soon as he stopped, he fell into a very deep sleep, not enough energy remaining inside him to keep even one eye open.

It was nearly night, the light fading from behind the curtain. I took a pillow and blanket from out of the closet and spread them on the floor next to the bed and lay down. I now looked at the ceiling, listening to Gabriel's breath rising and falling. Minutes, then hours passed by as I just lay there with my eyes open. Once, Doc gently opened the door to check on us. I glanced up at him. He pulled the bedspread around Gabriel's shoulders, then left the room. At midnight, I turned on my side and started to fall asleep. Doc had said the plane was leaving at noon the next day.

———————•———————

In the morning, I got Gabriel to walk with me to a bakery down the street, convincing him he needed to eat. We sat in the corner of the shop, near the display case full of bread and pastries. I ate half a Belgian waffle, Gabriel picked at the ends of a croissant. We each sipped cups of typically light, sweet coffee. On the way back, we took a side street where we came across a group of boys playing soccer in the road. The ball rolled to Gabriel's feet, and he kicked it up, bouncing it up and down off his knees several times before knocking it back to them. The kids oohed and aahed. Gabriel let a tiny smile crack across his face.

———————•———————

We arrived at HQ midmorning. I sat in the courtyard while Director Cole ushered Gabriel into his office and shut the door. About twenty minutes later, they emerged, and the director gave Gabriel a handshake and a tight hug. I followed Gabriel down the corridor to Doc's office. Doc took out his brown file folder and said he needed Gabriel and me to sign his final report. I saw the first page of the form, titled Medical Separation. Below the lines for the date and location was one for "Reason"; Doc had typed Psychological Disturbance. At the bottom of the last page, after all of Doc's typed notes, I saw Sheila's signature next to Doc's. I added mine and gave the pen to Gabriel. He didn't hesitate to add his own.

———————•———————

The taxi ride to the airport took about thirty minutes. Doc sat up front. Gabriel and I sat in the back. The driver had a BBC channel tuned on his car radio, and a song came on, "This Is the Sea" by

The Waterboys. In training, Gabriel had the cassette of the full album the song came from, and I had used my dual tape player to make a copy. As the sunlight flashed on the car window, images from training came back to me: Gabriel jumping up and down as we waited in line to get our room keys; sitting on the dock at night, watching the old fishermen cut across Lake Kivu; exploring the streets and markets of Bukavu as well as the surrounding mountains and forests; and of course, all the time I spent with Gabriel sitting on the banks of that training pond, soaking up as much knowledge from him as I could.

The airport was crowded but orderly. A TWA 747 sat on the tarmac, and there was no crazy, mad dash to get a seat on the plane. I walked with Doc and Gabriel as far as I could without a ticket. The stairs were wheeled to the plane and the doors opened. Doc took a couple of steps away from the two of us.

"So," I said.

"Yeah," said Gabriel.

We stood a moment, our eyes initially avoiding each other. Then I looked up at him. "You'll be fine," I said. "I'm sure you will." He nodded in agreement. "I'll write," I continued. "Knowing the Zairian postal system, you'll probably get the letter sometime in the mid-nineties." Gabriel laughed, in a way that almost seemed painful. My face started to tremble. "We'll miss you," I said.

Gabriel held out his hand. I shook it, and he placed his other hand on top of mine. "Take care of yourself, Michael," he said, his dark blue eyes piercing into mine. "And grow a lot of fish."

304

He turned, and he and Doc fell in line, moving toward the plane. When Gabriel reached the top of the stairs, he paused in the doorway. I thought he was going to turn around, his head started to move, but instead he took one final step forward and disappeared inside. I stood outside the terminal as long as I could and watched the plane taxi down the runway and lift up into the sky. It circled wide then headed west, rising higher and higher, growing smaller and smaller, until at last it just simply faded away.

# CHAPTER THIRTY-ONE

That long stretch of blank highway from Kikwit to Kitengo once again brought me a few hours of solace from all that had happened with Gabriel, Sheila, and I on our ill-fated vacation (we never did make it to the beach). As I steered my motorcycle to my village, making that final turn onto the wide sandy avenue, dozens of kids screamed and laughed and ran alongside me. As always, it was a welcome sight. I remember how great it felt to finally get back there, to pull up to my mud house with its dirt floor and no electricity or running water.

Time moved forward very quickly after that: Pumbu got married to Neva, and it was a huge two-day celebration in our village, pigs roasting day and night, the *munganji* dancers shaking and twirling in the sand almost nonstop. He finished his house and they moved in, and soon after, he began to build a small church on the outskirts of the village. As he became its only priest, the residents of Kitengo soon took to calling him Père Pumbu (Father Pumbu). His congregation was small at first, but steadily, it began to swell.

My work with the tilapia ponds continued to exceed my humble expectations. Just before Christmas, we had Vitesse's first harvest, and it was a big success. He added another pond, and soon, he was doing my job with me, traveling to other villages, teaching other farmers what he had learned about how dig a hole in the ground and "grow some fish." Baby Michael stayed healthy, and in fact, by the time I left, there were about a dozen more "Baby Michaels" in Kitengo and the surrounding villages, my name suddenly having become very stylish.

Sheila and I remained together, often planning "supply shopping" trips to see each other during the long three-month stints out in our villages. She was there by my side during many of my big events, and I was there with her when she broke ground on a large project of a half-dozen ponds built by the chief of her village. But days spun into weeks and weeks turned into months, until soon another year was nearly gone and our moment in Zaire was nearly at an end. A couple of months before we were due to return home, we took a trip back east to Bukavu, to where everything began. We spent a night at the training center, visiting with Ilunga and the rest of the staff, then hitchhiked north to Mount Kahuzi, a ten-thousand-foot inactive (we hoped) volcano. We made camp in a field at the base of the mountain, making a temporary tent from bamboo stalks and banana leaves. We were far from the main road and saw no one else around us as the sun started its crawl toward night, turning clouds circling the crest of the mountain into ringed purple streaks.

We sat side by side, knees to our chest, silently watching the sunset. Finally, Sheila spoke: "I can't believe in two months this will all be over."

"Me neither... Has it really been almost two years since our plane touched down? Seems like ten lifetimes ago."

"Mm," she said as the mountain shadow grew a bit bolder. And then: "I hope he is ok."

It took me a moment to respond. "I saw Doc in Kikwit a few weeks ago. He said Gabriel was moving back with his aunt in Virginia Beach. Said he heard Gabriel had been responding well to treatment so far... I sent him a few letters but haven't heard back yet."

"I don't think you will," she said. "I don't think either of us ever will."

"Really?"

"Yes. It would be too hard for him. I think he'll just want to push this far behind him, try as much as he can to forget about it. About us. About everything."

"Maybe... I'll still try to call him when we get home."

"Home," Sheila said, and rested her chin on her knees.

I looked at the side of her face, a wisp of her hair lifted by the evening breeze. "So... you're going to back to California?"

She almost purred in response. "Yeah... my sister is getting married in December." She turned to look at me, her gray eyes just catching the sunset. "You wanna be my date?"

"I've never been out West," I said. "Never been past the

Mississippi."

There was a long pause as we looked at each other, seemingly both of us trying to glean clues from the future. "You should come," she said. "Come visit. You might like it."

"I will. I'll 'go west.' See what happens."

She smiled without opening her mouth. "Yes," she said and turned to look straight ahead at the mountain now just barely traced by light. "We'll definitely have to see what happens."


As for Gabriel... I did what Razz suggested and took over the ponds he had started. They became the communal property of his village. But Sheila was right: I never heard from or saw him again.

I never did get to finally thank him, never got another chance to pay him back for all he did for me, the imprint of his helping hand never truly fading from my skin. Many times as I worked down in his valley, broiling and sweating underneath that big Bandundu sky, I would look up and think back to the moment I stood on the tarmac in Kinshasa and watched that TWA 747 fly away, taking Gabriel from everything he had dreamt about his entire life. In those moments, I wished I could have summoned all the magic powers that the people of Kitengo believed I had within me, and somehow transformed that plane into a perpetual energy machine, a vehicle with limitless fuel, so it could circle the earth for as long as it wanted. Then, each time the plane crossed a very specific spot on the globe, a small village in the middle of Africa, Gabriel would be able to look out the window and down to that valley below where two half-dug fish ponds sat diagonally to each other. The first time he passed by, he would be able to see the sides had been sloped at just the right angle (3:1) and the bottom had been dug to just the right depth (one meter). Next, he would see grass had been planted on the banks of the ponds and, soon after, each of the ponds filled to the top with water. He would see little flashes of silver, as the baby fish swam free in their new home, and then, after a few more trips around the world, he would look down and see the ponds nearly overflowing, three generations of fish packed into those ten-by-twenty-meter rectangles, practically bursting the walls. Finally, on a beautiful sunny day, early fall 1990, at the dawn of a new decade, on his last flight through the sky, Gabriel would look down with those piercing dark-blue eyes of his and see a crowd of excited people surrounding those ponds, those two ponds he had begun so many months earlier in such well-intentioned turmoil, and maybe he would smile, just a little bit, at what had become of his inspiration.

I know, because I was there. So were Sheila and Razz. So were Pumbu and his wife. Jackie and Vitesse and Baby Michael had traveled there as well. All the residents of Kitombe gathered down in that valley, abuzz with anticipation. They weren't disappointed. It was a huge harvest, a magnificent event, under that hot sun and wide sky. We pulled up net after net packed full of bright, silvery fish, those fish flopping and shaking as we poured them into buckets and weighed them on a hanging scale tied to a tree branch. Kilo after kilo. Pound after pound. It seemed never ending as each person happily waited in line to take their share. Some began to cook the fish right then and there, on the banks of the pond, in pans of palm oil, sizzling over hot coals dug into the ground. There was music, too, lots of it. I had brought my radio, and Zairian music played nonstop. *"Kwassa! Kwassa!"* (Dance! Dance!) the voices sang, and we did dance, forming lines and laughing, shouting as we swayed our hips, bumped our bodies, and threw our hands into the air while we passed around bottles of soda or wooden mugs of sweet, milky palm wine.

It was a wonderful moment, a culmination of so much. And as the afternoon sun began to sink lower in the sky, I went to the banks of one of the ponds and knelt down in the grass. Mevanda, the big-eyed girl who months earlier had helped me find my troubled friend, came and leaned her back against my shoulder. I noticed a smudge of dirt on her cheek, and I licked my thumb to clean it off.

A small flash of silver splashed in the pond, one of the baby fish left behind, causing circles to spread out over the water's surface. Mevanda looked down and pointed with her finger.

"Those are Gabriel's fish," she said.

I watched the ripples widen and fade and saw another fish swimming in the water. I held Mevanda a little bit tighter.

"Yes," I said. "They certainly are."

# END

# AFTERWORD

Well... I hope you enjoyed it.

While this story is based on personal experiences, it is a work of fiction. That means some things are true, some things are kind of true, and others I made up. Which are which?—I hope you see me grinning at you :)—that's for me to know, and no one else to find out. I blended everything together into a nice (and hopefully tasty) smoothie for you. Actually, the funny thing is that when I write something, the story itself often takes over as reality in my mind. Sometimes, I can't even tell the difference, so that when I read what I've written, occasionally I have to stop and ask: "Wait a minute, did that really happen, or did I make it up for the story?" It's a strange phenomenon, to say the least.

As far as "the organization" the characters worked for, I'm sure most people can figure out what it is based on, but it is actually a bit of a composite of a few different ones I've had experiences with. I did try a few fictitious names, but none of them felt right. So in the end, I decided the experiences the characters had would be more important than the actual organization they had them with. Hope I was right.

In the story, I give you a very quick index card–sized summary of the history of Zaire/the Congo. It is a fascinating country, a beautiful country full of nearly endless natural resources and wonderful people. It is also a country full of tragedy, unspeakable brutality and bloodshed, both self-inflicted and inflicted on them by other powers. If you are interested in learning more, I recommend the book *King Leopold's Ghost* by Adam Hochschild about the colonial era. For the power struggle between Mobutu and Lumumba in the early independence movement, I recommend *Lumumba: Africa's Lost Leader* by Leo Zeilig. Sadly, since the mid-1990s, war has been raging there almost nonstop, a war mostly ignored here in the West. If you want more information about that situation, there have been a few good articles in recent years about it. Best place to find them is you-know-where: simply Google "The war in the DRC."

When reading all this, however, I find it's important to remember that in the center of all this chaos and horror, there are real people, real families like Vitesse and Jackie, and noble souls like Pumbu, who are trying to live decent lives.

Finally, the goal of the projects done by many organizations like the one depicted in this story is self-sustainability, so that when and if these groups pack up and go, the skills and knowledge they leave behind can continue on their own. While it's true I have yet to return to the villages where I lived and worked, a colleague of mine, who was there at the same time as me, went back to Bandundu a few years ago to work on a different project with another organization. He reported back that the area had indeed remained largely isolated and insulated from all the destruction of the wars. He also went back to one of the villages where he had worked and visited a fish farm he had helped to set up over twenty-five years earlier. While the original farmer who owned the land had passed away, his sons had taken it over, and it was still going strong, *more than twenty-five years after he and "the organization" had left for good*. That is why people do things like this. As I stated in the story, if you look at the big picture, you can go insane. But if you focus on trying to help one person, one family, one village improve their lot in life, then it makes perfect sense and it makes everything you go through worthwhile.

That is something nice that I often try to think about.

—RL

# ABOUT THE AUTHOR

RUSH LEAMING lives in the Southeastern United States. He has done many things and lived in many places.

At various times in his life, he has been a/an: car wash attendant, bartender, dishwasher, adjunct professor, lab rat decapitator, shoe salesman, fish pond builder, a monster in a low-budget horror movie, music video director, refugee camp volunteer, film production manager, ESL teacher, star of a country music video, newspaper delivery person, Chinese wok assembler, nighttime hotel desk clerk, cement mixer, ballet manager, waiter, internet teacher, screenwriter, short film director, Cuban cigar mule, auctioneer, premed student, traffic pattern analyzer, photographer, landscaper, homeless, academic director, shepherd, lifeguard, audiovisual coordinator, recruiter for a prestigious government agency, and single dad.

Just to name a few…

His first novel, *Don't Go, Ramanya*, a political thriller set in Thailand, was published in the fall of 2016. He is currently working on his next novel entitled *Tales of a Starship Dishwasher*. Or maybe he is working on an Untitled Romantic Thriller. Or perhaps a collection of short stories. BTW, some of those short stories have appeared in *Notations*, *67 Press*, *Lightwave*, *The Electric Eclectic*, and *5k Fiction*.

www.rushleaming.com